WISDOM

What Reviewers Say About Jesse J. Thoma's Work

Courage

"Thoma writes very endearing characters, extraordinary people in normal lives. ...A slow burn romance with plenty of sparks and chemistry."—*Jude in the Stars*

"Set in the same universe as *Serenity*, Thoma has again done a great job of exploring difficult, relevant topics in an accessible way, whilst also managing to include a believable romance and some much needed elements of humour."—*LGBTQ+ Reader*

"I love a serious police procedural. Add in an enchanting romance with beautiful characters, and you have the perfect novel. That is exactly what I found in *Courage* by Jesse J. Thoma. I was hooked on page one, and was sad to leave this tale when I reached the end." —*Rainbow Reflections*

"*Courage* is a slow burn romance with plenty of sparks and chemistry. You can always count on Jesse J. Thoma to write solid but tender stories."—*Rainbow Literary Society*

"I LOVED that Thoma addresses the issues of police reform, Black Lives Matter, and 'defund the police' in a non-political way. She brings these issues into the story in a way that makes SO MUCH sense."—*Love, Literature*

"Jesse J. Thoma brings two stories to life in parallel, one being the work and dynamics of the new ride-along program and how the two protagonists deal with it, and the other the romance between the two. I loved both parts. ...Highly recommended for anyone looking for a good cop/social worker story who enjoys angst and tricky situations."—*Lez Review Books*

Serenity

"*Serenity* is the perfect example of opposites attract. …I'm a sucker for stories of redemption and for characters who push their limits, prove themselves to be more than others seem to think. This lesbian opposites attract romance book is all that, and well-written too."
—*Lez Review Books*

"I really liked this one. I liked the pace, the stakes, and the characterizations. The relationship builds well, there are likeable supporting characters, and of course, you're rooting for Kit and Thea even as your heart breaks for both of them and their situations. It's a sweet romance, and I appreciated that a lot of the issues Kit faces have nothing to do with her sexuality in a predominately male-driven, sexist profession."—*Kissing Backwards*

The Chase

"The primary couple's initial meeting is a uniquely amusing yet action-packed scenario. I was definitely drawn into the dynamic events of this thoroughly gratifying book via an artfully droll and continuously exciting story. Spectacularly entertaining!"—*Rainbow Book Reviews*

Seneca Falls—*Lambda Literary Award Finalist*

"Loneliness and survival are the two themes dominating Seneca King's life in Thoma's emotionally raw contemporary lesbian romance. Thoma bluntly and uncompromisingly portrays Seneca's struggles with chronic pain, emotional trauma, and uncertainty."
—*Publishers Weekly*

"This was another extraordinary book that I could not put down. Magnificent!"—*Rainbow Book Reviews*

"...a deeply moving account of a young woman trying to raise herself from the ashes of a youth-gone-wrong. Thoma has given us a redemptive tale—and Seneca isn't the only one who needs saving. Told with just enough wit and humor to break the tension that arises from living with villainous ghosts from the past, this is a tale woven into a narrative tapestry of healing and wholeness."
—*Lambda Literary*

Pedal to the Metal

"Sassy and sexy meet adventurous and slightly nerdy in Thoma's much-anticipated sequel to *The Chase*. Tongue-in-cheek wit keeps the fast-moving action from going off the rails, all balanced by richly nuanced interpersonal relationships and sweet, realistic romance."—*Publishers Weekly*

"[*Pedal to the Metal*] has a wonderful cast of characters including the two primary women from the first book in subsidiary roles and some classy good guys versus bad guys action. ...The people, the predicaments, the multi-level layers of both the storyline and the couples populating the Rhode Island landscapes once again had me glued to the pages chapter after chapter. This book works so well on so many levels and is a wonderful complement to the opening book of this series that I truly hope the author will add several additional books to the series. Mystery, action, passion, and family linked together create one amazing reading experience. Scintillating!"
—*Rainbow Book Reviews*

Visit us at www.boldstrokesbooks.com

By the Author

Tales of Lasher, Inc.

The Chase

Pedal To the Metal

Data Capture

Serenity Prayer Books

Serenity

Courage

Wisdom

Other Romances

Seneca Falls

WISDOM

by

Jesse J. Thoma

2021

WISDOM

ISBN 13: 978-1-63555-886-9

This Trade Paperback Original Is Published By
Bold Strokes Books, Inc.
P.O. Box 249
Valley Falls, NY 12185

First Edition: December 2021

CREDITS
EDITORS: VICTORIA VILLASEÑOR AND CINDY CRESAP
PRODUCTION DESIGN: SUSAN RAMUNDO
COVER DESIGN BY TAMMY SEIDICK

Acknowledgments

Wisdom is the final of the three Serenity Prayer books I set out to write. I'm incredibly grateful to Rad and Sandy for saying "yes" to these stories. As always, the entire team at BSB is a dream to work with.

To my editor, Victoria Villasenor, thank you for all you've taught me, large and small, and for making my novels infinitely better. Perhaps most of all, however, thank you for ruining every book that has disembodied hands and eyes and mouths wandering the pages.

To my wife, I'm a writer at a loss for words. Thank you for understanding the late nights of writing. Thank you for proofreading and listening to all my ideas, even the insane ones. Thank you for loving me.

Finally, to the readers. Thank you for picking up this book and the ones that came before. You have been and continue to be incredible. Thank you for every review (even the critical ones), email, and message. Knowing you're out there reading is a wonderful motivator to keep writing.

Dedication

To Alexis, my beginning, middle, and happily ever after.
To Goose, Bird, and little Purple Martin, you three fill
my heart with more joy than I thought possible.

Grant me the serenity to accept the things I cannot change
The courage to change the things I can
And the wisdom to know the difference.

PROLOGUE

"Put that away. You two are going to ruin this for me with premature celebration." Sophia Lamont looked away from the television long enough to glare at her brother, Davey, and best friend, Lily, before returning to the screen.

"It's in the bag, sis." David Lamont made a dismissive gesture and started to untwist the wire champagne top.

"Lily, stop him please." Sophia gripped her phone tightly and moved to the edge of the couch. What was taking so long?

"I'm with Davey on this one, hun. What is your campaign team telling you? I know they're blowing up your phone since you wouldn't let them over tonight," Lily said.

Sophia took a deep breath, put her phone down, and got up from the couch. She pulled the champagne bottle from Davey's hand before he could pop the cork. "I told you when I invited you over, we *do not* celebrate until every local network has called the race and I've received a concession phone call. Doesn't matter what anyone else is telling me. Those are my rules."

The idea of celebrating a success only to have it ripped away was almost enough to send her into a full panic attack.

"Fine, but I'm popping the top on this once you lighten up and realize you're going to make history tonight. I always knew you were going to be the one to make the family proud." Davey pulled her into a side hug.

"Did I miss the part where you haven't?" Sophia wriggled out of his embrace as she'd been doing since they were kids.

"A Black man with a criminal record." He gave her a look. "My trophy case is overflowing."

Sophia heard the sadness and anger in her brother's voice. It bubbled through her blood too. She struggled with what to say to relieve some of the pressure, but nothing came to her. It never did.

"That might be all the world bothers to see, but that's not all you are to me. You're also a terrible baker, an above-average cellist, and a pain in my ass." This time she sought out his hug.

"Well, my baby sister is going to fix everything that's wrong in the world, right, sis? Youngest state congresswoman we've ever had? First Black woman ever elected to the statehouse? Superwoman in a suit."

David's eyes were glistening. Sophia couldn't remember ever seeing him cry.

"You know he's right." Lily twirled a champagne flute between her fingers. "But I don't see you rockin' any type of spandex outfit under those beautiful clothes you pay too much for."

"I buy these clothes from you." Sophie swiped the champagne flute from Lily with a laugh and put it with the bottle. "Who's supposed to help get your business off the ground, if not your best friend?"

"And here I was wondering who's supposed to make sure you look halfway decent out there setting the world on fire, if not *your* best friend?"

Davey leaned on the counter and tried again to get a hold of the champagne bottle. "Maybe you should steal that smoking hot social worker's nickname. The one from the news a while back. What was it?"

"Captain Couture. Focus on the important details, Davey."

"I remember plenty of important details. She's also Valencia Blackstone's sister-in-law." Davey puffed out his chest.

"Oh, right, I forgot royalty was running in this race too. Do you know if she won?" Lily picked up her phone and started scrolling.

Sophia nodded. She allowed herself a small moment to imagine what victory tonight would feel like. What would it be like to work with someone like Valencia Blackstone if the results held?

"Captain Couture is probably the reason she won. She stood up for Valencia and suddenly people took notice. I wonder if Valencia will be fun to work with or an entitled rich idiot?" Davey grabbed a handful of snacks and popped some in his mouth.

Sophia glanced back over her shoulder at the television. She shoved her hands in her pockets to avoid picking at the fresh polish on her nails. "I have to get elected first."

Her phone rang just as an announcement flashed on the TV screen. Lily and Davey looked over her shoulder at the number. It was her opponent. She hadn't expected him to call and concede so quickly, although the results flooding in were almost enough to convince her the story was already written. She wanted to wait to celebrate until she'd been officially elected, but it looked like she already had. She felt a little weak in the knees. This was what she'd wanted since childhood, but it felt surreal all the same. She was about to take her place in history.

CHAPTER ONE

Sophia stood on the steps to the statehouse and leaned back on her heels to stare up at the beautiful marble building. It took her breath away as it did every day she climbed the steps to work. Since January when she'd been officially sworn in as the youngest state representative and first Black woman in the state's long history, walking into work had felt like a privilege. Since she was a child, she'd been dreaming of having an office here, doing the people's work. With that history however, both her own and political, came pressure to live up to the legacy she'd already imagined for herself.

She took another deep breath. The cold February air crackled through her lungs and made her shiver. Lily had come over last night and brought Sophia a new clothing creation from her spring collection, and while what Lily created was beautiful, it wasn't designed for warmth.

Sophia rushed down the hall to her office, wanting to get warm and settled before her day began. A member of her staff had texted her that both the Speaker of the House and the majority leader wanted to talk to her first thing. She was early, which might give her enough time to see if anyone had a clue what was going on. She hadn't been at the statehouse long enough to get called to the principal's office. Hopefully.

When she rounded the corner and walked through the door of her office, Rodrigo Cortez, who'd appointed himself her chief of staff, and Valencia Blackstone, her fellow freshman state rep, were leaning against her desk, laughing like old friends. She'd known Rodrigo most of her life. He made friends with anyone easily and quickly, whereas she'd spent hours on the House floor and in committee meetings with Valencia and barely gotten past pleasantries.

"Hi, boss. Here's your schedule for the day. You have constituent calls after your meeting with leadership. You've gotten fifteen requests to sponsor bills since you were sworn in so I blocked off some time this afternoon to look them over. I rejected two outright, but we should look over the others together. I have a pretty good idea of where you'll land on most of them, but it seems like the people elected you, not me, so I should let you do your job." Rodrigo finally took a breath. He held out a white paper bag with promising oily stains along the bottom.

Sophia put down her work things, snatched the bag, and peeked inside. "You didn't?"

"Of course I did." Rodrigo kissed her cheek. "My mother loves you."

Sophia pulled a homemade oreja from the bag and tried hard not to drool. She took a tiny nibble, careful to avoid getting the flaky pastry crumbs on her clothes before her meeting. The cinnamon and sugar flavor was followed by a hint of nutmeg. The nutmeg was a nice addition. It took a lot of willpower not to shove the whole thing in her mouth. The looming meeting was the only thing stopping her. She didn't mind looking like a post-snack Cookie Monster for phone calls later.

"You really should try one of these. She added nutmeg this week." Sophia held the bag out to Valencia. "Rodrigo's mother is a national baking treasure. But don't spread the word. We keep her quiet so there's more for us."

Valencia took one of the pastries and seemed far less concerned about getting pastry flakes everywhere. Sophia respected that.

"So why am I being summoned for a meeting with leadership?" Sophia dropped her treasure back in the bag and licked her fingers.

"How am I supposed to know? I just work here." Rodrigo batted his eyelashes dramatically.

Sophia didn't dignify his question with a response. He probably knew what brand and size underwear everyone in the building was wearing this morning.

"Fine, don't tell me. I'll savor the surprise." She scooted around Rodrigo and put her laptop on her desk.

"Valencia, were you here to see me or to get a morning dose of Rodrigo?" Sophia straightened a pen on her desk.

"Both, actually. Well, I was hoping to sweet-talk Rodrigo into getting a meeting with you."

"Don't sweet-talk him too much or his head won't fit through the door and he'll be stuck in my office forever. There aren't enough orejas for both of us to survive long." Sophia winked at Rodrigo.

"Honestly, I came to test the waters. He's less intimidating."

Sophia looked up quickly. She almost spit out the water she'd just taken a sip of. "Why in the world are you intimidated by me? You're a Blackstone. I imagine you have more than a few of our colleagues shaking in their socks."

Valencia waved dismissively. "That's about money. They want access to it or want to be seen as if they don't, even if they do. You're different. Everyone wants a piece of you because you, my friend, are the future of politics in this state. If you want to be."

Sophia tried to get the look on her face to reflect more "smooth political operator" and less "what the fuck?"

"So what do you want from her?" Rodrigo crossed his arms and moved next to Sophia.

He could be a bulldog when needed and Sophia appreciated his support now. She was still trying to find her balance after Valencia's directness. She was used to politicians being coy, although nothing in her interactions with Valencia had given her the impression that she was a typical politician.

"Whoa, I come in peace. We're both freshman reps looking to make our mark. I'm not going to lie and say I'm not ambitious and looking to fulfill the promises I made campaigning, but I also think there are opportunities for both of us if we work together."

Sophia sized up Valencia. She was wearing a suit that looked expensive enough to pay Sophia's rent for a year. Lily would probably drool herself into dehydration over the fabric alone, but it wasn't flashy. Sophia wouldn't have known it cost a fortune if not for Lily's lifelong obsession with fashion. Was the subtlety of her clothing and makeup choices a form of hiding her wealth? It didn't seem disingenuous and she certainly didn't need to walk around with a sign around her neck declaring her net worth. Her last name probably did that effectively on its own.

Valencia's campaign had been progressive, but lifeless, until her sister-in-law, Natasha Parsons, a social worker employed by the local police department, had vouched for her. Natasha had chosen to go into social work, but her family carried both wealth and respect, lending serious credibility to Valencia's campaign.

Sophia suspected she and Valencia agreed on many issues and could find common ground, but she was early in her first term and this wasn't the first request for collaboration from her colleagues. She was interested in practical projects with real world benefits. She wasn't interested in getting pulled into endless political grandstanding. It might take time, but she was willing to wait to figure out who had the same goal-oriented approach she did. "I was clear throughout my campaign, I'm willing to work with anyone who's interested in getting things done. I'm more interested in pragmatism and policies than partisanship. If you're similarly motivated, then let's keep talking." Sophia studied Valencia's face while she made the offer.

Rodrigo indicated his watch and grabbed the things Sophia never realized she needed until he handed them to her.

Valencia followed them out the door. "I'm not bullshitting you, Sophia. I think we could do good work together. I know what it's like to have people trying to get close to you for the wrong reasons. I'll show you I'm not one of those people. Mental health, substance use, and the criminal justice system are all areas I'm interested in. We'd both be in a stronger position to make real change if we worked together."

Sophia didn't promise Valencia anything more than to think about her offer. She shook out her shoulders and filed the conversation to revisit later as she followed Rodrigo down the hall toward the Speaker's office. He straightened a nonexistent wrinkle on her suit jacket and gave her a little push toward the door.

The Speaker of the House, Francis Spaziano, was a jovial looking White guy with too much belly and too little hair. Despite his constant smile and friendly demeanor, you didn't get to be in his political position with an infectious laugh. Even though they were in the same political party, Sophia didn't quite trust him.

"Sophia, come on in. Thanks for meeting with us so early this morning." Francis waved her in.

The majority leader, a nondescript White guy in a suit, was sitting in one corner of the office. Sophia took a seat opposite. Why was she so nervous meeting with her party's leadership?

"I know we had a chance to speak briefly at your swearing in, but we're thrilled you've joined us here in the statehouse. I'm speaking for the entire caucus when I say you're seen as a rising star in the party."

Why does everyone keep saying that? She gave him a quick smile. "Thank you. I came here like everyone else, to serve my constituents." Sophia shifted in her chair.

"Of course. Of course. But we also serve them by positioning ourselves well to increase our influence. You campaigned as someone willing to get things done so I know you're not a grandstander. Ambition isn't a problem. I support ambition. I *reward* ambition."

Sophia wasn't sure where he was going with his ambition plug so she stayed quiet.

"The governor is interested in using some of the capital of her first one hundred days to make a splashy policy announcement about tackling the drug crisis in our state."

Drug policy reform had been a central part of the governor's campaign. It wasn't surprising she wanted to focus on it now. Sophia was tired of the Speaker and the majority leader looking like cats with a fat mouse between their paws. The way they were looking back and forth at each other and then to her, she was starting to feel like she was the mouse.

"It's an issue in need of all the attention it can get. Perhaps I'll ask my staff to get in touch with the governor and see if I can join in her effort. As you said, I'm interested in supporting concrete action that will help my constituents. Thanks for the heads-up." Sophia uncrossed her legs but didn't make a move to stand.

The Speaker looked annoyed before his jovial expression returned. The majority leader laughed.

"Watch your back, old man. She'll have your job one day."

The Speaker waved as if dismissing a fly, but he shot a sideways glance at Sophia that reminded her why politics was a blood sport.

"The governor's put together a community design team to provide her with recommendations for innovative ways to reimagine a path forward. It's full of community members, not politicians, and they'll only be providing recommendations, but the fact that the governor convened it means she'll respect the opinions of the team. We got you a seat at the table."

Sophia took a moment to mull over what she'd been offered. It seemed like the kind of opportunity that wasn't handed to freshman representatives without some strings. She was no marionette.

"Walk me through why you picked me, why the governor wants me, and what's in it for you two?"

The Speaker shifted in his seat and adjusted the tuck of his shirt. "Isn't it obvious what's in it for you? I could ask any one of our caucus to join and they'd be jumping at the chance. You will be one of a select few on a team advising the governor and the only one from the statehouse. Your work will be hand-delivered to her. That kind of access and recognition isn't easy to come by. Not to mention the prestige of the design team itself. This is a first page of the résumé kind of opportunity."

Sophia nodded slowly. "Sure, but you asked me, which I appreciate. But, as an example, why aren't either of you taking my place on the team?"

The majority leader leaned forward in his chair and looked at the Speaker. "I told you we were going to like her." He turned to Sophia. "Do you know how many of our caucus wouldn't ask a single question and would already be out the door tweeting about having a chance to work on the governor's new initiative? Don't ever forget you're here to do the people's work. But, tweet the shit out of this once you're out of this room. You have to get reelected in a couple of years. And when that time comes, we're going to have your back. A star like you is good for us. For the party, I mean."

"He's right." The Speaker put his elbows on his desk and steepled his fingers. "I'm not used to people asking questions. Sorry. To answer your original question, what's in it for you is exposure to the governor on one of her pet issues. Make a splash and she's going to remember you. You'll be able to raise money based on your participation on the design team and proximity to the governor, and if she likes you, she'll campaign for your reelection when the time comes. You also get to work on an important issue and you have the chance to make some meaningful changes."

Sophia looked back and forth between the two men. They looked sincere. "And what about the other two questions? Why does the governor want me and what's in it for you two?"

"You're a young woman of Color, enthusiastic, a rising star. You're exactly who the governor wants on this team. It's made up of community members, but that doesn't mean the governor doesn't want someone from our line of work represented as well. As for us, we're politicians. The design team isn't tasked with making laws. Its purpose is to provide recommendations to the governor. You, however, are a lawmaker. If there's an idea that comes out of that team that can become legislative action, we want to hear about it."

Sophia felt like her brain was moving faster than she could keep up with, which of course wasn't possible. "So you're assuming the governor is going to take the recommendations from the design team and put together a bill she can introduce and force you to act on? That's the reason she wants me on the team? And you want me to undercut the governor and the spirit of the design team so you can preempt her by introducing your own bill? Essentially let the team do the work and then steal the ideas to get the credit?" Sophia stood and headed for the door.

"Hey, that's not what we're suggesting. Have a seat."

Sophia turned back, but she remained standing.

"Just keep us appraised of how things are going. Fair? You don't have to share things you're not comfortable sharing. But she can't sign anything into law without us, so we're all on the same team, right? You'll just be keeping us in the loop." The majority leader looked slightly chastened.

Sophia mulled her options. She knew it was too good an offer to be true. Say no and risk pissing off the governor. Say yes and there was the potential for these two to come asking for information she didn't want to provide. She smiled, her pulse racing at the nature of the game. Why were politics so much fun?

"I'll promise to represent myself and my constituents on the design team, and if you have questions about the process, please stop by my office anytime. Deal?"

The Speaker smiled broadly. "Agreed. There are a few additional things you need to know about the team."

The majority leader stood and leaned against the front of the Speaker's desk. "We've heard rumors the governor is including a diverse cast of characters on this team. Maybe she wants to look like she's getting opinions from all sectors. Whatever her reasons, don't let any stink in the room land on you. Gina Northrup and Tammy Potts are ones to avoid. You might be able to spin pictures of you and Tammy. Everyone loves a 'second chance' narrative, but the Northrup family is corrupt to its marrow. Give that one a wide berth. If you get tangled in that web, well, we warned you and we're not letting it swing back on us."

"Northrup, like Bartholomew Northrup?"

"His kid. Like we said, bad news. Stay away from her if you want to have a long career in this game."

On her way back to her office, Sophia ruminated on the two people she was supposed to avoid. She wasn't used to writing anyone off until she had a good reason to do so. She'd watched her brother get rejected over and over because society said he should be. She didn't dismiss the warning she'd been given, but she was a grown woman, she'd do a little research on her own. Now though, she had a date with a bag of orejas, Rodrigo, and her computer so she could figure out what the hell she'd gotten herself into.

CHAPTER TWO

R eggie Northrup waited for a break in traffic, then darted across the street. She felt her phone buzz in her pocket as she jogged. She checked it when she got to the sidewalk. It was her best friend and coworker, Ava, texting her to enjoy her "vacation" day.

Trade places with you. All you have to do is ask.

The reply came so quickly it didn't seem possible Ava could have typed it so quickly. *Not on your life, hotshot. Have fun. Stay out of trouble.*

"Asshole." Reggie looked at her phone as she mumbled, but she couldn't help but grin.

It was nice of Ava to reach out. While it was true she wasn't looking forward to today, maybe it would be a welcome break from her usual nine-to-five as a corrections officer. This morning she hadn't felt the weight in her bones that usually descended upon waking on workdays.

She looked at her watch. Still thirty minutes to kill. She cast around for a way to burn off some of the extra time and landed on a coffee shop two doors up the street. Downtown, in the shadow of the statehouse, wasn't part of her usual stomping grounds, and when she opened the coffee shop door she remembered why. Everywhere she looked were bland, nondescript, cookie-cutter people in business suits. Since they were so close to the statehouse, most of them were probably politicians. She hated politicians.

Looking at them gave her the same feeling she got when she walked down an empty, institutional, dimly lit hallway. The wall color and the feeling should both be called "business casual beige."

If she weren't so early for her meeting and the coffee didn't smell so damn good, she would have turned around and walked out. Instead, a non-business-suited interloper like herself ran smack into her since she'd stopped in the doorway. He flipped her off as he walked past.

Someone to her right laughed. Reggie spun around ready to growl at whoever was laughing at her, but was struck speechless by the woman grinning at her six feet away. Before she could get her head back on straight, another customer ran into her as he tried to get in the door.

"Do you like being a piñata or are you going to get out of the doorway?"

Reggie remembered how to move her feet and took a step toward the woman. She was wearing a suit, but it didn't look like it had come from the clothing warehouse for political action figures. The light pink shirt layered under the jacket beautifully complemented her dark brown skin.

"I wasn't sure if I'd be allowed to stay since there seems to be a dress code for this place." Reggie pulled open the sides of her nylon jacket and indicated her jeans and button-down shirt.

"You look all right to me. I don't think there will be complaints if you stay."

Reggie wasn't sure, but it seemed like the woman was flirting. Could that be true?

"If you're not meeting anyone, you're welcome to join me after you get your coffee. There aren't any free tables in here."

Reggie looked from the woman, to the open seat opposite her, to the counter. There wasn't much of a line despite how busy it was. She indicated she'd be right back and hustled to order. Had she lost her mind agreeing to share a table with a stranger? She'd have to talk to her. Generally, people reacted poorly to "none of your business" in response to questions.

She retrieved her coffee and looked across the shop at the gorgeous woman. They locked eyes, and seemingly of their own volition, Reggie's feet moved back toward her and her offer of company. Talking to a stranger couldn't be that dangerous. She'd never see her again. So what if she knew something about her? She wasn't one of the inmates she worked with, and hopefully she wasn't a politician.

She slipped into the seat across from her unexpected coffee date and introduced herself. "If we're going to share a table, obtained under what I can only assume was highly questionable means, I should at least know your name. I'm Reggie."

"Either a vicious rock, paper, scissors battle, an arm wrestling competition, or a dad-joke-off won me the right to this table, but I'm not disclosing which one. I'm Sophia. Nice to meet you, Reggie."

Reggie noticed Sophia hesitated a moment when she repeated her name back. It struck her as odd, but sometimes people got tripped up on the masculine name. More people would probably get tripped up if she introduced herself as Regina, the name on her birth certificate, looking like she did. She always thought Reggie fit the woman looking back at her in the mirror every morning, but she supposed her parents had no way of knowing what the naked, screaming, poop machine that entered their lives would be like as an adult.

"Did you really win the rights to this table with a dad joke?" Reggie used her coffee cup as cover to take a longer look at Sophia.

How did she manage an invite to sit at the table of a woman like her? Smoking hot felt too crass, but beautiful didn't come close to truly capturing all of her. Elegant, gorgeous, graceful? Nothing felt quite right. She'd have to ponder more later.

"I told you, I'm not giving away my secrets. What if I need to outfox *you* for a table sometime?"

Reggie tapped her chin. "My dad joke game is strong. However, I strongly suspect all you'd have to do is ask."

Sophia was taking a sip of coffee, but Reggie could see her smile behind the cup.

"So what do you do for work? You're wearing a suit like the rest in here, but like you, your clothes stand out from the crowd. Either you're like the rest with better taste, or you have a much more interesting job."

Sophia waved her finger as she set her cup back on the table. "Oh no, I'm not talking about work. That's too mundane. We can't go from dad jokes and flirting to work, but I will tell you about my clothes. My best friend, Lily Medeiros, is a fashion designer. She's selling her clothes online right now, but she's working on opening a shop. Maybe the next time you're in here, everyone will be dressed in a Lily Medeiros."

"For your friend, I hope that's true. She's clearly very talented."

"She would love to get her hands on you." Sophia put her hand over her mouth, then laughed. "For fashion purposes. Tall, built, hot butch face. A designer's dream."

Reggie nearly spit out her coffee. She swallowed and burned her throat on the too-large gulp. "Jesus. I see subtlety is your game. So if we can't talk about work, what did you have in mind?"

Sophia tapped her chin. After a moment's thought, her eyes lit up. "If you had to pick one animal that best described you, what would it be? Then I'll pick one for you. It will be completely superficial of course since I'm only going on what I can see and ten minutes of conversation."

Reggie smiled. "Okay. Yours is easy, in a room full of drab moths, it's easy to spot the beautiful butterfly."

"It's the suit, isn't it?" Sophia dramatically showed off her suit jacket and threw one leg out from under the table to show off the pants.

"Obviously." Reggie was distracted by Sophia's leg. She pulled herself back to Sophia's original question. "As for myself, I'm rather boring I think. I'd classify myself as a run-of-the mill dog. Not a small yappy one, but standard issue, big, protective, loyal."

"A bit slobbery, lots of tail wags, and kisses everything in sight?" Sophia took another sip of coffee but kept eye contact over the cup.

Reggie could feel her face heating but didn't break eye contact. "I suppose it depends on what's in sight."

"Something to file away for later. I like to think of myself as a giraffe. I tell myself I'm unique, reaching for the highest branch, and not afraid to kick the king of beasts in the balls when warranted."

Lucky for Reggie she hadn't taken another sip of coffee. She would have spit it across the table. "You shouldn't have encouraged me to get coffee, you nearly made me ruin that beautiful suit. I don't think I would have ever considered giraffe, but I like your description. And think what Lily could do dressing that long neck. It would be impossible to look you up and down, your neck alone would take fifteen minutes, but my, what a view."

"See, I knew it was worth taking a chance on you. A big handsome woman like you stuck in traffic, needing a rescue, and my lucky day, you're charming too." Sophia moved her cup back and forth from one hand to the other across the table.

"Well, I would be blind and dumb if I didn't attempt to charm a woman as beautiful as you." Reggie leaned forward and put her elbows on the table.

Where was all this forwardness coming from?

"And to think I was dreading this day." Sophia laughed.

Reggie was captivated by the sound of her laughter and the sight of her exposed neck as she tossed her head back.

"Thank you for making the morning something so much greater than what I was expecting."

"I wasn't looking forward to my morning either." Reggie looked at her watch. "Dammit."

Sophia tapped her phone, glanced at the home screen, and began packing her things. "I need to get going too." She hesitated, then held out her hand. "Give me your phone."

Reggie started to ask why, but Sophia put her hand on her hip and pushed her hand forward a little more insistently. Reggie unlocked her phone and handed it over. Sophia scrolled and typed quickly.

"Now you have my number. Just in case you ever feel like doing this again."

She looked shy when she handed the phone back to Reggie.

"What happens if we walk out that door and I turn into a gorgon? Or you find out I rob banks for a living? Or I don't return my library books on time?" Reggie stood up and grabbed her coat.

"You said you would describe yourself as a loyal, protective, big dog. Man's best friend is punctual with borrowed literature."

"Maybe I'm a hellhound then. How do you know?" Reggie followed Sophia out the door.

Once outside, Sophia turned and kissed her cheek. "I don't, Reggie. I don't really know anything about you. But what I do know, I like and I'd like to know more. That's why my number is in your phone. If you feel the same way, give me a call. Don't overthink it, Hellhound. I've gotta run, I'm going to be late."

Reggie looked at her watch again. "Dammit, me too. Thank you for coffee, Sophia Giraffe. I will call you. I'd like to know more too." She set off down the street toward the address she'd been given.

"I guess we're not rid of each other yet." Sophia caught up to her.

They walked in silence another block. When they arrived at the address Reggie was looking for, she and Sophia both pointed awkwardly toward the building.

"This is me."

"I'm headed in here."

Reggie looked back and forth between the building and Sophia. What were the odds? It was a weird coincidence, but it was a large building. Surely there were plenty of meetings starting inside.

She held the door and followed Sophia inside. They both made their way to the elevator and joined a large group heading up. The fifth floor button was already pushed so Reggie didn't have to request it. Sophia didn't ask for a floor either.

When the elevator doors opened on the fifth floor, Sophia exited ahead of Reggie.

"At the risk of stating the obvious, it's starting to appear we're headed to the same meeting." Reggie moved alongside Sophia again.

"Unless you're a hellhound after all and are only here to rob us all." Sophia gently elbowed her.

"Busted."

They were laughing as they pushed through the double doors into a small auditorium filled with about fifty people. To their right was a folding table manned by a no-nonsense looking Latinx man in a crisp suit and fantastic neon green glasses and a White woman in a Wonder Woman T-shirt and jeans who looked like she wished she had a different job.

"Check in over here, please." He waved them forward.

Reggie approached green glasses who meticulously straightened his pile of papers before acknowledging her. She heard Wonder Woman ask for Sophia's name, and Reggie nearly bolted for the door when she heard her reply, "Sophia Lamont."

It was not possible that she'd spent one of the most enjoyable thirty minutes with the most talked about, up-and-coming politician in the state. One who was no doubt looking to make a name for herself. Reggie knew all too well where that kind of ambition led. What the fuck was wrong with the universe?

"Name, please?" Green glasses was done shuffling papers.

"Reggie Northrup." The words felt dry coming out of her mouth.

Green glasses shuffled more papers and furrowed his brow. "Regina Northrup?"

"That's me." Reggie choked on the words.

Sophia snapped around and stared at her. The look on her face mirrored Reggie's internal turmoil.

Maybe I turned into a gorgon after all. Despite her own horror at actually enjoying the company of a politician, the thought that she caused Sophia such revulsion made Reggie sad. They admitted they didn't know each other. How could she have such a strong opinion? Reggie figured she knew the answer, he was serving time on cell block D, but she didn't want to believe it. How long would she have to continue paying for the sins of her father?

Sophia disappeared into the auditorium without another word. Reggie took the name tag green glasses handed her, borrowed a pen to scribble out "Regina" and replace it with "Reggie," and looked for a seat. She tried, unsuccessfully, to ignore the looks she was getting. Sophia didn't seem to be the only one less than overjoyed at her scoring an invite. What had the brass been thinking sending her here? What had the governor been thinking when she'd accepted?

She took a seat far away from anyone else. She'd developed a top-notch "keep away" posture honed from years of work at the state prison, and she turned it up to eleven. She was confident she'd be left alone, until someone took the seat next to her.

"Reggie, long time. I didn't expect to see a friend in this collection of strange bedfellows. You're a welcome sight."

Reggie closed her eyes and took a deep breath. She willed the woman to be gone when she opened them. She was not.

"Tammy Potts. I don't think our relationship can be described as friendly. What're you doing here?"

"Jesus, no one but my mother and the court calls me that. I'm on the outside now, Reggie. I always treated you with the respect you deserved while I was in your custody. Please, I ask that you return the favor when you're in my domain."

Reggie barely refrained from rolling her eyes. Tammy Potts was known to nearly everyone as the Zookeeper, one half of the most notorious drug-dealing duo in the city. She'd recently been Reggie's guest at the prison, but she was out now and had, if the rumors were true, rejoined her partner, Parrot Master, at the helm of their criminal enterprises. Although if other rumors were to be believed, while incarcerated she'd simply turned her attention to other branches of their business, namely the kind that ran drugs through the prison.

"Fine. Zoo, why are you here?"

"Special invitation from the governor. Who in this state has a better understanding of the impact of drugs on our community than me? And since everyone in this room hates me and I'm not overly fond of most of them either, you and I are going to have to stick close. The enemy of my enemy, and all that. Remember that tidbit of wisdom and consider me a friend."

Reggie shook her head. She'd be better off with no friends. She saw Sophia across the room. They locked eyes for a moment before Sophia quickly looked away. Reggie thought back to the meeting with the prison brass when they offered her this opportunity and she'd tried to turn it down. She'd only been in this damn conference room ten minutes and her worst fears had materialized. There was the trifecta of politics, gamesmanship, and too much riding on reputations alone. She had to find a way to salvage things or it was going to be a long few months. She wasn't sure how things could get worse.

CHAPTER THREE

R epresentative Lamont, you'll be joining the 'Policy In Action' group."

Bert, and his shockingly green glasses, directed her down the hall to a conference room jauntily labeled with the name of her group. She didn't comment on the fact that the policies currently in action were the ones they were supposed to be working to improve. The group should be called "Improving policies in action" or "Policies in action have failed so you asked us to figure out new ones, which no one else has been able to do for years."

She sat heavily in the remarkably comfortable conference chair. It was a significant improvement over the auditorium seat she'd spent the past three hours squirming in. Maybe her mood would perk up now that there would be adequate blood flow to her ass.

No sooner had she gotten settled than Reggie Northrup walked in followed by the Zookeeper. So much for an upward mood swing. Sophia didn't need a name tag or an introduction to know the Zookeeper. She and Parrot Master were infamous in the city, but Sophia's dislike was personal. A lifetime ago, Davey had gotten pulled into their orbit and had come out the other side with a criminal record.

Reggie waved as she sat down, but Sophia didn't have time to sort out that complicated situation right now. She went in search of Bert. He was still directing traffic in the auditorium.

"Why is the Zookeeper here?"

"Excuse me? The what?"

Bert's glasses and confusion made him look like a dazed grasshopper.

"The Zookeeper. She's a woman also assigned to Policy in Action and she walked into the conference room with Reggie Northrup two minutes ago." Sophia shoved her hands in her pockets to hide her twisting her fingers in knots.

"Oh. That's Tammy Potts. The governor specifically requested she be included. She was difficult to track down seeing as she just got out of *prison*."

Bert whispered the last word like it would escape and stampede around the room crushing everyone to death if he said it too loudly.

Sophia dug her knuckles into her temples and squeezed her eyes shut a moment. "Thanks, Bert. You've been really helpful."

Bert stopped her with his hand on her arm before she turned back to the conference room. "What did she do? To end up in prison, I mean?"

There was a mix of fear and curiosity in his eyes. Why did he think it was any of his business?

"I'm sure she'd be happy to tell you if she's comfortable. We have another break before the end of the day, right? You can probably catch her then."

Sophia returned to the conference room without waiting for his reply. She took her seat and pulled out her phone to text Lily.

Sophia: *The Zookeeper's here.*

Lily: *WHAT?!? Why???*

Sophia: *Don't know. Gov requested her. Went to make a stink about it but realized that's what people do to Davey.*

Lily: *But she's a drug dealer.*

Sophia: *That's what everyone said about Davey.*

The three bubbles indicating typing flashed for a long time. Sophia looked around the room and saw Reggie looking at her. She knew why she'd been warned to stay away from Tammy Potts, and she'd gotten her ass handed to her on that one. She was going to have to talk to Rodrigo about his less than thorough research on the Zookeeper. She should have known Tammy Potts and the Zookeeper were one and the same before she walked in the door. Now she was questioning what he'd told her about the Northrup family and what he may have left out. Maybe she should do her own research on Reggie's reputation. She smiled and was thrilled when Reggie returned it.

Her phone pinged.

Lily: *Sounds like we need to debrief in person. Usual place. Usual time. Love you.*

Sophia slid her phone back in her pocket. Her gut was unsettled at her reaction to the Zookeeper. They were going to be working together on this design team so she needed to set the personal aside. And more than that, as a lawmaker, she couldn't afford to get caught up in the assumptions and stereotypes the rest of the world settled on. She could feel the burn of her mother's disapproving frown as if she was pocket-sized and jumping up and down on her shoulder.

The rest of the room filled in until nearly all the chairs were filled around the table. Bert was the last to enter, and he closed the door behind him. Sophia looked at her fellow group members. She was the only Black woman, but she wasn't staring at a sea of White faces, which was a welcome change from nearly all her experiences in conference rooms like this.

It was hard to drag her eyes from Reggie because despite the warning, she was hot as sin. Sophia had a soft spot, or a hot spot, for women with short hair, hard bodies, and who looked like they knew where the emergency exits were and could get you to them if shit hit the fan. Reggie was checking all her boxes, and after coffee this morning she was funny and charming to top it off. If only she didn't have a political electric fence ten feet high around her.

Sophia continued her evaluation so as not to be caught staring at Reggie. She knew the Zookeeper so she skipped her. A young White woman was seated to the Zookeeper's right. She was whispering something to the Zookeeper and the two of them laughed. Sophia was surprised to see genuine affection between them. They looked like they came from different worlds. She immediately chastised herself. What was up with the snap judgements?

The woman's name tag said "Frankie." Sophia thought she remembered her introduction indicating she was a college student. She didn't have a chance to complete her assessment of her group mates before Bert called them to order.

"Okay, friends. Let's get started. We're Policy in Action. The PAC pack. The other two groups are addressing prevention and treatment. Before you ask, yes, policy will most certainly be relevant to those two areas. Whereas the other two groups are looking at concrete, actionable goals, we're looking big picture. We're looking to change a system. This is the group for big thinkers. If you're not in the right place…" Bert pointed to the door.

No one got up. For the first time since Sophia'd been blindsided by Reggie's identity, she felt the familiar thrill she always got when tackling a big, thorny issue, followed closely by the anxiety that somehow she might not measure up. As always, she did her best to squash it. She'd been picked for this. She took a deep breath, ready to get to work.

As she exited the conference room at the end of day one, Sophia wasn't sure what to make of the PAC pack except that Bert was an exhaustingly cheerful leader and there was a definite dividing line in the group on where they thought the future of drug policy was headed. One half of the group seemed interested in tweaking or modifying current policies and making incremental changes. The other half wanted to burn everything to the ground and start over, including Reggie, which for no good reason at all disappointed her more than it should. Then there was Gerald, a rather odd, late middle-age White man who hadn't updated his ideas of drug education since the nineteen eighties.

She hurried to the hole-in-the-wall taco shop she and Lily had been frequenting for years. It was where they went when they wanted to talk privately, away from Lily's extended family who owned and operated a restaurant Sophia felt like she'd grown up in.

Lily was waiting when she arrived. She'd already ordered and picked up their food from the counter.

"I need to hear everything about your day, but before we get started, did you tell Valencia Blackstone about my shop?" Lily gracefully wiped pico de gallo from her fingers.

"I did. She asked me about something I was wearing at work. What kind of friend would I be if I played coy with that information? Did she check out your goods?" Sophia wiggled her eyebrows.

Lily looked serious. "She must have because she called and asked if I would be willing to tailor any items myself. Then she bought almost everything I have available and asked if I'd design two custom pieces for events she has coming up."

"Is that a bad thing?" Sophia put her food down and took Lily's hand.

Lily shook her head. She started to say something, but it sounded like the words caught in her throat. She shook her hands out and took a deep breath. "You know how long I've been working to get this business off the ground. Most days it seems like it will never happen. But now, Valencia Blackstone bought my clothes. She bought *all* my clothes. Do you know what that means?"

Sophia pulled Lily into a crushing hug. "Yes, sweetie. I know exactly what it means. Your dreams are coming true and I couldn't be prouder."

Lily pushed Sophia away with a grin. "If this actually happens, and I'm not counting any chickens, I might finally have the money for the brick-and-mortar shop I've always wanted. I refuse to let anyone but you be my first customer. But enough about me, goodness, I talk too much. The Zookeeper?"

Sophia picked up her tacos and rolled her eyes. "I should probably start at the beginning. It's been one hell of a day."

She told Lily about her morning coffee flirt with Smoke Show Reggie before Reggie morphed into Ms. Bad Reputation. Then came the Zookeeper and her unease at how she'd reacted to her presence.

"Before you go on, I want to make sure I'm following. In the morning you meet the woman of your dreams, the girl daddy to your babies, the one to fill the other rocker on the porch in your retirement—"

"I don't believe I said any of that." Sophia waved her finger toward Lily while she took a sip of her soda.

"It was implied. So then, after your heart was broken by Bad Boy's mysterious past, you ran into one half of the duo that ruined

Davey's life? As an aside, can we talk about the fact that the most notorious drug dealer in the state is named Tammy? What do you think Parrot Master's name is? Norbert?"

Sophia shook her head and continued to eat.

"Fine, we can circle back to that one. It's worth pondering at a later date. My friend, you've had yourself a day. I sure hope the rest of your story includes leprechauns shitting gold nuggets to salvage some of this."

Sophia set her food down again and rubbed her temples. "More like passionate disagreement and intense opinions. The last part of the day, we were asked to think about current policies related to substance use and throw out new ideas to start from scratch or tweak what's already in place. Our leader, Bert, said all those new ideas would be our foundation as we move forward. Needless to say, as a group we don't all see eye to eye on the direction policy reform should move."

"Throw everything out and start from scratch. What's in place now clearly isn't working." Lily pushed her plate away and tossed her napkin on top of the basket.

Sophia frowned. "I don't understand how that's such a popular stance."

Lily looked surprised. "Even with Davey's experience? Okay. Where did your Reggie fall on the issue?"

"She's not *my* Reggie. She wants to tear it all down. Which surprised me because she's a corrections officer. The Zookeeper was team demolition, too. This young, smart, thoughtful kid named Frankie joined my side. It got heated. Bert, the facilitator, had to earn his money keeping us in order."

"Sounds exciting. Will they let me come and watch the next meeting? My sewing machine talks back sometimes, but it's usually pretty compliant. I don't get much excitement during the day."

Sophia reflected on the past twelve hours. Had it been exciting? She wasn't sure she'd classify it that way, but it had made her think, which was stimulating. And despite what she now knew about her, she couldn't stop thinking about Reggie and their coffee and flirtation earlier.

"I know that look." Lily separated their trash from the restaurant's flatware and dishes, a habit she'd picked up waiting tables at her family's restaurant. "This has that big brain of yours firing and the politician in you working. Policy making is in your blood so if there is a big bold change to be made, you'll figure out how to do it. But if that's not the right course of action, you'll scale back to what can be done, because you have the wisdom to sort out the difference."

"Oh, is that right? I'm glad you have that much confidence in me. Someone should." Sophia stood and linked arms with Lily.

"I have all the confidence in you. Don't get in your own way, trust your gut. You'll be fine."

They walked together, arm in arm, toward their houses, which were one street apart. The design team had already proven to be more rewarding than she expected, but also more of a challenge. Her official homework was to research an existing or new policy and bring that research to the next meeting to present. Her unofficial homework was to leave her personal feelings, those deeply held and newly emerging, outside the next time she stepped in the conference room. But how was she supposed to do that when everything political was so damn personal?

CHAPTER FOUR

Reggie groaned when the alert dinged on her phone. She had another design team meeting after work and hadn't done her homework. She'd been called to work double shifts to cover sick coworkers and had fallen asleep as soon as she'd gotten home. She wasn't going to make a good impression showing up unprepared tonight.

When she felt guilty for not devoting her full effort to the design team she only sort-of agreed to join, Sophia's face floated into her thoughts. If only they could rewind to the morning of their coffee date and…and what? She didn't want to go back and find out three minutes in that Sophia was a politician. Or have Sophia discover she was the daughter of Bartholomew Northrup. It was a bit of a gut punch, however, when the truth came out all around, and the magic of the morning was shattered by the reality of who they were in the real world.

"What's with the sour face? Toilets backing up again?"

Reggie smiled as her best friend approached. "If they were, you'd know because I'd be handing you a plunger."

"You know, Reg, what the world misses about you is your generous spirit. It's hidden behind your charming personality."

Reggie shrugged. "That's me, looking out for you. You know what they say about idle hands."

Ava raised her eyebrows. "Please tell me what they say about idle hands?"

"They're waiting for a toilet to plunge."

Ava leaned against the wall and bit her lip. Her body was shaking. Reggie could tell she was trying, and mostly failing, to stop herself from laughing.

"Jesus, Reg, there are so many places I could take that. You teed it up beautifully for me, but you also looked like you were in a shitty mood when I walked over, so I'll give you a break. What's got you tied up? Perhaps your lady friend?"

"She's not my lady friend. You remember what I told you she does for a living?" Reggie leaned her back against the wall and crossed her arms.

"She's a politician, so what? It's not like she's in charge of Satan's twitter feed or the one who designed one-ply toilet paper."

Reggie pushed off the wall and started walking down the hall. "How many politicians are we providing accommodations for right now?"

Ava caught up and pulled Reggie to a stop. "You mean are we hosting one specific politician, right? We also host murderers and other criminals, you know."

"That's my point. I don't want to socialize with them either. And not for nothing, there's some overlap between the two groups."

Ava held up her hands. "Whoa. Your lady friend really got all your hot buttons firing. What's the real issue? The fact that the last politician you cared about is locked up in our prison or the fact that as soon as your friend found out your last name she ran for the safer side of the street?"

Reggie balled her fists. "Who says I can't be pissed about both? Now can we talk about something else, please? I'm grumpy enough without adding this on top."

"Hey, you've got that design team thing tonight, right? Is that why you're..." Ava waved her hand in a slow circle in front of Reggie.

Reggie's shoulder's slumped and she nodded. "I was supposed to do some research on a current drug policy or a new one I'd like to propose and bring it to the group. I've been working so much I haven't done anything."

Ava lightly slapped Reggie's shoulder with the back of her hand. "Tell them about your work here. You don't need to do research for that."

Reggie would have laughed, but she could see Ava was serious. The group already knew she was a corrections officer. She wasn't going to stand up and bullshit her way through like a kid giving a report on a book she'd never read.

"Don't blow me off. The war on drugs. Mandatory minimums. How many of our guests here are with us as a result of current drug policies? Has their incarceration slowed the drug crisis on the outside? Have they been able to find and maintain sobriety within our walls? How many come back to stay with us again?"

Ava had a good point. When Reggie felt her cynicism and fatigue with the job creep in, it was almost always those arguments that niggled their way to the front of her thoughts. Those were the arguments that weighed on her and were making it harder to get up and punch in every morning.

"Thank you. I'd convinced myself I had to write a thesis on a new drug enforcement model or something. Why didn't they send you to this instead of me?"

Reggie had wondered that from the moment her superiors had asked her to take part. Ava, or almost anyone else, would have been much better received by the other members of the design team and were as knowledgeable, if not more so, as she was.

Ava patted her on the shoulder. "If you want to write new, good laws, who better to help than the daughter of a crooked politician?"

Later, on her way to the design team meeting, Reggie thought over what Ava had said. A dirty politician's clean kid probably would be good at making new laws, but in her experience, once you had the stain of a father's sins, redemption wasn't possible in the eyes of people who always had to consider reputation. Sophia's reaction to her last name was proof of that.

She took a seat at the conference table and was immediately distracted by Bert's glasses. They were neon pink today and looked bright enough to produce a sunburn.

"Bert's glasses might become the most interesting part of this experience."

Reggie hadn't noticed Frankie take the seat next to her. Seeing Frankie had been a bright spot at the last design team meeting. Frankie was a good kid. Reggie had gotten to know her when she'd come to visit her mom in prison every week for a couple of years.

"Depending on how today goes, it might be my only reason to come back."

"Nah, I know you better than that, Reggie. You'll stick it out even without eyeglasses catnip cause it's the right thing to do." Frankie bumped shoulders with Reggie.

"How's your mom, kid?"

Frankie's expression turned serious. "It's hard for her. Being locked up, she had to start over when she got out. That included all the work she'd done to get clean before. There are good people at Star Recovery though. My friend Kit's been working with her and she's doing well. It's not fair what happened to her."

Reggie shook her head. Frankie's mom was one of those who'd broken Reggie's heart every day that she'd been locked up. Prison wasn't the place for her. Society wasn't better off because she was behind bars no matter what the law said.

"I'm sure she's proud of you, being in college and all."

Frankie looked at her hands. "Yeah, she is."

The rest of the group filed in as they talked. Reggie saw Sophia enter the room and sit across from her. She smiled a hello. Either Sophia didn't see it or wasn't in a friendly mood.

"Do you know her?" Frankie extended her chin in Sophia's direction.

"No, not really. Only had a few conversations with her, why?"

Reggie was still watching Sophia talking easily with the man next to her. It would be easier to remember she was a dirty, rotten-to-the core politician if she weren't so distractingly beautiful and her lips weren't so full. What was wrong with her?

"I followed her campaign and I had an assignment about local government in one of my classes so I did some research on her. She seems pretty awesome." Frankie was threading her fingers together and not looking at Reggie.

"So talk to her. We're all equals in this room."

Frankie nodded. She looked like she was giving herself an internal pep talk. "I will. Thanks, Reggie. I'll do that."

Bert stood and his glasses drew all eyes forward. "Welcome back, everyone. Thanks for rejoining the PAC pack. We threw a lot of information at you last time, but now we're here to get to work. I hope everyone came prepared."

Bert looked around the room. Reggie sent a silent thank you to Ava for saving her ass. She saw at least one fellow PAC member squirming in their seat. Apparently, she wasn't the only one who'd had a busy week.

"Before we get to the juicy bits of our meeting tonight, I want to give you an overview of the process we're going to be using the next few weeks and for the design team overall." Bert shuffled through a stack of papers on the table in front of him, pulled one out, and gave it a theatrical wave.

"Today we will be laying the foundation for our work together. Each of you holds a brick, that we may, as a group, choose to add to our foundation. You will each have a chance to present shortly. They are our launching points so consider the ideas presented today carefully. We'll vote at the end on which to carry forward with us. Any questions so far?" Bert paused and looked around the room.

All the members of the team were looking around quizzically at each other, but no one spoke up.

"Fantastic. I'll move on. Over the course of the next weeks and months, we'll all work together to write a document containing a cohesive set of policy recommendations. The treatment and prevention teams will be following parallel paths to ours. At the end of our time together our recommendations will be combined with those of the other two teams. That combined document is what will be delivered to the governor."

"And then what? Does she have to follow our recommendations?"

Reggie wasn't sure which of the two women behind her had asked the question, but it was a question that had been on her mind as well.

Bert pushed his glasses up his nose and took a long moment before answering. He looked like he was choosing his words carefully. "The short answer is no. She doesn't have to do anything at all with the document presented to her. These are recommendations only. The more accurate answer is she asked you all to participate in this design team because she cares deeply about this issue and recognizes changes are needed in all the areas we will be exploring. Short of executive action, she cannot enact change unilaterally, but I believe if we give her solid recommendations, she has the will to work with the legislature to change the laws."

A little hum of excitement flickered in Reggie's chest and left goose bumps on her shoulders and up her neck. When was the last time she felt enthused about anything?

Bert straightened his papers again. "Reggie, why don't we start with you?"

Reggie started when she heard her name. Her stomach tensed. She replayed the bullet points she wanted to highlight. She could talk all day about her work and her frustrations with the job. She looked at Sophia, which annoyed her. Sophia was writing in a small notebook and didn't look up as Reggie started talking. That frustrated Reggie too, although it shouldn't have.

"I'm Reggie Northrup for those who don't remember. I'm a corrections officer. I work in the women's combined jail and prison unit."

Gerald, an older White guy, interrupted her. "Do you do youth tours? You know, those Scared Straight things?"

She bit back the retort about prison not being an amusement park. "No, tours are usually only for state regulators or legislators, medical personnel, things like that. People on official business in the interest of the facility, the staff, and the inmates."

"I think that's something we, as a group, should consider." Gerald looked around the room, making sure to look at everyone intently. "If kids knew what prison was like, they'd stay away from drugs."

Frankie and the Zookeeper laughed. Gerald looked offended.

"My fine fellow. Your premise is flawed as your assumption rests on the fact that children are unfamiliar with the realities of incarceration. In this, I fear that you are sadly mistaken." The Zookeeper rapped her knuckles on the table as if that settled the issue.

Gerald looked like he wanted to rebut the argument, but Bert indicated Reggie should continue.

"Right, so I see a lot of women come through for drug crimes, or with active substance use, or both. Instead of rehabilitation and return to society, I see discriminatory sentencing, exacerbation of substance use, and a war on drugs with plenty of losers but no hope of a winner."

Sophia put her pen down and closed her notebook. "So what's the solution, Reggie?"

Reggie folded her hands in front of her on the table and looked at Sophia. "I don't know, but the current system sucks. We can't keep throwing people in jail for having drugs on their person, or being high, or violating probation by drinking."

Sophia didn't break eye contact. "So legalize everything and make it a free-for-all? That would be anarchy."

Reggie shook her head slowly. "I never said that. But if you decriminalized and focused on treatment for those who wanted it, wouldn't everyone be better off?"

"What about the people who are already in prison? Do you let them walk out the door? Who's going to pay for treatment for everyone who wants it? And how are you going to convince my nana that buying heroin, cocaine, and crack shouldn't be against the law?" Sophia was popping the top off her pen and jamming it back on as she talked.

"Because addiction isn't a crime, it's a disease." Frankie's voice was quiet, but there was steel in her spine when she spoke.

Sophia's face softened. "I didn't get the impression last week you wanted to tear everything down, Frankie."

"I don't. But Reggie's right, jail isn't the right place for someone trying to get clean."

Reggie patted Frankie on the back. She met Sophia's gaze again. "If I had all the answers, I guess I wouldn't need the rest of you. I'm tossing my brick on the pile. There's a multimillion-dollar industry selling legal marijuana now. How many Black and Brown Americans will never have access to any of that money because of a criminal record for engaging in exactly the same enterprise? Except now young White men have taken it corporate and are raking in the cash."

Reggie saw rage flash through Sophia's eyes. "Don't lecture me about the plight of young Black people."

She held up her hands. "Sophia, I'm sorry. I wasn't trying to lecture. I'm telling you what I see on a daily basis."

Sophia waved her off. "The problem, Reggie, and I know you're not the only one who favors a complete tear down of current policy, is policy change needs legislation to have lasting impact and legislation requires consensus. The American public is not going to be on board with a full tear down. My nana and thousands like her in this state vote."

"Surely though, leaders lead, wouldn't you agree? A skilled and trusted leader can gain the confidence of her followers and convince them of a great many things." The Zookeeper leaned back in her chair and knit her hands behind her head.

"But there are some things that shouldn't be legal and some crimes that should still be punishable with prison sentences." Frankie was still sitting stiffly in her chair. "I don't care how much I admired a leader, I wouldn't want them trying to convince me, for example, Zoo, that you should have been allowed to start selling to me as a kid without punishment."

The Zookeeper put her hand on Frankie's shoulder. "I never would have. Parrot either."

"*You* wouldn't have. But not everyone in your business has the same moral compass. Selling to kids should be illegal. Can we all agree on that?"

There were nods all around the table.

"But how do you define a drug dealer?" Reggie had started to raise her hand. One look at Bert reminded her she wasn't in class.

The Zookeeper pointed at her and nodded. "A very astute question from my officer friend. There is no easy definition I think we would discover if we were to bandy this one about. Someone who sells drugs is too simplistic. What quantity? To whom? For what purpose?"

Bert stood and formed his hands into a T. "Excellent discussion. I want to make sure we have time for everyone to present, so let's table this for now. We have a lively group so I don't think this will be the last of our spirited discussions."

They finished the presentations before the dinner break. There weren't any more fireworks although Reggie could see the battle lines being drawn. She wished she and Sophia didn't disagree quite so strongly. It would be nice to have a point of connection instead of contention. She'd love an excuse to revisit their moments together over coffee instead of constantly being faced with the dividing lines between them.

CHAPTER FIVE

S ophia looked at her watch and stifled a yawn. How could it possibly be two a.m.? She'd been listening to public testimony on a proposed change in state law that would allow the possibility of a supervised opioid injection facility that, as proposed, would include medical care on site in case of opioid overdose and easy access to treatment referrals.

The change in the law and the injection facility had almost no chance of coming to pass, but that didn't mean Sophia and the rest of the members of her committee didn't need to listen to public comment. And man, were there comments.

The testimony was already in its twelfth hour and it looked like there were hours to go before they slept. Sophia admired the dedication of those still here, waiting their turn to voice their thoughts and get their opinion on the record. Democracy and civic engagement wasn't for the faint of heart, but to her mind it was the greatest form of self-expression. Agree or disagree with the arguments before her, she silently gave each member of the public a standing ovation for showing up and being heard. That said, she'd give an actual standing ovation if whoever was on deck brought her a cup of coffee and a donut before they took their turn at the microphone.

No luck with the liquid wake-up, but as the next person sat at the table and began their testimony, this one vehemently opposed to the idea of "promoting drug use" with a sanctioned injection site,

Valencia slid a note to Sophia. Maybe it was the late hour, or the extremity of the testimony, or the fact that she was having a moment of imposter syndrome and didn't think she should be in charge of lawmaking, but Sophia had a hard time fighting off a fit of giggles at Valencia's covert note-passing. It felt juvenile and collegial and more than a little silly.

Once Sophia was sure she wasn't going to inappropriately explode in a fit of laughter, she read the note.

Once this is done, if the sun hasn't risen, I'm going straight to Lenny's. Care to join me?

Sophia's mouth started watering thinking about the food truck that was well known in the city. Late into the night, Lenny, or one of his employees, would park the truck downtown and serve food to patrons stumbling from the bars after last call, individuals finding themselves out well after dark for business or pleasure, and on many occasions the bedraggled lawmakers at the capitol after a marathon public session like this evening.

YES!!

Sophia slid the note back to Valencia and refocused on the testimony. She wished her design team group mates were here. On balance, the testimony had largely been against the injection site. As she'd tried to point out, sweeping change needed legislation behind it to eliminate antiquated laws, free up funding that wasn't allocated to innovative programs, and in some cases legalize activities that were previously outlawed, and that required, for better or worse, public buy-in. A scorched-earth, start-from-scratch approach worked fine on paper, but this was the real world. Her world.

As soon as the testimony was complete at close to four a.m., Sophia darted to her office to grab her belongings.

Valencia, looking bleary, leaned against the wall outside her office door. "I've never seen a sign with Lenny's hours, but I'm about to find out how late he keeps that truck open. You still with me?"

Sophia shoved her purse on her shoulder and yawned. "I ran out of snacks six hours ago, and my heels are significantly lower than yours. I will race you to the front of the line and I will win.

If Lenny has already closed up, I'll borrow his truck and cook us something myself. My kitchen skills are about three out of ten."

"That's a perfect ten by pre-dawn standards. Less talking, more walking. Your fancy low heels aren't going to do you any good if you talk us both into starvation." Valencia bent down, dragged her purse by the handle along the floor, and finally swung it up on her shoulder.

The cool night air filled Sophia's lungs with life. Aside from a walk at lunch the day before, she'd been inside the capitol for twenty hours.

"What did you think of the testimony today?" Valencia paused at a street corner and checked for cars on the quiet street.

Sophia waited for the light to change and took a few extra steps to cross at the crosswalk. "It was good to see so many people show up to voice their opinions. I know a few people on my design team would have been disheartened to hear so many against the injection site."

"But not you?"

"I didn't say that, but how much would a place like a supervised injection site be helping anyone if it was constantly being protested or the subject of endless scrutiny, either from the media or public or political oversight? Would anyone be comfortable enough to use it?" Sophia put her hands in her pockets against the chill of the early morning and picked up the pace.

"So what's the solution? My sister-in-law's embedded as a social worker with the police department, and she knows firsthand that more needs to be done to help folks with the disease of addiction."

"I'm not sure yet. Care to talk it through with me and see if we come up with anything interesting?" Sophia searched Valencia's face for sincere interest or opportunistic excitement.

"Isn't that what you're doing with the design team?" Valencia looked guarded.

"We're not tasked with thinking legislatively. No idea is too big or small for the design team, but we saw firsthand tonight what happens when a proposal gets too far ahead of public opinion." Sophia shrugged.

"I'm game. I told you early on I wanted to work with you on something important to both of us." Valencia stopped in front of Lenny's truck and clapped her hands.

"Lenny, savior of hungry politicians, prince among men. Odes should be written to your greasy splendid offerings." Sophia chef kissed toward Lenny's truck, lit up and open for business.

She collected her hot dog and fries from the young guy manning Lenny's truck and turned to join Valencia for their curbside picnic when she ran straight into a uniformed, bemused Reggie.

"What are you doing here? You said you don't come downtown. You have my ketchup on your shirt." Sophia jabbed a finger at the red blob on Reggie's uniform shirt.

"Am I not allowed downtown?" Reggie reached around Sophia and pulled a napkin from the dispenser. She wiped the ketchup from her shirt. "Why are you at Lenny's at the butt-crack of dawn?"

Sophia stared at Reggie's chest as she finished dealing with the mess. "Work thing ended a little while ago. We were hungry. Why are you here?"

Reggie definitely caught her staring. That probably wasn't good, right?

"Me too."

"What?"

"Work thing. And hungry thing. Lenny's is worth the extra time to get downtown. Plus, it's about the only thing open that's worth the effort." Reggie hooked her thumbs in her belt loops and rocked back on her heels.

Sophia did *not* look at her crotch. Or, she didn't look as soon as she realized she *had* been looking, which was almost the same thing.

"I hope you don't mind the intrusion. As entertaining as the ketchup cleanup was, and at this hour nearly anything passes as entertainment, it seemed time to introduce myself. I'm Valencia Blackstone." Valencia held out her hand while perfectly balancing her food in the other.

Reggie took her offered hand. "Reggie Northrup. Were you at the same work thing?"

Sophia heard the disgust as the words came out of Reggie's mouth. What did she find so distasteful?

"Not a fan of politics? Or politicians? Democracy?" Valencia smiled at the last item.

Reggie laughed. "Oh, democracy's fine. The rest I could do without. No offense, ladies."

Sophia was offended. Politicians as an abstract concept were easy to make fun of, stereotype, and write off, but they were also the ones who ran governments and made laws. The good ones, the dedicated public servants who were committed to serving their country and their constituents for the betterment of all were the heroes of her childhood.

"Hard to have democracy without elected officials. It's sort of the point of all the voting, and a bit of advice you didn't ask for, perhaps you should reconsider when it comes to Sophia here. I'm a recent friend and colleague, but I think you will find her unimpeachable, even under the most exacting standards." Valencia raised an eyebrow and gave Reggie a pointed look.

Reggie rocked from foot to foot. "I'll remember that. Thank you. What was your work thing about? Or do you need to get home? It's late."

Despite herself, Sophia wanted to tell Reggie about the more than twelve hours of testimony. She told herself it was because they were both on the design team and it would be interesting to hear her perspective since their views differed so drastically. Why that had to happen at four a.m. under the stars wasn't something she had any interest in exploring.

"I called for a ride home. Sophia, can I drop you somewhere?" Valencia held up her phone.

Sophia looked at Reggie, though she couldn't fathom why.

"I'm parked around the corner if you don't have a car nearby. I don't mind driving you home."

Sophia handed Reggie her hot dog and lowered herself to the curb as gracefully as she could in the tight pencil skirt and matching top and jacket. She looked up at Valencia as Reggie took a seat next to her. "I'll be okay getting home, thank you. See you in a few hours for another round."

Valencia waved as a black town car pulled up. The well-dressed driver got out to open the door for her.

"There aren't two Valencia Blackstones in this city, right?" Reggie watched the car drive away.

Sophia shrugged as she took a bite of her food. "There might be, but she's the one you're thinking of."

Reggie stared after the receding car. "She's more human than I expected a gazillionaire to be, chauffer aside. So what was so titillating at the statehouse that you, regal giraffe of the congress, stayed until dawn?"

Sophia smiled around a mouthful of French fries and put her hand on Reggie's knee. "You remembered."

Reggie nodded and swiped a French fry.

Maybe it was the hour or her exhaustion, but she felt her guard lowering. She wasn't worried about Reggie's bad reputation or her political fortunes. Coffee and laughter and flirting were the memories pulled to the surface when she looked at Reggie tonight. Maybe it was dangerous to ignore, even for a moment, the reality of their situation, but until the sun crested the horizon, she was going to talk to Reggie, maybe flirt a little, and enjoy a damn spectacular view. She ignored the nagging voices of her parents clamoring for her attention, telling her to walk away, and took in every detail of Reggie's sinfully handsome face.

"I was listening to community testimony in front of my committee. It was related to a supervised injection facility."

Reggie wiped her fingers on a napkin and nodded. "Frankie mentioned that after the last meeting. I'm surprised no one proposed that for our team."

Sophia took the napkin from Reggie and moved to the trash can to throw away the garbage. Her fingers tingled where their hands connected. "Who says someone wouldn't have if you and I hadn't taken up so much time arguing with each other."

Reggie held her hands out. "Whoa, I want full credit. I also dragged the Zookeeper and Frankie down with me."

"Troublemaker and corrupting young minds. You should be ashamed." Sophia took her seat on the curb once again, a little closer to Reggie than she reasonably needed to be.

"I'm not the least bit ashamed I'd like you to note, for the record."

"So noted."

"I bet young Sophia was never a troublemaker, am I right?" Reggie turned to face her.

Sophia covered her face in her hands and shook her head. "The most trouble I got in was getting caught staying up past bedtime reading or sneaking more time on the computer researching a policy issue or politician I admired."

Reggie fell back on her elbows laughing. "I guess some people are born for their jobs. If politicians are necessary, I'm glad someone like you was elected to serve."

"Thank you. I think. What are you doing here so late? You said a work thing."

"Double shift and overtime. I couldn't leave until there was someone to relieve me. We were short-staffed. It was a long day." Reggie remained lounged back on her elbows but turned toward Sophia.

"I don't mean to keep you. We should go." Sophia started to stand.

Reggie put her hand on Sophia's arm. "I'm not in a hurry to put a lid on this day. Besides, when I sit with you and let you eat or drink you seem to forget you don't like me."

"I've never said I don't like you, Reggie. I can't think of a single thing at our coffee date that would have given you that impression."

Sophia tried for a playful disapproving look. She felt forty percent confident she pulled it off.

"You had no idea who I was then. I'm sure you've been warned to stay away from me. I don't need a board and all the pieces to be able to read the rulebook of this game."

Sophia cocked her head and studied Reggie. "Why *have* I been warned about you?"

What was the point of lying about something Reggie had already surmised? If she was direct, maybe Reggie would be too. She'd rather hear from Reggie what no amount of research could uncover.

"Look, you're going to get to know me through our work on the design team. You've already started over coffee and sidewalk hot dogs. Then you'll have to do what politicians do, weigh the pros and cons of perception versus reality, truth versus political narrative, ambition and ladder climbing versus anything that gets trampled as a result. How I fit in that narrative is up to you." Reggie scrubbed the short hair on the top of her head.

"Jesus. Don't think too highly of politicians do you? Or me, it seems." Sophia stood up, looked around, then put her hands in her pockets.

Reggie stood too and pointed up the street. "My experience with politicians is that they want to be reelected and they want to retain power. There are a lot of ways for a lot of people to get hurt in the pursuit of those goals."

Sophia stopped walking and pointed her finger at Reggie's chest. "Let's clear something up right now. Maybe you've had a string of crooked politicians in your life or maybe everyone behaves badly around you, but I'm not one of them. I'm here to serve. That's my top and only priority. Yes, getting reelected is important because it is furtherance of continuing to serve. You want me to give you the benefit of the doubt, I ask that you do the same for me."

Reggie smiled. "I don't know you well enough to pass judgment. But I can tell you that I like that you are far and away the smartest person in any room you enter and that everyone knows it. I like that you'll go toe to toe with anyone if you disagree with them. And I especially like that you see yourself as a giraffe."

"You know other animals stay close to herds of giraffes because they're tall enough to see danger coming from far away. They're an early warning system for more vulnerable animals closer to the ground. Even those reaching for the highest branches can be looking out for the ones below them. It's possible to do both." Sophia glanced at Reggie who was nodding with a pensive look.

When they got to the car Reggie opened the door for her. Sophia slid into the passenger's seat and felt her exhaustion overtake her like a deluge. She struggled to stay awake on the short drive to her house. If she didn't have to give Reggie directions she likely would have embarrassed herself by snoring over the music.

Reggie walked her to the front door and waited for her to get inside safely before bounding back down the walk and driving away. Sophia appreciated her chivalry. As she crawled into bed, thoughts of Reggie intruded. They'd still argued tonight and clearly saw politics from very different perspectives, but there had also been moments of fun.

Despite warnings and her own misgivings, she worried she might like Reggie. How was that possible? And surely that was a notion she shouldn't even entertain. Right?

CHAPTER SIX

How many pairs of glasses do you suppose that man possesses?" The Zookeeper leaned close to Reggie's ear. Reggie shooed her away. She could think of very few scenarios where she'd want someone whispering in her ear, and none of them involved the Zookeeper. She had noticed Bert's glasses as soon as she'd walked in, though. They were orange today with green polka dots. The man had a flair all his own.

Frankie sat down and nodded toward Bert. "Bert, where do you get your fabulous glasses?"

Bert adjusted his glasses and smiled shyly. "My wife makes them for me. She's an artist, but we both like bold colors."

"Tell your wife she's brilliant." One of the other group members gave a soft round of applause.

Bert blushed. "I certainly will. Are we ready to get started? We have a lot to do today, but first, we need to select cochairs for the group. Before you nominate yourself or someone else, be mindful of the fact that it's an extra time commitment and the cochairs will work closely together outside of the regular group meetings. I'll be relying on both individuals to move our agenda forward as we continue down the road together."

The Zookeeper raised her hand. "I'd like to nominate Sophia and Reggie."

Reggie turned and stared at the Zookeeper. What was she thinking? Of all the qualified people in the room, why would the

Zookeeper pick her? Out of the corner of her eye she saw Sophia looked nearly as shocked. Was it because Sophia was put forward or because Reggie was?

"Seconded."

Reggie didn't catch who was going along with the Zookeeper's crazy idea.

"You beat me to it."

"That's who I would have chosen."

"Feels like a no-brainer to me."

Was there a group text she'd been left off of? Bert looked a little stunned too.

"Okay, well to ensure any shy members of the group have a chance to weigh in, I'm going to pass out the ballots I created. Please write down the names of the two individuals you'd like to see as cochairs."

After ten minutes, Bert announced the results. "With overwhelming support, Sophia and Reggie, congratulations, you've been elected cochairs should you choose to accept."

Reggie looked at Sophia who held her hands out to the sides as if to say "why not." That was enough for Reggie. She was already in this and she'd be lying if she said being forced to spend more time with Sophia didn't hold some appeal.

"I accept, although for the record, I think you all are nuts." Reggie looked around the room at her PAC teammates.

"I'm in too, but I agree with Reggie, any one of you would have made a wonderful cochair."

"Maybe we just want more opportunity to watch you two go after each other. It's kinda hot." Rhonda, a Latinx, self-described butch dyke who'd just turned ninety, winked at Reggie.

Laughter and chatter erupted and filled the room.

"It appears, Bert, that once again you are on the precipice of losing control of the ship you're captaining." The Zookeeper leaned back in her chair and linked her fingers behind her head.

Bert rapped his knuckles on the table. When that didn't work he took off his glasses and waved them above his head. "All right, we have our cochairs, it's time to get to work."

Reggie offered to man the marker as they recapped the ideas generated at the last meeting. She zipped between two large pads of paper hung on the wall. One was for new policy proposals and the other for current policies in need of change.

Once she had captured their lists, everyone was given a marker and they all went up and added their initials to their top three priorities. Reggie could feel the energy and excitement in the room when everyone returned to their seats and surveyed the results. It was hard not to be swept up in the feeling.

Bert clapped his hands. "Wonderful. Look at the progress we've already made."

The top vote getters were ambitious. Decriminalization, expanded treatment and improved access, criminal justice and sentencing reforms, racial equity initiatives. Some of the items on the list were so broad Reggie wasn't sure how they were supposed to operationalize them, but that was probably what the rest of the meetings were for. This meeting was for the big picture. They could narrow their focus and come up with specifics as they moved forward.

She saw Sophia frowning as she looked over the group's new list of priorities. Reggie didn't see Sophia's initials next to the broad, ambitious, and likely controversial items on the list. If this was the direction the group was headed it was probably going to be hard for Sophia. What would their cochair meetings be like if Sophia disagreed with the fundamental direction of the group?

"For the rest of the time today, we're going to break into small groups. You're going to be in these groups for much of the rest of our time together working on one of these topic areas. So please look them over now and choose your top two. Indicate your first and second choice on the paper in front of you and hand them in to me. After lunch I'll split you out into your groups." Bert stood at the head of the table with his hands resting on the back of his chair looking like the coolest kid at a model airplane collector's convention.

After lunch, Reggie held the door as everyone shuffled back in the room.

As Sophia passed through she put her hand on Reggie's shoulder. "Are you free after the meeting today to talk about cochair business?"

Reggie swallowed hard. That couldn't possibly be as suggestive as it sounded, right?

"Sure. I have some time."

Sophia smiled widely, making her whole face light up. "Great. Bert said we'll need to meet outside these team meetings pretty regularly. Maybe we can set up a regular meeting time."

Reggie nodded. What was she getting herself into?

"You all right?" Frankie poked Reggie as they retook their seats. "You look like you ate something funky."

Unbidden, an image of Sophia eating a hotdog surrounded by the soft light of a streetlamp popped into Reggie's mind. She looked at Sophia across the table, who smiled shyly back. Could she possibly know Reggie was thinking about their chance meeting a little over a week ago?

Frankie poked her again, harder this time. "Stop staring at pretty ladies like you've got no game. What group did you put first?"

Reggie grumbled and thought about not answering Frankie for her cheek, but the earnest look on Frankie's face broke Reggie of those thoughts.

"Treatment." Reggie adjusted her sleeve. "I know everyone will probably expect me to go with criminal justice reform."

The Zookeeper made a "pfft" sound, joining the conversation. "Who better to advocate for expanded treatment than one who sees where those unable to access treatment too often find themselves? I believe Frankie and I, in our own way, could speak to your expertise in this arena."

Reggie was having a hard time with the fact that she sort of liked the Zookeeper, one of her former inmates and a notorious drug dealer. She had an "it's complicated" relationship with a well loved and respected politician and a budding friendship with a criminal. This design team was turning out to be quite strange.

Bert announced the groups and Reggie was assigned her first choice. Her group consisted of herself, Frankie, the Zookeeper, and Sophia. They gathered in the corner of the room Bert assigned to them. There were three other groups, each with four members working on racial equity, criminal justice and sentencing, and decriminalization.

"I wouldn't have thought you'd put treatment at the top of your list." Reggie leaned toward Sophia as they sat down.

"I'd have said the same thing about you. To answer your unspoken question, there is room for legislating in all the categories on the board, but I think perhaps this area of focus has the most room for compromise. With a title like 'decriminalization' the horse is already out of the barn on the direction everyone is moving, don't you think?" Sophia was leaning close to Reggie as she spoke quietly.

"Are you two ready to share with the rest of the group?" The Zookeeper crossed her legs and looked back and forth between them.

Frankie scowled at the Zookeeper, but Reggie could see there wasn't any bite behind it.

"Oh leave them alone, old lady. Just because you and Parrot Master have been together since the ice age doesn't mean the rest of us don't like to flirt sometimes." Frankie nudged the Zookeeper lovingly.

"We're not flirting."

All four of them laughed at Reggie and Sophia's simultaneous denial.

"Shall we commence?" The Zookeeper flipped to a new page in her notebook and balanced it on her knee. "I'm open to counterarguments, but it would seem we have two streams of inquiry at our disposal, access and treatment itself."

"I agree. The question is, do we tackle both or focus our attention on one or the other?" Sophia tapped the end of her pen on her chin.

"Both."

Everyone looked at Frankie and waited for her to continue, but she stared back like she'd said all that needed to be said.

"I agree with Frankie." Reggie looked around for a pen and paper she knew she didn't have. "What good are expanded treatment options without improved access? And enhancing access is great, but there isn't enough high quality treatment for everyone who wants it *now*, never mind if it becomes an option for more people down the line."

"Both it is." The Zookeeper jotted something in her notebook. "Our young friend Frankie has already been working to expand access to treatment in my neighborhood, over by the library. You've also been working with Star Recovery the last few years, right?"

Frankie's cheeks turned red at the Zookeeper's praise. "This is something that means a lot to me. Thea, at the library, and Kit, at Star, have been great to give me so many opportunities. If we're going to split into two and two, I think I'd like to work on the treatment arm."

Reggie wasn't aware of Frankie's work in the community, but she could see the passion for it in Frankie's eyes. She tried to think whether she'd ever felt that way about her work, or anything in her life. If she had it was long gone now. Melancholy nipped at the heels of that realization.

"Do either of you feel a strong desire to join Frankie on the treatment arm of our endeavor?"

Sophia shook her head. "I'm fine with either."

"If you want to work with Frankie, that's fine with me." Reggie glanced at Sophia.

The Zookeeper took another note and nodded. "That's settled then. On to the next order of business. How shall we structure our time together during these formal gatherings?"

They spent the rest of the time figuring out the best way to divide up work and make use of the time they met as a group. At the end of the meeting Reggie had a better understanding of exactly how much work the design team would entail and that over the next few months she was going to be spending an inordinate amount of time with Sophia. Whether that was an enjoyable experience, for either of them, remained to be seen.

"It seems like we're going to be seeing a lot of each other. Perhaps we can call a truce and agree to give each other a chance?"

Sophia seemed to read Reggie's mind.

"I'll agree to those terms." Reggie extended her hand.

Sophia laughed but took her hand. Sophia's hand was smaller than Reggie's and felt much too nice as it slid into hers. At the risk of giving a weird limp handshake, Reggie gripped gently. Sophia's hand was soft and didn't deserve a rough squeeze.

The shake was over too quickly and Reggie wanted to pull Sophia's hand back and hold it longer. What was wrong with her? Those kinds of thoughts certainly weren't going to help their long hours working together go smoothly.

"Can we start with dinner?"

"Excuse me?" Reggie rubbed the back of her head.

"To celebrate our truce and talk about any of the fifty things that are now on our to-do list. The Zookeeper runs an efficient meeting. She should have my job. Or our job as cochairs."

Reggie put her hand to her forehead.

"Forgot about that, huh?"

"Completely. Maybe we should kick off our truce in a bar."

Sophia grabbed her bag, grabbed Reggie's hand, and pulled her toward the door. "Now you're talking. What are you waiting for?"

Reggie looked down at their joined hands. *My sanity, to start with.* Not for the first time, she wondered what the hell she was thinking. But she wasn't thinking, which was a problem. This was how she felt when she was around her dad as a teenager, swept up, enamored by the fun and excitement of his political career and connected friends, blind to the reality. She couldn't let that happen again. She looked down at their joined hands again and then up at Sophia, who was smiling at her and looking more beautiful than ever.

She couldn't let herself get swept up and swept away, but here she was, being led to a night out by a beautiful politician. It was just drinks, right? What was the harm in that? She wanted to facepalm, but there was no way in hell she was going to pull her hand out of Sophia's grasp so she did it mentally. Once again, what the hell was she thinking?

CHAPTER SEVEN

A s soon as Sophia stepped into the evening air outside the office building, she started to second-guess her spontaneous invitation. Why exactly had she invited Reggie to drinks of all things? And why were they still holding hands? She carefully extricated herself from the latter and tried to decide how rude it would be if she rescinded her invitation so quickly.

Reggie looked off balance with their current arrangement too, which instead of hastening Sophia's run to the off-ramp, made her want to stay on the road they were on. She wasn't such a sucker to her wild emotions that she was willing to take Reggie's hand again, but she'd be perjuring herself if she swore under oath that the thought hadn't crossed her mind. Reggie was hot as the devil was devious and Sophia had eyes and a pulse. Even her nana would get palpitations if Reggie took her hand to help her to her seat in church.

"Am I letting you pick our watering hole?"

Since they were no longer holding hands, Reggie had shoved hers in her pockets and had her shoulders turned in against the chill of the evening.

"You are, and you're not going to guilt me into picking a crappy bar because you didn't wear a jacket. Not to sound like my mother, but why didn't you bother to check the weather on the way out the door this morning?"

Sophia sounded exactly like her mother, and she winced internally. She'd never missed a chance to point out a failure.

Reggie smiled a lopsided grin. "It's in my truck. In my defense, I had no idea wandering downtown with you after the meeting would be an option. I would have dressed appropriately."

Sophia cocked an eyebrow and tried to keep the chuckle from her voice. "Do I want to ask how you would have dressed if you had known?"

"I guess we'll never know." Reggie kept a completely straight face. "So, have you decided where you're taking me?"

Sophia thought about her choices and felt her anxiety rise. They were downtown, close to the statehouse. It was Saturday but politicians didn't always work Monday through Friday nine to five. If she went to any of the popular places close by, she would almost certainly run into a handful of people she knew.

She looked over at Reggie and felt guilty thinking of what it would mean to be seen with her by people in political circles. The Speaker and majority leader had warned her to stay away from Reggie. She'd been dragging her heels on looking into Reggie now that she knew her. It felt wrong, but it also left her too far in the dark for her comfort. Everyone knew the infamous story of the Northrup name. What she didn't know was how Reggie fit in the pages of that particularly dubious book. She made a note to ask Rodrigo on Monday.

Reggie said she didn't like politicians so maybe it would be better to avoid the political cesspools anyway. That was the kind thing to do, for Reggie.

"Do you mind a little bit of a walk? We can stay close by if you're too cold."

"I'm tougher than I look. Hellhound, remember?" Reggie didn't take her hands out of her pockets but still flexed her arms dramatically.

"Okay, tough guy, let's go."

Sophia led them away from downtown a few blocks to a hole-in-the-wall establishment that was more restaurant than bar. It served Cape Verdean cuisine, the bar stocked drinks popular on the island, and it was owned by Lily's parents. It wasn't until they walked through the door that Sophia considered what bringing Reggie here of all places would mean. There were going to be questions to answer. A lot of them.

She was barely in the door before Mrs. Medeiros was out of the kitchen and fussing at her. Somehow Lily's mother had always known when Lily, Sophia, or Davey entered fussing distance.

"Sophia, you haven't been around in too long. Are they working you too hard now that you are responsible for improving all of our lives? I know it's a big job, but you still have to make time to come by so I can feed you. Come sit, your table is always available."

Mrs. Medeiros stopped short as she turned to pull Sophia toward the table she'd been eating at since she was a child. Sophia turned to see Reggie looking like she'd suddenly remembered she needed to be anywhere but here.

"Sophia, where are your manners. Who is your friend?" Mrs. Medeiros had her hand on her hip and a scowl that anyone would do well to avoid.

Sophia shuffled her feet. "Reggie Northrup, this is Mrs. Fatima Medeiros, the owner of this establishment."

"It's very nice to meet you, Mrs. Medeiros."

"Oh, please call me Fatima. Come, let's get you settled down. I'll bring out some food."

Reggie looked over her shoulder as Mrs. Medeiros led her toward the table Sophia always occupied.

"Don't worry about her, she's been eating here since she was in diapers. She knows the way to her table. I'll get you two settled and then I promise I'll disappear. I'm not too old to understand when my company's not needed."

Sophia saw Mrs. Medeiros wink at Reggie.

"Mrs. Medeiros, it's not like that. It's a work thing."

"Of course. It always it." She stopped in front of the table Sophia thought of as hers and offered another round to the current occupants if they picked up their food and found somewhere else to sit.

"You didn't have to do that."

Mrs. Medeiros kissed her cheek and wiped the table. "It would be weird to see you sitting anywhere else in here. I still think of you,

Lily, and David doing your homework in here after school before your dad came to pick you up. I'll be right back with something for you to eat. Any food allergies, Reggie?"

Reggie shook her head, still looking a little overwhelmed.

Sophia took her seat and motioned for Reggie to sit. "I promise the food's fantastic. As long as you're not a very picky eater or a vegetarian you'll be happy. Sorry, I promised a bar and we ended up here."

Reggie looked around. She carefully examined all the details Sophia had stopped noticing a long time ago. Looking at them now was like taking a detailed inspection of a years old, well loved tattoo. The wooden tables had long ago lost their matching chairs and now had an assortment of colorful seating scattered through the dining room, no two chairs matching any other. The bar was made from a single slab of the most beautiful wood Sophia had ever seen and was always shiny and clean, even on the busiest nights, and the kitchen, partially open to the dining room, always reminded her of the feeling of Mrs. Medeiros's embrace. Comfort, love, and warmth came from that kitchen whether you were family or a perfect stranger.

"This is so much better than a bar. Especially one of the ones downtown that try way too hard."

Soon, Mrs. Medeiros brought out heaping plates of food, and Sophia's mouth watered like Pavlov's dog after so many years of watching food arrive from that same kitchen. Never mind that it smelled amazing. Mrs. Medeiros could probably present her with a muddy tire and her mouth would salivate at this point. Reggie looked in a similar boat. For the briefest moment, Sophia wished Reggie looked at her the way she was looking at the plate of food in front of her, ready to devour it.

"I guess we should get to work." Sophia picked up her fork and looked at Reggie above a bite not yet taken.

Reggie shook her head vigorously. "Nope, not yet. I'm not talking about Bert, the Zookeeper, the design team, drugs, my job, any of it while I'm eating anything that smells this good. You can ask me about something else or we can talk about the weather."

Sophia put her fork down and drummed her fingers together above her plate. "Hmm, this sounds promising."

Reggie looked a little alarmed, but she eventually smiled and leaned back in her chair and took another bite.

"Is Reggie your full name?" She already knew the answer from the Speaker and majority leader, but it was a softball warm-up toss.

"No. Regina. My parents had high hopes for a queen and instead they got me."

"I don't know, you'd look pretty good with a crown." Sophia waved her fork toward Reggie's head. "Middle name?"

"Am I going to get home and find you've cleaned out my bank account? You'll never guess my security questions."

Reggie was smiling so Sophia knew she was joking and wasn't taking offense at what some might consider personal questions.

"I'll tell you mine first. It's Rose and I'm named after my two grandmothers."

"I should make up a story about my name so it doesn't sound as ridiculous as the truth. My middle name is Louise. My parents argued about what to name me, and neither of them would give on their preferred name. So they flipped a coin to see which would go first and which would be middle. My mom won so I'm Regina. Dad got stuck in the middle."

Sophia leaned forward on her elbows and took a long look at Reggie. She examined her face in great detail. She had high cheekbones and beautiful blue eyes, but her chiseled features and short, neatly cropped hair gave her a sexy androgyny.

"Lou doesn't suit you. I'm glad your mom won."

Reggie laughed. "I thought with that inspection you were going to tell me I had food on my face or something."

"That too." Sophia leaned over and wiped a bit of sauce off Reggie's cheek.

She pulled away quickly. She could have just pointed. Now her fingers felt tingly and she didn't know what to say. There was no way she'd wipe sauce off the face of the majority leader, Valencia, or any of her other colleagues.

"Thank you." Reggie put her finger to her cheek.

"There's still food on your plate, and it's your turn to ask a question."

Reggie sat up straighter and her whole face lit up. "When you were a kid, what did you want to be when you grew up?"

Sophia tilted her head and gave Reggie a grin. "You may not want to know the answer to this one. I've always wanted to be a politician."

She hid a laugh behind her napkin as Reggie's mouth practically fell open.

"What kid wants to be a politician? How does a little kid even know what a politician is?"

"This kid, to answer your first question. As for your second, I learned all about civics sitting at this table. Mrs. Medeiros's mother came to America from Cape Verde and always believed in America's goal of forming a more perfect union." Sophia stared over Reggie's shoulder, lost in memory.

"The American Dream isn't a political story though, right?"

Sophia laughed, the humorless kind that comes from deep pain. "Oh, the American Dream myth is incredibly political, but I'm not talking about that. Maria Santos believed in the ideals of America. Democracy, freedom, opportunity, equality. She's the one who opened my eyes to the fact that America is a work in progress."

"But why politics? There are lots of areas to make a difference and push the country forward. "

Sophia gripped her napkin tightly in her lap. "Of course there are, but I didn't want to have a career along any of those paths, I wanted to be a politician."

Reggie looked like she was trying to read the *Iliad* in Mandarin. "But why?"

"Because marching and organizing and lobbying gets you to this point, if you're lucky and damn good at what you do." Sophia moved her hand along the table. "But to get across the finish line, you need your reforms enshrined in law. I want to cross the finish line."

"You want the credit." Reggie sounded sad.

"No." Sophia put her hand down on the table a little harder than she meant to. "If there is good policy to be made or if there is a way to move the country or the state or the city, or even one person closer to our more perfect union, then I sure as hell don't want to trust someone else to do the right thing and get the signatures on the page. I will never put my name on a bill if it means I can't more effectively shepherd good policy into law."

Reggie cracked a smile. "You better be careful, Representative Lamont, you might make me into a believer and you know how I feel about politicians."

Sophia took another bite and shook her fork at Reggie. "I think I know you well enough now. You're a stubborn fool not easily convinced. I'm not going to be deceived by some sweet talk over dinner. Now you tell me, what did you want to be as a kid?"

Adorably, Reggie's cheek's pinked. "A stop sign."

Sophia coughed to clear the water that traveled down the wrong pipe. "Excuse me?"

"You heard me." Reggie smiled. "I liked that my job was to tell people what to do to stay safe and they'd have to listen without arguing. There was no other way to interpret my message, and if you didn't follow the rules you got in trouble."

"Is that why you became a corrections officer instead? They seem a little the same."

"No." Reggie lost her joviality.

"Care to expand on that? I didn't mean to upset you."

"No." Reggie looked down at her food and seemed to avoid eye contact.

Sophia flailed about for something to say.

"We're not quite done with dinner yet, so I get one more question. If you and I could be having this meeting anywhere in the world, where would we be?"

Reggie looked up from her plate with a twinkle in her eye. "Are you hoping I'll start flirting with you again?"

Sophia rested her head on her hand and batted her eyelashes dramatically. "Now why would I want to do that?"

"Truthfully, you probably don't." Reggie's expression clouded again.

Some of the spark between them dimmed. What wasn't Reggie saying? Once again, Sophia made a note to talk to Rodrigo on Monday.

"Well, I guess it's good I wasn't seriously asking you. Now, answer my question."

Reggie looked around the restaurant and then back at Sophia. She moved her hand across the table so theirs were almost touching, but didn't make contact. "I'm pretty happy just where I am."

"Oh, smooth talker, you are trouble."

"I told you you should stay away from me."

Sophia was flustered. Reggie would turn anyone's head and she'd brought her here of all places on what felt much too much like a date.

"Should we finally get to work?"

Reggie touched her hand this time. "I didn't mean to make you uncomfortable."

"You didn't."

Reggie looked at her like she was full of shit. "I'm ready to get to work. Do you prefer the job where we figure out how to provide better access to substance use treatment or the one where we're in charge of wrangling that unruly group of people in Bert's PAC pack?"

Sophia put her head in her hands. "Why did we let the Zookeeper draft us into the cochair position? It's going to be so much work."

"She wouldn't be any good at her job if she couldn't get people to do things they weren't sure they wanted while convincing them it was their idea and in their best interest."

Sophia thought of Davey. She rummaged roughly through her bag looking for a notebook and pen. She gripped the pen tightly as she uncapped it and prepared to take notes. "The Zookeeper and Parrot Master are very talented at getting people to do things they don't want to do."

Reggie looked quizzical but didn't push. Sophia appreciated it.

"I think we should meet weekly if you're open to it. There's a lot of our own work to do, but I suspect we're going to have a lot to keep on top of with all the other groups as well. If some weeks there's nothing to talk about, we can always cancel." Sophia wrote notes as she talked.

"Or we can come back here, eat more delicious food, and you can tell me, if money was no object what's the most outlandish thing you'd buy." Reggie pushed back from the table enough to stretch out her legs.

Sophia stopped writing and took in Reggie's long torso and legs. It felt like a tease, but she could tell Reggie was trying to get comfortable after a long day of sitting.

"That's easy, I'd buy—"

Reggie sat up and held up a finger. "No. No answering. That's a question for a week when we don't have anything to talk about. Right now we're up to our tits in work. There's no time for that kind of nonsense."

If Mrs. Medeiros wouldn't have come out of the kitchen and scolded her in front of the entire restaurant, she would have thrown her napkin at Reggie for her insolence.

They agreed to meet once a week until they got a feel for the demands of the design team and their cochair roles. Sophia was worried it wasn't enough, but for now it would do. When she thought of what spending so much time with Reggie meant for her, personally and professionally, she started to sweat. Not the feminine glow kind of sweat women supposedly did that was delicate and sexy. This was the pit stain flop sweat that gave away the bad guy in an interrogation. Except she wasn't doing anything wrong, so she had nothing to worry about. That's what she kept telling herself, so why did it feel like a lie?

CHAPTER EIGHT

The cold air felt invigorating cycling in and out of Reggie's lungs as she completed mile four of her morning run. She usually ran along the river, but this morning she deviated from her routine and found herself skirting the park that fronted the library. The park was quiet this early, but as with any public space, it was never truly empty.

She crossed a footbridge and headed for a bench beside a giant oak. She pulled to a stop and rested beside the bench, taking a sip of water she carried with her. She looked around the park and at the library bordering one side. Although the building was large and should have been imposing, its lineaments were surprisingly inviting. Frankie had spoken glowingly of the head librarian. Perhaps it was time for Reggie to finally renew the library card she'd had on her to-do list for ages.

She was about to resume her run when she heard someone shout her name. She turned and saw the Zookeeper strolling across the park headed in her direction. A man was with her, but he stayed away when the Zookeeper approached.

"Reggie, you are far from home at an ungodly hour. Surely heart health is not worth rising before the dawn?"

"Is that why you came over? To check on my cardiovascular fitness? I thought you went to law school, not medical school."

The Zookeeper took a seat on the bench and motioned for Reggie to join her. Now that she had stopped moving, Reggie was getting cold, since she was dressed for running, not chitchat, but it seemed rude to refuse the invitation so she sat.

"Law school was a lifetime ago, and we all make mistakes when we're young and stupid."

Reggie turned to look at the Zookeeper. "I think there are a few lawyers, probably a judge or two, who don't see your law school years as the point you lost your way."

The Zookeeper smiled and waved her finger in Reggie's direction. "That's because their thinking is constrained by the rule of law. I expect better from you. Come with me."

They walked along the path through the park a couple of minutes before the Zookeeper stopped them. She pointed to a woman sitting on a bench under a much smaller oak.

"That woman there trades sex for drugs, sometimes money. She doesn't have stable housing. She's been through detox at least three times but wasn't connected to outpatient treatment services so relapsed every time. She's at high risk to be the victim of a violent crime, contract an infectious disease, or die of an overdose."

"Why are you telling me this?"

"Because, I want you to answer whether a lawyer is better able to help her than I am? If you can answer that, then you know why this park, and not a courtroom, is my territory." The Zookeeper leaned against a tree, crossed her arms, and waited for Reggie.

Reggie looked at the woman on the bench. Her heart felt heavy for her pain. No person should have to struggle so deeply to survive day-to-day. She'd heard the rumors about the Zookeeper and her flock of lost souls, but it seemed like an urban legend. What could be in it for the Zookeeper?

"What you have to offer her might depend on whether your rumored flock exists."

The Zookeeper's eyes lit up. She pushed off the tree and clapped Reggie on the shoulder. "Neuronal activity forming new pathways. You give me hope. Yes, my flock does exist. The woman you see is part of it, in fact. She's the Ostrich. They all have animal names to protect them, and I am the Zookeeper."

"I did wonder where you got that name."

That was one of about ten thousand mysteries solved about the Zookeeper.

"So your flock exists, so what? Why isn't she better off in the system? Don't you supply her with the drugs that may one day kill her?"

"Because the system doesn't work. Out here, I can keep her from encountering those who mean women on the street harm. I can control the quality and quantity of the drugs she consumes, which she's going to buy from someone anyway, and there are doctors I trust who work on a concierge basis if I request such services." The Zookeeper ticked things off as she spoke.

"Okay, but that only helps the people you know. Couldn't you do more using your law degree?" Reggie glanced back at the Ostrich.

The Zookeeper waved dismissively. "I fear the point has entirely escaped you. Tammy Potts, esquire doesn't get invited to be part of the community design team, no matter how good she is. The Zookeeper's input, however, is sought out. There are infinite ways to make a difference in the lives of people significant to you."

Reggie wasn't aware this side of the Zookeeper existed. How many people knew it did?

"I did not choose our design team group lightly. I put my effort into things that are meaningful to me." The Zookeeper pointed to the Ostrich. "Sophia is a politician and a rule-bound thinker. I need you to expand your mind as we work together."

Reggie shook her head and took a step back. "I'm not okay with any proposals that are illegal."

"I haven't suggested anything of the sort, nor is it my intention to do so. I'm asking you to consider solutions you hadn't considered viable prior to this conversation."

"So instead of a square peg round hole problem, you want me to consider maybe applesauce is the solution?"

"Yes." The Zookeeper pumped her fist excitedly. "I knew you were the woman for the job."

"How crazy are you planning on getting with your proposals that you had to interrupt my run and freeze me half to death?" Reggie rubbed her arms to try to warm up.

"I am letting young Frankie take the lead on our team's proposals. I'm simply laying the foundation for a positive reception." The Zookeeper was looking across the park at the library.

Reggie wished she could read the Zookeeper's mind. What did the library have to do with all this?

"So why did you leave law? And why go from upholding the law to breaking it? Your business cost you dearly, too. You wouldn't have been under my care if not for your product." Reggie shifted from foot to foot and blew in her fists in an attempt to keep warm.

"Perhaps we can dig deeper on that subject another time, Officer Northrup. I fear I have delayed you long enough. I wouldn't want to be the reason you strained a muscle on your return trip home. Before we part, however, rest easy, I am doing well in my recovery. I had access to treatment options many in your care do not. I'll see you again presently."

Reggie was left watching the Zookeeper rejoin the man who'd been waiting patiently outside the radius of their conversation. The two of them linked arms and made their way back across the park. Reggie took another look toward the bench over her shoulder, but the Ostrich had also moved on.

She tried to make sense of her conversation with the Zookeeper. What had she meant by needing to expand her mind and employ flexible thinking? The Zookeeper clearly didn't know anything about her if she thought there was any way Reggie was going to bend or get creative with rules. That wasn't who she was or what her last name allowed. Her father had seen to that. But thinking in terms of applesauce...well, maybe she could do that. There was still a recipe to make the sauce, even if you intended to use it to darn socks. Anything was better than doing things the way they'd always been done.

The Zookeeper had said Sophia was constrained by the law because she was a politician. What kind of upside-down world did the Zookeeper live in? Was Sophia the one upstanding politician in the state? Reggie had certainly never met another.

She wanted to believe in Sophia, but believing was a risky business. Believing led to hope, and hope, in her experience, led to letdown. She didn't want to be let down by Sophia, so it was safer to never let herself start believing. Or hoping. The problem was when she thought about her upcoming meetings with Sophia, her heart gave a little flutter. A very happy, hopeful flutter, and that seemed like a very dangerous thing for her heart to be doing.

CHAPTER NINE

Sophia put her head on her desk or, more accurately, put her head on the huge pile of papers stacked on her desk. Her eyes were starting to glaze over and she was only two hours into her marathon reading session. Not that she was complaining. She was living the dream. It was just that this dream, at this moment, was a little dry.

Someone tapped her on the shoulder and she knew it was Rodrigo from the earthy cologne and the welcome thud of the coffee cup hitting her desk.

"I should take a picture and post it on your official page so your constituents can see how you're really repaying their vote for you."

Sophia flipped him off without raising her head. He took her hand and moved it to the coffee.

"You wouldn't need this so badly if you weren't spending all night out with a hot corrections officer. Don't think I won't set a curfew for you if your poll numbers drop even a quarter percentage point."

Now Sophia looked up. "It was a work meeting and it didn't go that late."

"Well, as long as it was a work meeting I guess it doesn't matter that you were flirting with the daughter of Bartholomew Northrup in front of God and everybody." Rodrigo had his hand on his hip and a frown on his face.

"Bartholomew Northrup? So it's true?" Sophia held her hand up to stop the outburst she could see gathering steam in Rodrigo's body language. "I know it's true, I guess it was easier to ignore if I didn't actually hear the words out loud. I suppose that explains why she doesn't like politicians."

"More like explains why you need to keep away from her. I don't care how much she heats up your lady parts."

"Excuse me? I don't care if we've known each other since kindergarten. We're at work. Knock that crap off. If you want to be helpful to me, help me catch up on the research I should have done already. Find out what you can about Reggie Northrup, not her father."

Sophia thought about the few times Reggie's father, unnamed, had come up. She'd shut down, so clearly uninterested in visiting that part of her life, at least not with a relative stranger. She didn't seem like the heir to a corrupt political dynasty, more like the apple trying to roll far from the shadow of the tree that bore it, but maybe she was seeing what she hoped to see. She had been warned about Reggie for a reason, right?

Rodrigo was still looking at her disapprovingly but she wasn't interested in hearing more from him. Although how he knew about her having dinner with Reggie would have to be addressed at some point. It was probably Lily's brother Will's doing. She hadn't seen him tending bar, but if he was there, then everything she ate or said, Rodrigo would know about. There were downsides to keeping your friends from toddlerhood close to you.

She shooed him out the door. "Go find out what you can about Reggie. I have reading to do."

The pile of policy papers didn't become any more appealing or exciting after Rodrigo left. Sophia wasn't sure what was wrong with her today. Usually she loved reading through exactly these kinds of documents.

She picked up her phone and pulled up her brother's number. She looked at the mountain of work on her desk, quickly calculated how far into the night she'd have to work if she took a long lunch now, and dialed.

"Hey, Davey, free for lunch?"

"Hey, sis. You have good timing. If you can get to the job site and can stand to get those fancy clothes of yours dirty, I've got a lunch pail of food I'm willing to share."

Sophia knew what Davey packed for lunch, since it hadn't changed since he was seven. But she hadn't been a big fan of peanut butter and banana sandwiches even then.

"I'll bring my own lunch, thanks. Can I bring you anything?"

"Nah, I'm good. See you soon."

Sophia grabbed her purse and dropped her phone inside. She pulled on her jacket as she swung the door closed. She felt bad not letting Rodrigo know she was heading out, but she was still annoyed at him from his insinuations about her, Reggie, and her and Reggie. He could entertain himself until she got back.

Davey had recently found employment with a construction company that hadn't been overly concerned with his criminal history. The owner, Josh Marsden, said he was a believer in hard work and second chances and if Davey was interested in the first, he'd extend him the opportunity for the second.

When Sophia arrived, Davey was laughing with a group of guys dressed in work gear and dirt, just like he was. It wasn't until she got closer that she realized one of the "guys" was a woman. She mentally slapped herself for assuming the work crew would only be men.

"Oh, hey, Sophia, there you are." Davey waved her over. "Soph, this is my boss, Kit Marsden. Kit, this is my baby sister, Representative Sophia Lamont."

Sophia rolled her eyes at Davey. "Sophia. The way he introduces me, he makes it sound like our parents named me 'representative.'"

Kit laughed. "I know a thing or two about the glow of a proud family member. My cousin Josh embarrasses me at every opportunity. Are you the Sophia my friend Frankie has been gushing about? From the community design team?"

Sophia nudged a rock with the tip of her shoe. For a big city, the world was pretty small right now. "I don't know about the gushing, but I am on the design team with Frankie."

"The Zookeeper's part of the team too, I hear. I'd consider buying tickets to that show. I volunteer with Star Recovery and have a few years clean and sober under my belt. If there's anything I can do to help you guys, get in touch. Frankie knows how to reach me, or you can leave a note in David's lunchbox." Kit clapped Davey on the back and smiled. "I'll let you two get to lunch. I know the breaks go quick when you have someone you want to spend time with. It's nice to meet you, Sophia."

Sophia watched Kit lope off and couldn't help comparing her to Reggie. While Kit was undeniably attractive, she didn't measure up to Reggie, in Sophia's opinion. It's not that there was anything missing when she looked at Kit, it was more that there was something *there* when she was around Reggie.

"She's great, isn't she?" David nodded toward Kit. "She had a really bad drug problem, but she's gotten back on her feet now and runs this business with her cousin."

Sophia frowned. "Probably helps that she's a White woman and had a family business to fall back on."

"She would tell you that herself. And apparently, the Zookeeper kept her out of trouble when she was practically living on the streets drowning in her addiction." Davey led them to a couple of buckets, which he flipped over so they could sit.

"Are there by some chance two Zookeepers in this city?"

Davey shook his head. "Not that I'm aware of. It surprised me too. But you've always hated her more than I do."

That surprised her. Sophia thought it was a universal Lamont family hatred that bubbled in her blood.

"Do you know I'm working with her now? On the design team?"

"I heard Kit. Do you use your polite indoor voice when you talk to her or the one you saved for me when I was goofing up as a kid?" Davey licked peanut butter off his finger and took another bite of his sandwich.

"How do you think I feel working with her, after what she did to you?" Sophia jammed the lid back on the seltzer she'd brought and twisted it closed tightly.

"You're never going to get that bottle top off if you don't grip it a little lighter, Soph. Look, I know it's easier to be mad at a person than, I don't know, the universe, society, 'the system,' but you should redirect from the Zookeeper."

Sophia glared at Davey.

"It's true. At the trial, it made sense to blame everything on Parrot Master and the Zookeeper so I'd look like a victim of their drug dealing, but it's not really what happened. Mom and Dad tried to keep you out of it since you were still a kid. You know how they were anyway, more interested in blaming me for my failure than getting you involved. You hadn't screwed up yet and were the last hope for the family."

"I wasn't that much of a kid." Sophia kicked a rock and scuffed her shoe.

There wasn't any point arguing with the rest of Davey's assessment.

"No, you've never been much of a kid, and you were probably a better lawyer at sixteen than the ones that defended me." Davey put his arm around her.

"Why do you suddenly feel the need to come clean and defend the Zookeeper?" Sophia helped herself to one of Davey's apple slices.

Davey swatted her hand away. "This commission for developing policies or whatever it's called, it sounds like it can make a difference. The Zookeeper can help. I'm not here to argue she's a morally upstanding person, but she's brilliant. She's a lot like you if you broke bad. It's why I was attracted to her and Parrot Master in the first place."

"Please don't compare me to a drug dealer too loudly."

Davey smiled the big goofy grin Sophia loved so much. "You're a politician. Take it as a compliment."

Sophia punched him in the arm. "Take it back."

Davey shook his head so she punched him again. He laughed, like he always did, and she grew annoyed, as she always did.

"So what's the real story if you weren't corrupted by the Zookeeper?"

"Soph, come on. The outcome's all that matters. That's what impacts my life now. Who cares what caused it." Davey slammed his lunch pail closed.

"I care, Davey. You lost your scholarship and your chance to find a job in a symphony. I'm in a position to do something about what happened to you so the pattern doesn't repeat. But I can't do anything if I don't know about it." She reached out and took his hand. "I can't believe you haven't told me the truth all these years. Do you have any idea how much that pisses me off?"

"Of course I do. I wanted to tell you, but then it got longer and longer since it happened, and it seemed like a weird thing to bring up at Thanksgiving. Fine."

Sophia waited out Davey's predictable habit of taking forever to warm up to a story. At the rate he was going he was going to run out of lunch hour before he got started.

"There's not much to it. I was a typical college kid, buying drugs for my own use. Stupid, yes, but not something half my dorm wasn't doing. It sounds dumb, but it helped the music flow better. Got me out of my head. The night I was arrested, the Zookeeper asked me to bring some pot back to the dorm for a guy who lived down the hall. They had a standing arrangement or something. When I was arrested I had what I'd bought plus the other guy's stuff on me so I was charged with possession with intent to distribute."

"The prosecutor made you out to be the drug dealer for your entire dorm." Sophia felt her face grow hot.

Davey nodded. "It was my word against the preppy captain of the chess club. Walking by that guy's door was enough for a contact high, but they wanted to make an example of me. Suddenly everyone forgot I was there on a music scholarship and played cello in the orchestra. I was a Black dude who sold drugs."

Sophia looked at the ground and took a deep breath. She once again grieved for a society that didn't allow Black people, especially young Black men, to have the kind of "kids will be kids" moments afforded young White people.

"I'm pretty sure the Zookeeper helped my lawyer strike a deal and keep me out of prison for years."

"Really?" Sophia looked Davey in the eye to judge if he was serious.

"Ask her yourself, but you aren't going to convince me it's not true. They were talking about five, ten years, and then out of nowhere it's down to six months. A couple of days later, the prosecutor is on the news with a flashy arrest of one of the big-time dealers who worked for Parrot Master. I saw the Zookeeper right after I got out and she said she was glad the prosecutor came around on my case. Then she mentioned the other thing like they were connected." Davey stood up and stretched.

"You need to get back to work?" Sophia stood up too.

"In a few minutes. Wanna walk around the block?" Davey tucked his lunch pail and led Sophia onto the sidewalk.

"You've blown my mind a little, Davey. I guess I have to be nice to the Zookeeper now." It was still complicated. If Davey hadn't been doing the Zookeeper a favor, he wouldn't have had the extra pot on him. But because of her, he'd only done six months instead of years. The Zookeeper was like a hologram. What you saw depended on what angle you took a peek.

"You're always nice to people, Soph. It's one of the best things about you."

"So what do you think we should do?"

"With what? Your designer's showcase? Find ways to make people's lives better. There's probably a lot of things you can't change. Okay, fine, move on. That fight's for another day. But I bet there are plenty of things worth fighting for, like down on the mat, final round, go for the knockout, worth fighting for. That's where I'd say you put your money and your mouth."

"Jesus, Davey, you do paint a picture. And you think I'll just know these worthy causes?" Sophia pulled her jacket a little closer as they turned a corner and walked into the wind.

"Of course." Davey put his arm around her. "You're the smartest person I know, and you have teammates, so you don't have to do it alone."

Sophia leaned into her brother's embrace. "To be honest, I was hoping you'd just tell me what we should write in as our recommendation for the governor, but your pep talk was nice too."

Davey gave her a squeeze and released her as they got back to his job site. "Policy and changing the world are your domain, sis. I'm counting my blessings to have this job and a sister like you."

Sophia kissed him on his grimy cheek and waved as he headed back to work. She couldn't believe he'd kept so much of the detail of his arrest from her, but she was glad to have the context now. She thought about the captain of the chess club and wondered what happened to him. Had he needed or wanted treatment? Had he gotten it if he did?

What about the other kids buying drugs in Davey's dorm? And what about those in the Zookeeper's flock? Or those that fell through the cracks? What about, what about, what about? Her mind raced with questions as she walked back to the capitol. She couldn't wait until she next met with Reggie. They had so much work to do.

CHAPTER TEN

R eggie sipped her coffee and waited for Sophia. They were meeting at the same coffee shop where they'd met for the first time. Reggie didn't feel any more at home than she did the first time, but she did feel a thrill of anticipation every time the door opened.

Since her meeting with the Zookeeper, Reggie had taken pages of notes, trying to follow her suggestion and think outside the constraints of the current system. She still wasn't entirely sure what the Zookeeper had meant by that, but there was some weird stuff in her notebook. If Sophia laughed at her she was blaming it on the Zookeeper.

While Reggie was lost in thought she missed Sophia's arrival. When she sat down at the table Reggie nearly jumped out of her boots.

"Don't sneak up on me." She slammed her pen on the table.

"Good afternoon to you too." Sophia crossed her arms.

Reggie shuffled her papers. "Sorry. You surprised me."

Sophia didn't look convinced but seemed willing to let it go.

"Ready to get to work, or do you need something first?" Reggie pointed over her shoulder to the counter.

"I'll be right back."

"And I'll find my manners while you're gone. I know I have them around here, somewhere." Reggie peeked under her notebook.

Sophia ruffled her hair on the way by.

When she returned Reggie was ready to apologize again, but Sophia jumped right into work mode. Reggie was disappointed there wasn't any flirtatious banter, but she'd probably blown that chance when she'd snapped at Sophia.

"Look, before we get started, I'm sorry for the rude way I said hello."

Sophia cocked her head and smiled. "I don't believe you said hello at all."

"Right, well, hello. It's very nice to see you. I'm not used to being so lost in thought people can sneak up on me. That can be a little dangerous at work."

"I handle prickly, grumpy people all day at work. You don't scare me." Sophia folded her hands on the table.

"Just how is it you handle them?"

Sophia winked. "Shall we get to work?"

Reggie shook her head then dropped it to the table dramatically. "Fine."

Sophia tapped a pen on the back of her head. "Up you go, I need you to talk to me about that notebook full of scribbles you're sleeping on."

After an hour, Reggie got them coffee refills. When she worked with Sophia it was easy to forget about their lives away from the table. Sophia was so beautiful she stunned Reggie every time she saw her. Women like her should only exist in movies or imaginations, but it was her intelligence that was especially attractive. Sophia, Reggie was learning, was in a league of her own when it came to strategizing, thinking of all sides of policy, and working a problem. It was fun to work with her even if she was always three steps behind.

"Since that night we had an early dawn hot dog party, I've been thinking about the supervised injection site. It's a non-starter, at least right now, and I'm not interested in writing it into our recommendations, but are there other, less dramatic things we could suggest that would hit the same target?" Sophia took the offered latte.

"Why couldn't we suggest it? It doesn't seem that different from the politics of needle exchanges when they were first suggested.

They were controversial, and getting those programs off the ground was a huge lift. The opposition was loud and unrelenting, but think of all the lives that have been saved. How is a supervised injection site different?"

Sophia nodded slowly. "Sure, I get that needle exchanges were controversial, but at the end of the day, reducing the chance of deadly disease transmission by making clean needles available was the extent of the services provided. Inviting active substance users to come to a specific location staffed with medical personnel with the express purpose of using illicit drugs seems altogether different."

"But the end goal is the same, right? Both programs are intended to reduce the negative consequences for the one using the drugs and to a lesser extent the community at large. One through disease transmission and the other by overdose prevention." Reggie leaned forward, her elbows on the table.

Sophia took a sip of coffee and sighed. "It doesn't matter, Reggie. The public testimony on the injection site proposal was eighty/twenty against. It never made it out of committee."

"But what do you think about it? People change their mind when leaders they trust explain to them why they should reevaluate their beliefs."

"I think, politically, it's a non-starter, at least for now."

"If you want to know why I dislike politicians so much, this is why." Reggie's knee was bouncing at the rapid pace of her heart, which had started double-timing the more strenuously she and Sophia disagreed.

"I know." Sophia looked down at the table.

When she looked up, her expression was sad. Reggie felt guilty. It wasn't Sophia's fault Reggie found the constant calculations and transactional nature of politics repugnant. It was the world Sophia lived and thrived in so decisions she evaluated came through that lens.

"It looks like you have more in that notebook. Surely you sketched the blueprints to common ground in there somewhere."

Reggie slowed her knee and relaxed her shoulders. "Hey, I don't think we're doing this right if we don't disagree. If there were easy solutions to this stuff someone else would have come up with them already. Didn't they tell us during the orientation we're supposed to argue?"

Sophia smiled. "I think they did, but honestly I was pretty distracted by you that day. Well, you and Bert's fabulous glasses."

Reggie laughed. "His glasses are half the reason I show up every week."

"I wanted to steal the last pair he wore. Maybe I'll see if Lily wants to branch out into eyewear."

"They would have looked much better on you."

It was easy to picture the vibrant glasses against Sophia's dark brown skin. Reggie didn't like the idea of anything covering Sophia's expressive brown eyes, but those glasses had been so inviting and fun, she could imagine them enhancing Sophia's playful side that she'd only seen during their discussions of giraffes and in the pre-dawn hours. She'd happily rip the glasses from Bert's hands if she could see more.

"Share your thoughts. Don't hold back."

Reggie froze. What was Sophia asking of her?

"Your notebook. What did you write down for us to talk about today?"

Sophia must have picked up on her confusion.

"Of course." Reggie tapped the notebook and flipped back and forth between pages a couple of times to reorient herself to what she'd written and to get her head back in the game.

Now it was Sophia's turn to look confused, but she didn't say anything while she waited for Reggie.

"The first thing I think we should figure out is where folks find roadblocks to access. I can think of a couple, but we're going to have to talk to people who have firsthand experience. Second, what kind of treatment should we be expanding access to? I don't know who to ask there." Reggie checked things off on her notes as she talked.

"These are good. Keep going." Sophia was taking her own notes now. She scooted around the table closer to Reggie.

"The last thing is where, or how, would we expand access? I don't think we'll put up flyers on telephone poles, although I wrote that down, along with singing telegrams, and bus and gas station ads. We have to get the word out somehow."

"Singing telegrams?" Sophia looked like she was holding back laughter.

"It's applesauce." Reggie tried to wave it away and move on.

"If you say so. Okay, so where are the roadblocks, what is the access needed for, and how do we communicate? I'd also add why's it needed because any change in policy is going to need to have a sales pitch to the general public. You don't have to like it. You can say it's dumb politics, but you have to get people on board if you want it to work." Sophia wrote *WHERE, WHAT, HOW, WHY* in big letters across the top of a new page in her notes.

"That seems easy enough. Shouldn't be a problem to knock this one out. What do you think, a couple of days? We did the hard part in coming up with big block letter headings." Reggie pointed to Sophia's notes.

Sophia moved her chair even closer to Reggie. She leaned over and circled the same words she'd bolded at the top of her page in Reggie's notes. "There, now you've identified keywords too. We're on a roll."

Reggie sat back and put her hands behind her head. "All in a day's work."

She was rewarded with a poke in the stomach.

"I met Frankie's friend Kit at my brother's construction job site the other day. I think she might be a good person to start with for a couple of these questions. She might not be able to answer them or might not want to, but she might be able to point us to someone who can."

"The prison system should go under the 'where' category. I can be our source on that one. Treatment options dry up as soon as someone's behind bars. I think it's one of Parrot Master and the Zookeeper's most lucrative business arenas." Reggie leaned over to Sophia's notes and added *Prison* under the proper heading.

Reggie pulled a blank sheet of paper from her notebook and started a list of the people they wanted to talk to and the questions they wanted to ask.

"I wonder if we should talk to Natasha Parsons. Do you know who I'm talking about? She's that social worker who works for the police department, the one who made the news for stepping in front of about a hundred police to stop them from shooting a mentally ill guy?"

"You're right. She'd probably have some fabulous insight for us. Valencia Blackstone, you met her at Lenny's. She's her sister-in-law. Might be good for an introduction."

Natasha Parsons went on the list.

"You're the only person I know who keeps notes on paper." Sophia looked over Reggie's shoulder as she wrote.

"You're taking notes on paper. The Zookeeper does too, at the meetings." Reggie pulled her notes closer to her and pointed at Sophia's handwritten sheet.

"True. I left my iPad in my office, and I admit I still like to do things like diagraming on paper. Can't imagine the Zookeeper likes to put much on electronic devices waiting for snooping hackers to take a peek at her underworld super highway."

Reggie shrugged. "I'm not interested in going all digital. I'm rather analog myself, so pen and paper suit me."

Abruptly, Sophia stood. She touched Reggie on the shoulder. "Add whoever else we should talk to initially to our list. I'll be right back."

Reggie watched Sophia weave between tables, then turned back to the list. She could have added a slew of community organizations but decided to keep their initial contacts minimal. Each person they talked to would likely lead them to another contact.

She did add the Zookeeper to the list. If she minded her flock as she said then she would certainly know the flaws in the system operating above board.

As she finished and surveyed their work, Sophia returned. She set a plate containing a single, enormous chocolate chip cookie on top of the pile of notes strewn across the table. She retook her seat which wasn't right up next to Reggie's, but still she adjusted to close any remaining distance.

"This is to celebrate a first rush of success."

"Are you sure it's not because you want to watch me drool over a cookie? Chocolate chip cookies are my favorites." Reggie kept her hands in her lap so she didn't make a fool of herself diving for the cookie.

"I wouldn't be altogether upset to watch you drool, but maybe not over a cookie." Sophie looked at Reggie out of the corner of her eye.

Reggie opened her mouth to say something but closed it again. What was Sophia implying? Not what Reggie thought, right?

"Cookie?" Sophia broke the cookie in half and slid half to one side of the plate.

Reggie picked up the cookie and inched closer to the edge of her chair. Their shoulders were touching and she could feel the heat of Sophia's body. The sweetness of the cookie was mixing with the subtle scent of Sophia's perfume. It was making Reggie's head spin.

She'd seen beautiful women before and not lost her head. She'd worked side by side with intelligent women before and not been knocked off-kilter. What was it about Sophia that had her barely recognizing herself or her reactions? Why was she giving a second thought to someone in a profession she swore she'd never interact with again?

Reggie told herself it was because she believed in the work and that was more important than past hurts no matter how deep. She looked at Sophia who smiled at her with a dab of chocolate stuck to her bottom lip. What if while the past was buried deep, new feelings were allowed to grow? What could befall her then?

CHAPTER ELEVEN

P lease tell me that your mother's on another creative kick and she's mixing spices I'd never think had any business falling in love until I took my first bite." Sophia didn't look up from the report she was reading at the gentle knock on her doorframe of her open office door.

"I admit to not having the slightest idea what it looks like when spices fall in love, but I suspect you weren't expecting me." Speaker Spaziano filled up the doorway, looking amused.

Sophia jumped to her feet. "My chief of staff's mother is an outstanding baker. What can I do for you?"

The Speaker sauntered into her office and lowered himself into one of her guest chairs. He motioned for her to sit as if she were the guest. "How's the design team going?"

Sophia's heart thudded in her chest and her stomach clenched. The question wasn't unexpected, but that didn't mean she wouldn't welcome a trapdoor in the floor or the ability to teleport.

"The work has been gratifying and the team is engaged, diverse, and thoughtful. I'm confident the recommendations we produce will satisfy the governor's mandate."

"Yes, of course, I'm sure it's wonderful, etcetera, etcetera. Now what about what I really want to know?" He leaned forward in his chair and smiled his big jovial smile with a sinister edge lingering at the corners.

"You'll have to be more specific." Sophia took a breath to settle her heart rate.

"Very good, Sophia. Never give away more than you need to. You're a natural at our game. The other lesson you'll learn is never give anything away without getting something in return."

"And what is it you have to offer me?" Sophia raised an eyebrow and waited him out.

"I like you, Sophia. You're an ambush hunter, just like me. I'll give you this one because we play for the same team and I hope our relationship is only beginning. If you can deliver the legislative win we spoke about I'll see to it that you're elevated to the number three position in the House in the new legislative session." He sat back.

Sophia took a few breaths, then stood and came around to the front of her desk to buy herself some time. "Sir, we already have someone in that leadership position."

He waved his hand. "Not a problem, I'll take care of my end. Now, what can you tell me about our legislative possibilities?"

Sophia counted to ten to avoid telling him to go to hell. Reggie's boogeymen was alive and bribing her in her office. A tingle ran up her spine when she thought of Reggie. What did the Speaker know about Reggie?

"We're still in the early stages of our proposal development, but there are some promising avenues that may develop from the recommendations we send the governor. I told you I'd keep you informed as relevant information surfaced and I will." She glanced at her watch. She had a meeting in three minutes, and hopefully Valencia would be early.

"And what about the two undesirables I warned you about? I know you've been spending an inordinate amount of time with the Northrup woman."

She stood and crossed her arms, fury flooding her veins. "She has a name, they both do, and I'm not sure I'm comfortable with the fact that you're keeping track of who I'm spending time with."

Speaker Spaziano stood and stepped closer, his smile gone. "I don't give a fuck what you're comfortable with. I'm not handing a leadership position to someone I can't trust, and if you're affiliating with that piece of garbage family, then I can't trust you or use you to help me or the party. I told you some stains don't wash off, and I don't like to be seen getting that dirty. Get me what I want, Sophia, and keep one eye over your shoulder. In our business, someone's always watching. Do the right thing for your career here. It's a no-brainer."

Sophia sank heavily into her chair as soon as he left. She wasn't sure if she wanted to laugh or cry at the absurdity of the situation. A leadership position was a dream and yet, it was far too good to be true, right? And what about Reggie?

Valencia knocked, causing Sophia to jump.

"You were expecting me, right?"

Sophia waved her in. "Yes, sorry. My morning has gone off the rails already. It's throwing me for a bit of a loop."

"My cat puked up something electric blue and stringy this morning, and lucky for me the puke pile was exactly where I put my feet when I get out of bed in the morning. I think it's a full moon so we have twenty-four hours of this crap ahead of us."

Sophia laughed. "Your telling me that shouldn't make me feel better, but it does."

"That's why I told you. My husband's morning didn't start out all that well either with me screaming out curse words and hopping around the bedroom." Valencia wiped tears from her eyes as the two of them laughed.

The moment of levity allowed Sophia to make a decision. Trust had to start somewhere. "Before we get started, hypothetical only here, how would you feel about being offered something like a prime committee assignment or a leadership role in exchange for pushing through legislation that will make someone else look good and potentially give them the credit for someone else's work?" Sophia worked hard to keep her hands still and nervous fidget-free.

"That's tricky. On the one hand, it seems like a cut-and-dried bribe, right? But those assignments go to folks who get results or deliver for the party, so there may be some shades of gray." Valencia looked thoughtful.

"I'd want to know what was expected in return once the new assignment or leadership post was handed out." Sophia tapped her chin as she thought.

"And is the initial legislation something you believe in or something you're *told* to sponsor?" Valencia looked energized. "It does feel hard to shake off the bribe vibe though."

"It does, doesn't it? Thanks for playing along. My design team cochair strongly distrusts politicians, and I've been trying to think of scenarios like that one through her eyes. I know how she'd view the arrangement. Shall we get to work?" Sophia returned to her desk chair and pulled out a notebook and pen. Reggie's habit of paper note taking was bleeding into her life now too.

After about thirty minutes of brainstorming practical substance use policy changes, Valencia tossed her pen on the desk and stretched. "What's the deal with this, anyway? Aren't these the details you're working out with the design team? Why do you need me?"

Sophia adjusted the sleeves of the beautiful new suit jacket Lily had made her. "The design team will provide recommendations and guidance to the governor. What she chooses to do with that, I have no idea. If she sticks it in a drawer, I'd like to be ready with this." Sophia pointed at the work they'd been doing. "And if she comes out with something destined to fail?" She indicated the notes on her desk again.

"And if she wants legislation she can put her name on?"

Sophia smiled. "Then I guess it won't be such a bad thing that you and I will already have something amazing ready to go."

"Just like that? You and the design team do the work, but then you'll let me take credit next to you?" Valencia looked skeptical.

"The design team will get credit for the work it does, but the work stops at the doors to the statehouse. In here, you and I are working on something different, and to the extent that I can control it, we both get credit or it gets buried."

"Even if you're offered one of those hypothetical leadership positions to kick me to the curb?" Valencia winked.

Sophia choked on the sip of water she'd taken. If only Valencia knew. Would she take credit for the bill if it meant a meteoric rise?

"Even then. What good is any leadership position without the respect and support of those you lead? Bribery isn't the way I'm hoping to rise."

"Good enough for me." Valencia rubbed her hands together and picked up her pen. "Let's get back to work."

Sophia looked down at her notepad, and the faintest hint of what she hoped would be a solid bill. What would Reggie think of this meeting, where she was using what she knew would be considered the safest and least progressive ideas of the design team to craft this bill? The thought of Reggie made her chest tighten with feelings she wasn't sure she could or should examine closely. She didn't want to be looking over her shoulder constantly when she was with her and the unpleasant reminder that she should was unsettling. Perhaps she should be more disheartened by the attempt to bribe her. She was relieved Reggie hadn't been there to witness it, not because she was ashamed of her own behavior, but because she wanted Reggie to see her as separate from, better than, the politicians she despised. The fact that she wanted Reggie to see her in that light was playing with fire since Reggie's favorable opinion could very well get her burned.

CHAPTER TWELVE

The doorbell rang and Reggie jumped up to answer. She looked forward to her once-a-week game night with Ava although it was Ava's turn to pick the game so they could end up playing endless rounds of Candyland.

Ava breezed in carrying a game box and a brown paper bag. Reggie was curious about both, but her stomach won the day.

"What's in the bag?" She reached for it.

"Absolutely not. I was nice to you tonight and brought the train game, so keep your grubby hands off this bag until I give the green light."

"You really should get a job where you're allowed to boss people around. You're really good at it." Reggie tried one more time for the bag but was swatted away.

"My job is bossing you around." Ava batted her eyes at Reggie.

"Well, you're very good at that too. I'll get us beer. You set up the board."

Reggie returned to a prepped game board, dealt cards, and the most extravagant donuts she'd ever seen. She didn't think it had taken her that long to find the bottle opener.

"Are those from that place downtown that always has a line halfway down the block?" Reggie picked up a donut and examined it. "What are those things on top?"

"Fruity Pebbles cereal, I think. That place would put anything on top of one of these. We should try making donuts and dumping whatever crazy thing we can think of on top and calling it gourmet food."

"What makes you think either of us can bake?" Reggie gave the Fruity Pebble concoction a sniff.

"Bake? We can't bake. Or at least I can't. But I'm great at making weird stuff up. What about a Jell-O mold and banana donut? Or a donut lollipop with a cherry on top?"

Reggie laughed. "Why would anyone want either of those?"

"Who knows? Why did I buy these? Is it good?" Ava pointed at the donut.

"It smells all right. The colors are weirding me out a little." She took a bite and chewed slowly. "That's actually delicious. Your moldy Jell-O doesn't stand a chance."

Ava stuck out her tongue and snatched the donut from Reggie. She took a bite and her eyes got wide. "You're right." She handed it back. "Guess I'll have to stick to kicking your ass at board games."

They played the first fifteen minutes mostly in silence. Reggie was content to focus on accumulating the cards she needed to rack up points. Maybe Ava was still dreaming up donut flavors, she wasn't sure.

The game board was a map of the United States, and to score points you had to play train routes connecting cities throughout the country. As she lay down another route stretching her connected trains farther and farther across the country, her mind meandered back to the design team and her argument with Sophia. She looked at the map and thought of the ways substance use had impacted the entirety of the country, but not equally or equitably.

The negative consequences of substance use often didn't strike equitably either, although addiction cared little for the boundaries of race, class, gender, or any other category of human distinction.

"How many people do you think would be left in our prison if drugs weren't illegal, or at least they were decriminalized?" Reggie absently played her turn.

"Everyone, unless you're thinking of letting all the folks currently serving time out. But each year the number would drop. After a few years, maybe only half? But you know as well as I do that sometimes disorderly conduct charges or resisting arrest charges are actually related to drug use. I bet those would go up a lot if cops or prosecutors couldn't go after someone another way."

Reggie leaned back and sighed. "I hadn't thought of that. It would take time for a culture change in the police departments too. Otherwise the heaviest, most vulnerable users would continue to suffer the most and end up with us anyway."

"Hey, look what's happening with our police department. They have those social workers now. That's something. What's going on with you lately?" Ava put her cards down and leaned forward, her elbows on her knees.

"What do you mean? Nothing's going on with me."

She reached for more cards, but Ava stopped her. Reggie was surprised to see concern in Ava's expression.

"I've watched you get more and more closed off, especially at work, and now you've got this design team, which seems to have rattled you all around. I know you've never really liked the job, but it seems to be worse lately. So, I ask again, what's going on with you?"

"Oh come on, we're all closed off at work. Do you spill your life story to the women locked up with us? That's always been our rule. You act like you live at work, sleep at work, have no life outside of work. The less they know about you the better."

The words tasted sour coming out of Reggie's mouth. It was the hardest part of the job, refusing to allow the possibility to form bonds based on shared life experiences. When she'd taken a job in corrections she hadn't been fully aware of the toll it would take on her mentally.

"Protecting ourselves doesn't mean we become robots or lose the ability to feel anything. You always have me to talk to. You know that, right?"

Reggie nodded. She did know Ava was always there for her, but she had no idea what to say or where to begin. It wasn't a part of the job she'd ever heard her coworkers talk about. She'd taken the job initially to ensure her father paid his debt to society, but now the emotional burden of the job weighed so heavily she felt like the one doing time. She never even saw him, and more than once she wondered if she was doing penance of some kind by choosing a career in law enforcement. Maybe she'd felt like she should have to pay for his sins. She hated it.

"So tell me about the design team then, but not the boring world changing parts. I want to know about the woman who's rattled your insides enough to make you stomp around work and talk to yourself when you think no one's around." Ava nudged Reggie's knee. "She comes up every time you tell me about the meetings, so don't lie to me."

Reggie thought of Sophia. She felt lighter and she smiled. She frowned as soon as she realized her mistake. "There's nothing to tell. Sophia and I are paired up working on our part of the policy proposals, of course she comes up."

"Fine, if I win this game, you have to tell me the truth. Deal?" Ava held eye contact like they were having a staring contest.

"You always win." Reggie looked at her cards and then the board.

"Then fess up now and save yourself the misery."

"Pick up your cards. Let's play." Reggie pointed at the board and focused intently on her next move.

They played in silence for the next twenty minutes. Reggie put up a valiant fight, but in the end, as always, Ava was victorious. Reggie didn't know why she always lost. She'd tried various strategies, but Ava was the superior player. Tonight it meant confessing something she wasn't sure she was ready to admit.

Ava waited patiently as Reggie fidgeted in her chair. "Sophia is my partner on the design team and we argue about almost everything, but we can't seem to stop flirting either. Beautiful doesn't do her justice. She takes my breath away."

"This is fabulous." Ava clapped her hands. "You can still feel human emotion just like a real boy."

Reggie flipped her off.

"You can't ask me to do that kind of thing if you really like this woman." Ava pointed at Reggie's middle finger. "You've been on a few work dates and still think she's gorgeous, so ask her out on a real date. If she flirts back with you while you're working she's going to say yes."

"That's not what I'm worried about." Reggie walked to the window. She looked out over the view of the river. "She's a politician."

Ava came to stand beside her. "So?" She looked at Reggie, clearly confused.

"So, she's a politician. As a rule, I'm not interested in politicians. They're bad news."

"I think that rule's already broken, hot stuff, and I don't think they're all bad. I hear Abraham Lincoln wasn't horrible. Lots of people liked Reagan and Obama. Probably not the same people, most likely, but still, people liked them."

"Lots and lots of people liked my father too. That doesn't mean he was a good person and not rotten to the core." Reggie slammed her hand on the window frame. "Politics draws in corrupt people and leads good people to make constant calculations in their life, political calculations that rarely take into account anyone but themselves."

"Wow. I'm going to sidestep the pile of daddy issues because I'm not a shrink and I don't want to get any on my shoes, but my unprofessional opinion is you might want to exorcise those at some point."

Reggie glared at Ava who held up her hands defensively.

"I know, I know, he's an asshole and was a terrible father. But here's my last question for you. When you look at Sophia, do you see the political boogey monster you just described? Is that how she makes you feel?" Ava tapped Reggie in the center of her chest. "Try letting this lead for a while. Or at least thaw it out."

Spontaneously, Reggie pulled Ava into a hug. She tried to pull out of it immediately since it was an unfamiliar feeling, but Ava held on.

"Thank you for the advice. I'll consider seeing if Sophia would be interested in some more flirting. But I still think politicians are the worst."

Ava gave her a gentle shove away to break the embrace. "I wouldn't expect anything else, you stubborn ass. Now go get us more beer and let's play another round. Maybe you'll finally win on your hundredth try."

Reggie flipped her off again on the way to the kitchen. "I think you only win because you cheat."

"It took you long enough to figure it out."

Even if Ava was secretly cheating, Reggie didn't care. It was a small price to pay for such good friendship. She thought about Sophia and her stomach danced. Was she brave enough to ask her out? Maybe not yet, but she could suggest their next working meeting was back at Fatima's restaurant. She couldn't change Sophia's profession, but was she willing to fight for a chance to see what a step beyond flirting might look like? Only time would tell.

CHAPTER THIRTEEN

Sophia hung up the phone and rolled her neck. She'd blocked off the afternoon to make constituent phone calls and answer letters and emails, but she rarely sat for such extended periods of time and her back and neck were screaming.

Rodrigo walked in with his arms full, looking stressed. He always looked stressed late afternoon when she was making phone calls and not attending to the hundred other things on her to-do list. Especially when he knew she had to be out of the office promptly and she was running behind schedule.

"Should I get a standing desk?"

"I thought you were taking care of the needs of the people, not interior design. If you're done being productive, I've got other things to fill your time." He dropped the armload of papers onto Sophia's desk.

She took a closer look at what he'd deposited and saw it was draft legislation. She'd have to speed-read if she was going to make it to the design team meeting on time this evening.

"Can you take care of lunch and clear my afternoon tomorrow? I don't think I'll get through all of this tonight."

"Already done. I know you want to get out of here in time for your side hustle and to see your sexy woman." Rodrigo fanned himself.

"My side hustle is the design team the leadership asked me to join, and she's not my woman." Sophia put her hand on her hip.

Rodrigo mirrored her gesture. "Speaking of leadership, the Speaker's been asking for an update on the design team. I've been stalling him like you asked, but that's only going to work for so long. And, Sophia, sooner or later he's going to find out about Reggie. Just because she's not your woman doesn't mean you don't want her to be. I for one am going to enjoy the hell out of the show, but I suspect your bosses will not."

"You're not invited to the show." Sophia came around her desk and sat on the front edge. "There's nothing for leadership to get upset about. Reggie and I are cochairs, we have to spend time together, which is what I told him the last time he asked and I'll tell him every time he asks going forward. But I do need you to tell me what you learned about her."

She felt dirty even thinking of getting a briefing on Reggie and her family. Why should political calculus come into play with who she spent time with? It certainly didn't when she was alone with Reggie, but there was a part of her that worried that could come back to bite her. What kind of person did that make her? Exactly the kind Reggie thought she'd be because of politics.

Rodrigo shut the door. "Bartholomew Northrup is a real gem. He's in prison after getting convicted on racketeering charges, but he's been accused of assault, bribery, and murder."

Sophia waved him off. "I know that part. What did you learn that's not available with a Google search?"

"For years he was the gatekeeper through which politics flowed in the state. If you wanted something done, you courted him. If you needed a favor, you'd better have something to offer in return. He was transactional and always came out on top. Regina Northrup is his only child. Her mother died of cancer shortly after Regina graduated from college." Rodrigo ticked off items on his fingers as he went.

"Reggie." Sophia gripped her desk tightly. "She goes by Reggie, not Regina."

Rodrigo looked at her like she had three heads. "Did you hear the rest of what I said?"

"I heard it. He's a terrible man. No wonder Reggie thinks politicians are corrupt assholes. Anything about her?"

"Nothing concrete. But Sophia, she's his *only* kid. She was with him at plenty of events as a teenager and young adult and she knows all the players. There's a reason people don't trust her. Whether it's true or not, she's seen as his heir to the family business."

Sophia threw her hands up. "But she's not in politics. She abhors the whole business."

Rodrigo put his hands out as if offering peace. "I'm only the messenger. You asked what I'd heard."

"You know this is why people hate politics and politicians, right?"

"Sure, and rightly so. You know why they love them? Because they make their lives better by passing good laws, like the one on your desk." Rodrigo tapped his wrist. "You're going to be late if you don't start reading."

Sophia waved him out and flopped back in her chair. She flipped to the first page of the bill and scanned it without processing any of it. She pulled out her phone, debated, and texted Reggie to say hi.

She smiled when Reggie responded right away. When it was the two of them, Sophia had a hard time remembering why associating with Reggie was politically risky. She'd chosen a career that did not reward risk taking, but maybe her personal life deserved a different metric. Who was she kidding? Politicians weren't allowed personal lives outside public scrutiny. No wonder Reggie was disgusted. Politicians were in endless pursuit of elusive approval from thousands of faceless strangers often to the detriment of those closest to them.

That was a thought for another time. She looked back at the bill on her desk. She concentrated, mostly, for three pages. She stole a look at her watch and realized she was going to be late to the design team. She packed up as quickly as she could and double-timed it to the now familiar building.

The buzz in the room was almost as electric as Bert's two-tone neon leopard print glasses. She didn't have a chance to ask what had everyone so excited before Bert got them started.

The first half hour was devoted to progress updates from each of the teams. The longer Sophia listened, the more uncomfortable her chair, clothes, and air in her lungs became. What was everyone thinking? Was she the only one who thought smaller steps was the way to go? Was she wrong to think that way?

After the updates, they broke into their smaller teams. Sophia considered faking an illness and heading home. She wasn't up for another showdown with Reggie after what she'd just heard. When she saw Reggie across the room setting up a chair for her, she knew she couldn't sneak out the door. It wasn't part of her makeup to avoid her duty, but even if it were, Reggie was like a bonfire and she was a helpless moth drawn to her flame. At least Frankie and the Zookeeper were working on their own part and were setting up at the conference table.

"That was intense." Reggie indicated the rest of the PAC members. "I'm all about reform, but even I think some of that is an ocean too far. You must be close to a panic attack."

Her shoulders relaxed from ear level and she nodded, grateful that Reggie already understood. "I haven't squirmed or sweated that much since I forgot my homework one time in third grade."

Reggie considered her intently. "I can see a young, panicked Sophia without her math papers. You wouldn't dare blame it on the dog I bet."

"No way. When it was time to turn in our homework, I turned in a one-page apology letter. I was convinced I'd blown my chance of moving up to the fourth grade."

It wasn't hard to conjure that feeling again. She'd had it at various times throughout her life. Being perfect was impossible, but damn if she didn't try and then feel defeated when she fell short. Perfection was the most important virtue her parents had tried to instill in her and Davey.

"What do you think Brenda Seeley's going to say when she stops by?"

Reggie was shuffling through her notebook so missed what Sophia was sure was a shocked expression.

"The governor's coming here? When?"

"At some point tonight. Were you not here yet when Bert told us?"

Sophia had met the governor a couple of times since she took office. They were both women of color in their first terms, looking to fulfill their campaign promises and serve their constituents. Of course the governor answered to a larger following than Sophia, but at least on paper their political priorities aligned. The place they differed was how comfortable they were making a splash.

Sophia wasn't shy about her pragmatism. She'd been derisively given the "moderate" label more than once, but she preferred to think of herself as a problem solver and a realist. Governor Seeley fell a bit left on the spectrum and was a skilled partisan. Sophia admired her political chops and calculated risk taking. She hadn't gotten elected governor by playing it safe. There was probably a lesson in her rise to power, but Sophia wasn't sure Brenda Seeley was the one she'd choose to emulate.

"I must have missed Bert's announcement since I got here a few minutes late. I'm interested to see what she has to say, since she's the one who put all of us together."

"We better have our best stuff polished up to show her. Do we have any best stuff?"

Sophie caught Reggie looking her over and not exactly discreetly.

"Should I be offended you don't think either of us is 'best stuff'?"

Red crept up the side of Reggie's neck. "The governor's on her way, I don't have time for flirting. Stop fishing for compliments. I'll tell you how beautiful you are later. Besides, when it comes to this." She looked at her notes, then turned the notebook upside down and examined it again. "We may still have some work to do."

"Didn't crack it since I last saw you?" Sophia tapped Reggie's notebook with her pen.

She'd foregone her laptop and iPad when she came to the design team or met with Reggie. It felt odd and also freeing to jot things down on paper, she hadn't done it in so long. She didn't know anyone aside from Reggie who still took notes by hand.

"I probably cracked a thing or two, but I haven't solved the drug crisis since the last time you saw me. I'll have to stand up and bat my eyelashes and give her my most winning smile to prove my use to her." Reggie directed her over-the-top eye flutter at Sophia.

"The First Gentleman is sure to be insanely jealous." Sophia mocked swooning.

Reggie gently poked her in the knee. "Hey, don't get distracted by the sights. I told you we don't have time for flirting, we have work to do."

Sophia rolled her eyes and poked Reggie back. "Fine, go ahead then, you show me yours."

The pink migrating farther up Reggie's neck was adorable. Sophia would have paid four pennies for her thoughts in that moment.

"I've been thinking about the Zookeeper."

"That's disappointing." Sophia sat back, away from Reggie, and crossed her legs slowly. She enjoyed that Reggie watched.

"Not like that. I was thinking about the time she was an inmate at my prison." Reggie looked over at the Zookeeper and looked hesitant to continue. "I can't tell her part of the story. Some of it's her business to tell or not, but my point is her main business didn't slow down because she was locked up. If anything, I think her being behind bars might have made it easier to run one branch of their business."

"And you allow that?"

Sophia didn't mean to sound quite so accusatory.

"We don't *allow* anything of the sort. But you try to stop drugs being smuggled in when someone like the Zookeeper is involved in logistics and planning. She's got guards on her payroll, visitors, you name it. She's set up an entire subsidiary operation that runs through every cell in the prison. As fast as we can lop off one rotten limb, a new branch sprouts."

"So what does that have to do with us and the work we're doing? Don't the inmates have the choice to get treatment while they're with you?"

"That's the thing, aside from twelve-step volunteers and religious and psychological counseling, there's not any type of formal drug treatment offered. No medication-assisted therapy, which is badly needed. A court order said corrections facilities have to provide it, but states all over the country have been slow to roll it out, and individual facilities are already low on funding." Reggie wrote a few notes in her notebook and underlined "MAT" and "Corrections."

How was what Reggie saying possible? Surely those arrested for drug crimes should immediately be offered drug treatment if they wanted it. Wasn't prison supposed to be about rehabilitation?

"That's wrong on every level. It shouldn't be easier to get heroin than methadone in prison."

"Oh, she'll sell you methadone too if you want it." Reggie hitched her thumb over her shoulder toward the Zookeeper. "But your point is taken."

There was more Sophia wanted to say and ask, but before she could the conference room door opened and Governor Seeley stuck her head in. She smiled brightly and waved as everyone stopped and stared at her.

"Don't let me interrupt. I want to chat with Bert for a moment and then I'll come on by and chat with each of you if that's okay with everyone."

Sophia was impressed with her charisma and easy command of the room. She didn't ask for all eyes to land on her, they did because there was nowhere else that demanded more attention.

"When I walk into a room, where do people look?"

"What?" Reggie turned her attention back to Sophia.

"Nothing, never mind. We should keep working. She'll be over soon." Sophia glanced once more at the governor talking to Bert and then refocused on Reggie.

"I don't suppose I can speak for everyone, but the moment you walk in a room, you're the most compelling thing in it, to me. If that's what you're asking." Reggie looked like she was going to take her hand but pulled back before their hands touched.

"No matter what anyone says about you, you are very sweet, Reggie Northrup." Sophia did what Reggie had not and joined their hands briefly. "But you told me no flirting."

The moment their hands touched and Sophia leaned toward Reggie, the governor appeared. Reggie quickly pulled her hand from Sophia's.

Sophia stood quickly to greet Governor Seeley. Reggie jumped up next to her.

"Representative Lamont, so wonderful to see you. I was thrilled to hear you had joined the design team." The governor shook with one hand and clasped Sophia's shoulder with the other. "And, Ms. Northrup, wonderful to have you. Corrections is an important piece of this puzzle. Tell me about the work you two are doing." She pulled up a chair and waved them both back to their seats.

Sophia let Reggie fill the governor in on their area of focus and initial brainstorming. While Reggie talked and the governor listened, Sophia studied. She watched how Governor Seeley listened intently and kept eye contact. She could tell by Reggie's body language she was engaged in the conversation.

Being a good listener was an important skill for a politician because even when you didn't care a lick what someone was telling you, you still needed to make sure they felt heard.

"I applaud the work you two are doing. I hear from Bert you've both been elected cochairs of this Policy in Action group. Congratulations." The governor held up her finger, silently asking for a moment, and leaned back to get a whispered update from a staff member who materialized behind her. "Sorry for the interruption. I was offering much deserved congratulations."

"Thank you, ma'am. I'm looking forward to the process unfolding over the coming months." Sophia practiced the targeted eye contact.

"I've heard great things about you, Ms. Lamont. If you call me Brenda, is it okay if I call you Sophia?" The governor waited for Sophia's nod and then continued. "Sophia, I watched your campaign and have heard the chatter about you. You'll probably have my job one day if you're interested."

Sophia hoped she didn't look as shocked as she felt. "Ma'am, I'm not sure what you mean."

"Please, false modesty and demurring only works when you're not ready to announce something. Behind closed doors you need to always be ready to go for the throat. This is me giving you advice as a crusty old lady who was once young and eager, like you, not as the governor, okay?" Brenda patted Sophia's knee.

Sophia dared a glance at Reggie. It looked like a thunderstorm had rolled in over a party yacht three tequila shots out to sea.

"Thank you, ma'am. I'll keep that in mind and remember to pack my brawling bras when I dress for work."

Brenda laughed a full-throated, fill-up-the-room-with-joy laugh. More than a few design team members turned their way. Sophia saw even Reggie smiled.

"I like you, Sophia. I hoped I would. I can help you go far while I'm the most powerful politician in the state, but I want something from you."

Of course she did. Why didn't Sophia see that coming? Politics was always transactional, that was part of the fun. The trick was making sure you got more than you gave. Now Sophia had to come out on top.

"I'm listening." Sophia made sure her face was neutral and indifferent.

"When the design team is wrapping up, I want you to join forces with the other cochairs. I want you to get the final proposals compiled and I want you to draft legislation that gets through both chambers and onto my desk. I want something out of this design team that I can sign into law. I know that's not the purpose of what you're doing here, but how about we save everyone the months of grandstanding and chest thumping that would be necessary if I took the proposals from this team and rolled out a plan of my own. You talk to my office and get something done so the two of us can announce it the day the design team wraps." Brenda clapped her hands once as if that settled it.

Sophia was having a hard time ignoring Reggie's increasing agitation. She wondered what Brenda truly thought of Reggie's presence on the design team or her obvious displeasure now. Sophia was fairly confident Reggie looked like a three-year-old about to lose her mind over spilled apple juice because she had a front row seat to the political give-and-take she seemed to loathe, but Brenda likely had no idea.

"Reggie, do you mind asking Bert if we have any homework for our next meeting?"

Although Reggie looked reluctant, she nodded and headed to the front of the room to talk to Bert. Sophia needed to feel free to do her job, not worry about what Reggie was going to think of her.

Sophia turned back toward Brenda. "What's in it for me? You get the bill and fulfill a campaign promise, but what do I get?"

"Ah, good, much better than meek and mild, but not a very good question. You get your first piece of substantial legislation, sponsored by you. Not only that, but you help me fulfill one of my first one-hundred-day wish list items and fulfill one of your campaign promises to get things done. On top of that, you have the thanks of a grateful governor."

"So you'll owe me." Sophia pointed between Brenda and herself.

"I didn't say that." Brenda shook her head. "You're not as green as you look, rookie. Do we have a deal?"

"I'll do my duty as cochair of this group and I'll keep in touch about legislative action."

Brenda looked like she wanted to say more on the topic but let it drop. She glanced over her shoulder at Reggie talking to Bert. "A last piece of advice, off the record, Sophia. Be careful with that one. She's bad news. Getting mixed up with her doesn't lead to the chair behind my desk."

The frustration bubbled up fast and hot.

"Is it her that's the issue or her family name?" Sophia took a breath to keep her tone level.

"One and the same in our line of work, perception is reality. Be careful. There are some stains you can't wash away. Maybe she's a Boy Scout, maybe not. Are you willing to put your career on the line to find out?" The governor raised an eyebrow and stared at her for a long moment.

"Thanks for the advice. I don't have a choice while we're on the design team, but I hear you and I appreciate the warning."

Sophia did appreciate the warning even if she wasn't comfortable with the message. She had to find out what Reggie was being punished for if it went beyond what her father had done. Whatever was bad enough to blacklist Reggie didn't seem like the kind of thing she'd be mixed up in. Reggie was kind, charming, and thoughtful, the opposite of most politicians. Maybe that's why they didn't want her around.

The governor took her leave with a promise to keep in touch about the design team's progress. It sounded more like a teacher promising to keep track of the progress of a mandatory book report than a friendly check-in, but Sophia knew it was all part of the game.

Reggie was still talking to Bert, which gave Sophia a chance to evaluate her without getting caught. Her insides quivered when Reggie laughed at something Bert said. She didn't figure that was supposed to happen with a work colleague. She thought of not seeing Reggie again after the design team was finished and immediately felt downhearted.

She put her head in her hands a moment and tried to clear her thoughts. The governor was asking for legislation from the design team simply so she could say she'd worked toward a campaign promise. The Speaker and majority leader wanted first crack at the outcomes from this group so they could poach the glory from the governor's agenda. No one cared what the recommendations actually were or where Sophia landed on the issues. She was caught in the middle, expected to play a role she wasn't sure she was appropriately cast for.

Then there was Reggie, who should have been like touching a hot stove, but instead was heating her in all kinds of other ways. She took another look at Reggie who saw her and smiled. Sophia's stomach misbehaved again. Jesus, this had been quite a meeting.

CHAPTER FOURTEEN

R eggie paced her kitchen watching the clock tick closer to the time she'd have to decide whether to get out of the house or be late to meet Sophia. Would she dare blow her off completely? No, she wasn't mad enough for that.

It had been two days since the last design team meeting, and the time and distance hadn't tamed the fire in Reggie's belly from watching Sophia and Governor Seeley go tit for tat on the outcome of the design team's work.

The governor had asked Sophia to do her a favor, and instead of spitting in her face, Sophia had asked Reggie to step away.

"I guess someone's face was spit on." Reggie shoved her feet into her boots and stomped to the door. "Great, now you're talking to yourself. Pull it together, Northrup."

She called Ava on the way to meet Sophia.

"So, did you decide to go?"

Reggie thought Ava sounded more entertained by her plight than was appropriate for the situation. "I'm going, but I'm not going to think she's pretty when I get there." Reggie gripped the steering wheel harder.

"Bullshit on that one. Reggie, rules are good. Look at our job. We live for rules, even the dumb ones, but this no politicians rule might make you miss out on something great right in front of you."

"I don't actually like living for the rules. Our job sucks. But the no politicians rule *is* a good one." Reggie glanced at her notebook on the seat next to her to double-check the address. "The governor asked her for a favor and then she asked me to leave. Do you know how many times that same scenario played out for me as a kid? My dad conveniently had some errand for me to run as soon as a friend of his came by asking for a favor? Political favors aren't usually in the public interest, especially the kind that need to be finalized without an audience."

Ava sighed. "I know your dad's a monster. I've had the displeasure of spending way too much time with him. It doesn't mean Sophia was agreeing to sell the governor one of your kidneys. Maybe the governor needed a cooking class recommendation because she's terrible in the kitchen. Have you thought about doing something radical and talking to Sophia about why she's the worst?"

"Shove it, that's a terrible idea." Reggie was smiling and she knew it was bleeding into her voice.

"I'm full of terrible ideas. That's why you're friends with me."

"Your Jell-O mold donut *was* a terrible idea. You're right though, Sophia could be the female version of my political nightmare and I'd still think she's gorgeous." Reggie navigated into a parking spot and turned off the engine. "But hormones and body reactions are out of our control."

"Give her a chance, man, for the love of God. And, Reggie, if you didn't work with me and all of our rules, what would you do?"

Reggie was silent a long time. Admitting out loud what she'd only ever told her mother, even to Ava, felt precarious. "I've always wanted to be a teacher."

"Political science, I assume?"

"I'm hanging up now. I'll consider calling you next year." Reggie picked up her notebook and pen and got out of the truck.

"Hey, Reggie? You'll make a wonderful teacher. Now go unstubborn your ass and talk to your lady." Ava made a loud kissing noise through the phone before she hung up.

"She's not my lady," she mumbled. She glanced at her watch. She was still a few minutes early but decided not to wait. She and Sophia were meeting Frankie's friend Kit Marsden to ask her some questions for their design team planning.

Kit had asked them to meet at her job site, which was an active construction site. She'd told them to head for the company truck and she'd meet them there, so that's what Reggie did. When she came around the truck bed she was greeted by a slender, attractive, butch White woman, and a handsome Black man with a friendly smile, who looked so much like Sophia that Reggie did a double take.

"Are you Reggie Northrup? I'm Kit Marsden."

Reggie saw the man with her do a double take himself.

"Are you the one my sister Sophia goes on and on about?" He examined her more intently.

"That probably depends on what it is she's going on about. I'm perfectly willing to plead the Fifth if necessary." Reggie put her hands in her pockets and let Sophia's brother take her measure.

"No need, I think she li—"

"Davey, whatever you were about to say, please remove yourself from my business."

Reggie looked up and locked eyes with Sophia. As promised, her body betrayed her and thoughts raced from "beautiful" to "stunning" to "hot damn." She looked down quickly to hide her smile and nudged a rock with her shoe.

"Kit, I'll see you later. Reggie, it was nice meeting you. My name's David Lamont, in case my sister disowns me after this and I don't get to meet you again. She's not so bad. Give her a chance."

"Davey."

Reggie heard a warning growl she'd never heard in Sophia's voice. David must have recognized it too because he scooted across the construction site double-time.

"Sorry I'm late. I see my brother's stuck his nose in my business, as big brothers love to do."

Even though she'd chased David off with a growl, Reggie could see how much Sophia loved her brother. It practically radiated off her as she watched him retreat back to work.

"Nice to see you again, Sophia." Kit extended her hand. "I know David's his own man, but in case you're the worrying kind of sister, he's been a great addition here. We get a lot of newcomers who think this is the job for them, but you'd be surprised how many wash out on the first day. I hope he decides to stick around."

"I certainly am the worrying kind. He says it's the quality that would least recommend me. I won't speak for him, but as his sister, I appreciate that you didn't write him off the minute you saw his application. Most people do when they see he has a record." Sophia looked at Reggie. "He doesn't try to hide it, but I'd still appreciate it if you'd keep that to yourself. I'm only willing to share now because I think it's relevant to some of the questions we might want to ask Kit."

"You can trust me."

Kit looked curious as she watched the interaction between the two of them. Reggie felt like there was more to the look than mere observation, it looked like recognition, but she couldn't be sure.

"If Josh, that's my cousin and the owner of the company, made hiring decisions based on past mistakes, I sure as hell wouldn't be here. He's a pain in my ass, but you won't find a better man walking the earth as far as I'm concerned. He's also the worrying kind, so I thought I recognized the look." Kit pulled some folding chairs from the bed of the truck. "You said you had some questions about my work at Star Recovery?"

Reggie took the offered seat and sat across from Kit. She thrilled when Sophia set her chair closer than was necessary. It was a warm late March day, so the fresh air felt nice, especially since Reggie was now sitting next to the hottest woman she'd ever been this close to.

"Yes, we do. You said you were familiar with the design team from Frankie, right?" Sophia crossed her feet at the ankles and dust kicked up and covered her expensive looking heels.

Kit nodded. "She's been talking of almost nothing else since it started. The Zookeeper's participation still baffles me, but I suppose I can see the value if I step back. She and I have a complicated history."

"You and half this city."

"Fair point." Kit got up and rummaged through a cooler in the truck. "Can I get you some water?" She held out a water bottle to each of them.

Reggie took the offered drink. "We're working on policies to improve access to treatment. I'm sure you see a lot of the barriers through your work at Star. Can you shed any light on the topic that can help us?"

"Where to begin." Kit took a sip of water. "Access has to be easy. You can't set up shop in a storefront somewhere and expect everyone to hop on a bus and find you. Star's well known in the community, but we still have to get out and meet folks where they are."

"Do you mean literally meet them on a corner or in their home, or meet them where they are mentally in their journey to sobriety?" Sophia was taking notes and only looked up when she asked Kit to clarify.

"Both, actually. But just then I meant physically. A few years ago, Frankie helped organize what she called 'family dinner' at the library where my wife is head librarian. The park out front is Parrot Master and the Zookeeper's territory."

A look of serenity crossed Kit's face when she mentioned her wife. Reggie hoped to love someone enough someday to get that look with a passing thought.

"Anyway, Frankie convinced all parties that one night a week, the library would host community organizations and a huge party, and Parrot Master and the Zookeeper would put a closed sign on the park for a few hours. In the middle of the neutral zone is a Star Recovery table. We get people all the time who ask for help and say they never would have known to seek us out."

"It's not possible to have a folding table set up on every street corner, and Parrot Master and the Zookeeper aren't going to shut down their business willingly all that often. Do you have ideas for how you get access out into the most vulnerable communities?" Reggie wrote "diffuse access points" in her notebook and underlined it.

Kit shrugged. "I guess that's more your department. I'm not a politician or on fancy committees. I can only tell you what I see and what I know from my own experience. If I'd walked past a place to sign up for rehab one of the times I had a brief moment of motivation at the height of my use, who knows, maybe I would have found my way out sooner."

They talked to Kit a little bit longer, mostly about her past drug use history and ideas for easier access to treatment. Getting folks in the door was often only the first step in the recovery journey, but sometimes the largest. Long term care and follow-up could be the entire focus of another design team group.

"One last question before we go." Reggie folded her chair, collected Sophia's, and followed Kit to put them away. "If you were in charge, would your goal be to get rid of drug use, or reduce the harm from use?"

Kit looked from Reggie to Sophia. "You're never going to rid the world of drugs. Trying is a fool's errand. What we can all get better at is caring about the *people* who use those drugs. Addiction is a disease that inflicts suffering indiscriminately. I've always thought of it as a tornado sweeping up everyone and anything in its path. Why, as a society, wouldn't we try to do everything we can to reduce the harm that tornado inflicts?"

After thanking her for her time, they walked off the construction lot together. It was early evening and daylight savings meant sunset wasn't yet upon them.

As if by mutual consent, they both turned away from their vehicles and walked away from the work site and the return to their lives. At the corner, they turned again and Reggie was amazed at the change in scenery. This street was tree-lined with neatly appointed single family homes. It was a far cry from the bustling city block where her truck was parked.

"It feels like we're a world away." Sophia looked over her shoulder then left to right. "Where did this little piece of suburbia come from?"

"It's one of my favorite things about this city, it's so small that transitions that would take twenty blocks in other places happen street to street here." Reggie indicated around them. "I wonder what's around the corner."

Sophia had an adventurous twinkle in her eye. She took Reggie's hand and didn't let go. "Let's find out." She gave Reggie's hand a tug.

Reggie feigned indecision.

Sophia pouted. "Do you have somewhere to go?"

"Nowhere I'd rather be." Reggie let herself be led down the street.

The feel of Sophia's hand in hers was causing all of her nerve endings to stampede from her brain back to her hand like a herd of wild horses running free and joyful in the wind. She hoped the evening and this street never ended.

"Are you still mad at me for talking to the governor like a politician the other day?"

"No, you're hard to stay mad at. I was mad at you when I drove over to our meeting today. But now you're holding my hand and I can't stay mad at you when you're touching me." Reggie looked down at their joined hands. "But yes, I was mad at you for being a politician with the governor."

"Reggie, I'm a politician all the time. It's my job. That keeps coming up as a sticking point for you."

"Out of curiosity, if I unstuck, where would I go?"

Sophia held up their joined hands in an "I don't know" motion. "It's hard to argue there seems to be something here, when we stop loudly disagreeing about everything and think of each other as Reggie and Sophia, two people who might like each other."

"I do like you, Sophia Giraffe."

"And I like you too, Hellhound. Try to remember you like me the next time I'm talking to another politician." Sophia changed their hand position so their fingers intertwined.

"I'll try. Can you try to be less obvious with your skulking around, trading favors next time? I have bad memories associated with that kind of thing." Reggie tried to kick a rock but stubbed her toe instead.

"I wasn't trading any kind of favors." Sophia pulled her hand away. "Whatever kind of experience you've had, that's not the type of person I am. I asked you to go talk to Bert so you didn't glare at the governor so long that her security tagged you as a threat."

"I'm sorry. I didn't mean to put you in an awkward spot with the governor." The words came out in a whoosh. "Can I have your hand back? Tell me what happened. I'm touchy about anything like that. You see how people react to my last name. I have reasons I'm the way I am." Reggie reached for Sophia's hand. She sighed with contentment when Sophia reached back.

"Any chance you want to tell me about those reasons since they keep butting in every time we're together?" Sophia gave Reggie's hand a little wiggle.

"Sure, but not right now. I'm walking, holding hands with a woman who, if I'm being honest, takes my breath away a tiny bit. Why would I want to ruin that?" Reggie kept her eyes purposefully forward, but she could feel Sophia looking at her. She was rarely, if ever, ready to talk about her father with anyone.

"Can't think of any reason at all to ruin something like that. But if you're short of breath, how are we going to continue our adventure? Should I step away so you can recover yourself?" Sophia started to take a step to the side.

Reggie pulled her closer. Sophia caught her toe on an uneven patch of sidewalk and tripped into Reggie's arms. Their faces were a novella's width away from each other. The feel of Sophia in her arms and her breath on her lips was making it hard for Reggie to breathe.

"I should scold you for your poor manners causing me to trip, but your chivalry preventing my fall more than makes up for it." Sophia leaned forward slowly and at the last moment turned her head and kissed Reggie's cheek.

Reggie sighed in contentment and displeasure at the kiss. Had Sophia intended to kiss her lips at first? It seemed for a moment as if she had.

Sophia extricated herself from Reggie's arms and continued down the sidewalk, pulling Reggie with her. "I want to see what's around the next corner, don't you?"

"Isn't that why we're on this walk?"

"Well, then, a little more walking, a little less distraction." Sophia winked at her.

"I can't imagine why I'm distracted, but I'll try to pay more attention to the trees and the sidewalk. I won't give the source of my distraction any more attention so I don't ruin our walk."

Sophia poked Reggie in the ribs and laughed. "Maybe you don't know much about women, Reggie, but we don't generally like to be ignored."

"Shh, this very attractive woman I like quite a bit said I'm too distractible, so I'm trying to concentrate. Do you mind?" Reggie made a show of looking at a tree as they walked past and scrunched her face into an exaggerated look of focus.

"You like to live dangerously, don't you, Hellhound?" Sophia squeezed her hand.

That got Reggie's attention. Sophia took her arm and moved it over her shoulders. She slipped under and snaked her arm around Reggie's waist.

"I don't want you getting so distracted you wander off on me. I'm enjoying myself."

Reggie felt like her heart might thunder out of her chest. Could Sophia feel it beating wildly? Maybe she did like to live wildly. She certainly felt wild right now.

CHAPTER FIFTEEN

Lily had her hands over Sophia's eyes as she guided her forward. "Only a few more feet. There's a bolt of fabric leaning against a chair on your right, don't trip on it."

"You have your hand over my eyes. If I trip it's your fault and I'm taking you down with me. No one will be able to explain how you and I ended up tied in a bolt of fabric together on the floor." Sophia shuffled along a little more slowly.

"A fantasy come true," Lily whispered seductively in Sophia's ear.

Sophia shivered away the heebie-jeebies. "Ugh. You find the worst times to do that to me. Let me see this big surprise already."

"I know I'm not the one you want whispering in your ear. Can I come on a double date with the two of you next time? I'll bring an extra napkin to clean your chin when you drool all over yourself."

Sophia shook herself free from Lily's grasp over her eyes. She had a sharp retort at the ready when she took in where they were.

"Is this... Did you finally... Am I standing in... Lily, really?" Sophia opened her arms for a hug.

Lily nodded and hugged Sophia tightly. They rocked back and forth as they embraced. "I finally did it. This is my place. I have a shop of my own. Can you believe it?"

"Of course I can because you're amazing. If you get one of those little bells over the door it's going to be ringing constantly." Sophia held Lily at arm's length, then pulled her back for another quick hug. "I'm so happy for you."

"Can I tell you about it? I mean, what I have in mind?"

Lily walked around the small store explaining her vision and the layout of her dream clothing boutique. Sophia knew she'd been planning for this day since childhood.

"So, what do you think?" Lily popped the top on a bottle of champagne that she'd magicked from somewhere in the near empty room.

"I think it's amazing. I can't wait to make my first purchase. But I also have to set the record straight. I do *not* drool over Reggie." Sophia sat against one blank wall and patted the floor for Lily to join her.

"I say you have since the moment you saw her and Mama told me you brought her to the restaurant."

Sophia knew bringing Reggie to Mrs. Medeiros's restaurant would raise questions she didn't know how to answer, but she didn't regret it. She waved her hand as if shooing a pesky fly. "I don't want to sidetrack from all of this." She pointed around the room again. "Tell me more."

Lily shook her head and pointed at Sophia. "Oh no, you don't. I know what you're doing. You know everything there is to know about this place. We have plenty of time to talk about you. So get talking."

There was a long silence while Sophia tried and failed to sort out her jumbled feelings. She thought about her walk with Reggie in the fading daylight and her confusion about Reggie's dislike of politicians. How the feelings of attraction and revulsion could orbit one person, she didn't know.

"Do you know who Bartholomew Northrup is?"

"Sure, who doesn't. Corrupt son of a bitch who's in prison for being a corrupt son of a bitch." Lily looked confused by the seeming subject change.

"Well, everything you've heard about him is only the half of it. He took bribes, doled out favors, took regular payments from local businesses to stay on his good side, helped move drugs throughout the city, and apparently also had a violent side. He's suspected in numerous assaults and is a suspect in at least one murder. That's Reggie's father."

Lily looked interested now. "Whoa. She lost the parenting lottery. He sounds like a joy to introduce on father-daughter day at school."

"She's hinted that they aren't close and he's the reason she doesn't like politicians." Sophia spun the champagne flute between her fingers.

"Can you blame her? What's really going on here? Who cares who her father is?" Lily took her hand.

"What do you mean who cares? Everyone cares. I'm a state rep. Bartholomew Northrup is in prison for being a corrupt politician."

Lily pulled her hand away. "Are you planning on dating him? Has Reggie killed anyone? You're going to have to lay it out for me, Sophia, because I really don't understand. You're into her, aren't you?"

Sophia nodded and looked down at her hands. "I don't think Reggie's corrupt. Of course not. She's caring, kind, thoughtful, completely the opposite of her father from the sounds of it. But she was a teenager and around him a lot at the end, right before he was arrested. People talk. They say she should have known what was going on, and there's even talk that she'll take his throne one day, if she hasn't already."

"Oh, bullshit. What throne? He's a crooked politician, not a king and he's in jail where he belongs." Lily reacted so strongly her champagne sloshed over the edge of her flute. "She was a kid. How much did you know what was going on with your parents when you were that age? How much did you give a flying fuck? You're really going to let the opinion of other people decide whether or not you get a chance at happily ever after? Maybe you crash and burn with Reggie or maybe it's meant to be, but you'll never know if you're too scared to find out. This is one of those times you flick the ghost of your mother right off your shoulder. She has no business giving you advice."

Sophia put her drink down, stood up, and started pacing. "There are a lot of factors here. The Speaker has already warned me about what could happen if I'm seen getting too close to her, and the governor is expecting a lot from me. Not to mention she made her opinion about Reggie pretty clear as well. My reputation is at stake. A lot of people vote based on nothing more than reputation."

"I'm going to cut you off." Lily stood too and put her hand on Sophia's shoulders. "What happens in your stomach when you look at her?"

"It misbehaves."

"And what do her eyes do when she first looks at you?"

"They dance like the sun on the ocean at dawn."

"And you brought her to Mama's place, which is like bringing her home to meet your family. From where I'm standing, it seems like those are the only factors that matter, sweetie. Do me, and you, and Reggie a favor and ask that woman on a date. I say this with as much love, respect, and affection as possible, but politics can fuck itself in this instance. Now, I'd like to tell you about a love story, a wedding, and some beautiful clothes I've been asked to make by Valencia's sister-in-law."

Sophia stared at Lily, not sure what to say. Could she put aside politics and the risks to her career and focus on what she wanted? The concept seemed foreign. She'd always looked at minefields to achieving her goals and looked for ways to mitigate them. Blindly strolling ahead seemed reckless. What if she took a chance and she and Reggie didn't work out but her career was irreparably harmed? The career she'd been dreaming of and building since childhood. What if she shunned Reggie and she was the one? Was any career, even her dream career, worth that? What if she drowned herself in a pile of "what-ifs"?

Sophia picked up her drink and linked arms with Lily. This problem didn't have to be solved in the next few hours. Tonight she wanted to hear Lily's love story. Love stories were hard and wonderful. They took work and choices and faith. Her faith was shaky. She'd never questioned her commitment to her career and her dreams. Bedrock was not supposed to move beneath your feet, especially not for someone who purported to hate everything you held closest. But how was she supposed to give up on something that was supposedly wrong and yet felt so right?

CHAPTER SIXTEEN

R eggie unpacked her tablet and water bottle on the bench next to her and looked around in contentment. She'd taken the bus from her house to the park and was now seated in front of the library she'd admired prior. Now she knew Kit's wife was head librarian which made her want to venture in all the more.

Spring was in full bloom and although her allergies were threatening to force her to dig her eyeballs out of her head so she could scratch all the way at the back, the park was glorious. She had a weekday off and was determined to spend as much of it outside as possible. Ava had to work, which made hiking less appealing, but sitting in the park felt luxurious and she was going to make it productive.

With a deep breath, she unlocked her tablet and opened a search tab. She typed in "teacher credentials." She tapped around a few of the search results before realizing she needed to narrow down. She redid her search to only show credentialing requirements and teacher training programs nearby.

The more she read, the more she was aware of a strange feeling deep in her belly. It was so foreign she had trouble recognizing it at first. After a while it was impossible to mistake for anything but the bone deep thrill of finding your way after wandering lost for eons.

"Making a career change?"

Reggie nearly swung her tablet around to vanquish the invader. Instead she took a breath, stood, and gave herself a pace of space.

"Jesus fucking Christ, Zoo. What are you doing sneaking up on me like that? What are you doing here?"

"This is my territory. Perhaps I should inquire after your presence here, but it's a beautiful day and the park draws all quarters of our city. You are always fondly welcomed on my stomping grounds." The Zookeeper came around the bench and sat down. She picked up the tablet and examined the page Reggie had been reading. "You would make a fine teacher, Reggie. Corrections never suited you."

Reggie hesitated then returned to her seat on the bench. She left as much room as she could between herself and the Zookeeper. "How do you know I'm not doing research for a friend?"

"Psychologists, barbers, bartenders, and drug dealers are good at reading people. We're good listeners and we understand how and why people tick. Plenty of people have and will say things that make me particularly unscrupulous given my profession and willingness to manipulate for profit, but I try to do good where I can, perhaps especially after my own brush with complete vulnerability, first to substances and then in your care. Whether you see it or not, I have my own moral code." The Zookeeper handed the tablet back.

"Your flock?"

"A relevant example, yes. No one associated with Parrot or myself preys on the weak. Commerce is commerce, but there are red lines and those cannot be crossed. Even when I was under your watchful eye, my flock was protected." The Zookeeper pointed around the park. "I'm always watching out for them."

"I asked you this once before and you said we could dig deeper another time. So I'll ask again, couldn't you have done more for them as a lawyer?"

"I thought so, as my admittance to the bar attested." The Zookeeper looked far off in the distance, her face losing its usual hard edges. "But as a lawyer you're constrained by the rule of law and someone else's moral code. I found it frequently didn't line up well with my own. I could have, within that rule of law, done a great many things that would've left me sleeping uneasily at night."

"I don't buy it. You could've been a public defender. Or an immigration lawyer. Gotten child predators off the streets. Certainly, your moral code points in the same direction as the men and women working to help domestic violence victims and vulnerable children."

Reggie didn't know why it mattered to her what the Zookeeper did for a living, what business of it was hers? Maybe at the end of the day she wasn't comfortable being the kind of person who was friends with a drug dealer. Would she consider the Zookeeper a friend? Colleague? Coworker? Was there a label that fit the Zookeeper?

"Why do you think I protect my flock? I abhor violence against the innocent and the vulnerable. But I assure you, I can do far more out here than in any courtroom. Being overworked and underpaid in the service of as many as I could cram into my schedule was never a sustainable career path for me."

Reggie stared at the Zookeeper and shook her head slowly. "I don't understand you, Zoo."

The Zookeeper stood and patted Reggie on the shoulder. "That's okay, you don't have to. The important thing is I know myself. Time under your watchful eye allowed for a deeper inner gaze for which I'm grateful. You know the real reason I couldn't be a public defender?"

Reggie shielded her eyes from the sun as she waited for the Zookeeper to enlighten her.

"I love my man and I love money. I would've had to give up both to embrace the law. That wasn't my true love. I can't change who I am, but I can still fight for the things that are important to me, out here." The Zookeeper gestured around the park. "On my own terms, without having to answer to anyone or work around any red tape. I tip the scales of justice in the direction it should lean. Out here, I'm able to sweep away the debris that clutters up the legal system."

Reggie stood and followed the Zookeeper's sweeping motion with her gaze. "I'm worried you're talking about due process. I still don't know what to make of you."

"Few do. Before I leave you to your reading, a word of advice. Your father may have you walking a path similar to my law degree. You chose a divergent path to his, whether your heart was in it or not. I had Parrot as a beacon to a better path forward, in a manner of speaking. I wonder, if you looked around, whether there might be someone to help you achieve that clarity? It seems as if you're looking." She pointed at Reggie's tablet.

Reggie looked at her shoes as her cheeks heated. "Sophia?" She looked up but the Zookeeper was loping across the park away from her. "Do you mean Sophia?" Reggie called out, but the spring breeze seemed to fling the words back in her face.

She sat back on the bench and picked up her tablet. She looked down at the teacher degree program she'd been reading about, then at the Zookeeper's retreating form. Did she know something Reggie didn't?

Reggie nearly jumped out of her seat, for the second time that morning, when her phone alerted her to a new text message.

It was from Sophia. *What are you up to?*

Getting philosophy lessons from the Zookeeper and rethinking my life.

The typing bubble displayed on Reggie's screen for so long she thought Sophia might never write back. Finally, her phone rang.

"If you tell me you're running away with the Zookeeper to become a drug kingpin I will swear under oath I never knew you. And I'll be a little jealous."

The sound of Sophia's voice made Reggie feel like someone had whispered on the back of her neck. "You'd rather be the one running away with the Zookeeper?"

"Have dinner with me tonight."

There was silence on the line as Reggie waited for Sophia to take it back, but she didn't. "I'm not sure a rogue like me deserves dinner with a lady like you, but I accept before you rethink your offer. Where are you taking me?" Reggie pumped her first silently and spun around in glee. A pissed off pigeon squawked at her.

More silence on the line.

"My invitation was impulsive. I hadn't thought past the asking." Sophia sounded unsure.

"You took me somewhere important to you when we went to Fatima's restaurant. Can I do the same this time?" Reggie could sense Sophia's hesitation, but it didn't drag on long.

"Thirty seconds after asking you out and I've already lost control of the date. Sweep me off my feet and take me to your favorite restaurant. You already know where I live. You can do things properly and come pick me up."

After she hung up, Reggie packed up her things and strutted her way out of the park. She had a date with Sophia. Not a working date, but an honest to God, datey date.

She hadn't been on a date in so long she couldn't remember how long it'd been. Dating meant putting yourself out there and being emotionally vulnerable. Her stomach tightened and her chest squeezed. It felt like the park air called for allergen reinforcements to invade her nose and eyes. Why was it so hard to breathe?

Reggie pulled her phone out and checked the time. Ava should be getting off work. She dialed.

Ava answered on the second ring.

"I need help."

"What's wrong? Where are you? Are you hurt?" Ava sounded close to panic.

"I have a date." Reggie took some deep breaths that everyone said were supposed to help but were making her throat itch.

Ava hung up on her.

Thirty seconds later, she called back. "You scared the ever-loving shit out of me because you're freaking out about a date?"

"Are you going to help me?"

"Of course I am, but next time say hello first and let me know you're not dying. Did she ask you or did you grow a pair and ask her?"

Reggie moved the phone away from her ear so as not to blow an eardrum from Ava's exuberance. "How do you know who the date's with? Maybe I met someone at the park today."

"Did you meet someone at the park today?"

"Only the Zookeeper."

"I'm hanging up and not calling back if you tell me you're having dinner with the Zookeeper. Otherwise I'll meet you at your house in an hour."

Reggie could hear Ava unlocking her car and tossing her work bag into the passenger seat.

"Sophia asked me on the date, but I'm picking the place. I'm thinking of getting food from Carmen's, but I don't want her to think I'm weird. Come over and talk me out of my own head on this." Reggie had been walking briskly enough to be breathing hard although she'd probably be hyperventilating breathing in clear mountain air. She slowed down and ran her hand through her hair. She'd met Sophia plenty of times for the design team, there was no need to get so worked up. The rest of the way home she vacillated between excitement and nerves. Maybe Ava could remind her she still had access to the full range of human emotions and it was worth taking them out for a spin.

Once she got home, Ava was waiting for her and made short work of getting her ready and staving off her self-sabotaging thoughts. Sophia was a politician, so what? Reggie was used to keeping her thoughts and feelings locked up tight at work, but she could turn that off, right? It was surface reassurance at best, but for the moment it was enough.

Reggie checked the mirror one last time before she headed out the door. She gave Ava a hug. "I'm trying to talk myself into feeling more freaked out, but I'm mostly happy. Thank you for giving me that."

"I think that beautiful woman waiting for you is probably the reason for that goofy grin, Romeo, but I'm glad I'm here to see it. Off you go before Carmen runs out of food." Ava shoved her out the door and pulled out her own key to Reggie's place and locked up.

Reggie took the front steps at record pace and leapt into her truck. She tapped the steering wheel impatiently at a red light and drove a bit faster than she probably should have on her way to Sophia's place. As she parked, the nerves returned, but they didn't feel overwhelming this time. They were the pleasant jitters when something exciting and meaningful was about to happen. They increased as she approached the door and knocked.

When Sophia answered the door, the nerves disappeared. Everything disappeared except Sophia.

"You look…I'm at a loss for words. You are so beautiful."

Sophia looked down at her shoes and clasped her hands together. Reggie stroked Sophia's cheek and gently lifted her chin.

"If there are any mirrors in that house, you know I'm telling the truth." Reggie took Sophia's hand and led her to the truck. "I can take you to any restaurant in the city if you'd prefer, but if you're up for a bit of an adventure, I'd like to take you somewhere a bit different."

"You can take me to a restaurant next time. I love adventures." Sophia accepted Reggie's help into the truck and held onto her hand longer than was necessary after she was settled.

Reggie raced around to the driver's side and tried to steal a glance at Sophia without her noticing. Sophia busted her right away. They both laughed.

"Why do I feel like a teenage boy on his way to prom with the hottest girl at school?" Reggie started the truck and pulled away from the curb.

"You'd be a terrible prom date. You have no tux, I have no corsage, no tiara." Sophia scooted as close as her seat belt would allow, her hand within touching distance of Reggie's thigh.

"I wasn't a very good date in high school either. I'll see if I can do better tonight."

"So far, so good."

Reggie pulled over in front of a row of attached storefronts whose best days were behind them.

Sophia gave her a questioning look. "Are you lost?" She looked up at a street sign.

"Not lost, hungry." Reggie pulled her closer. "Still up for an adventure?"

"Depends on what you're going to say next."

"Picnic with the Zookeeper. Frisbee golf. Drag queen bingo. Anything sparking an interest for you?"

She ticked answers off on her fingers. "Absolutely not, what the hell is that, that's always fun, but I know for a fact it's not bingo night." Sophia unbuckled and put her hand on Reggie's knee. "Try again or I'll be forced to hitch my wagon to another caravan and hope to find my way home."

"There is a very good Italian restaurant right through that door." Reggie pointed to a sketchy looking storefront that looked like anything but an Italian restaurant. "I'm planning on buying you dinner." She wasn't nearly as interested in dinner now that Sophia's hand was on her leg, but they couldn't sit in the truck all night like this.

"Last chance, Reggie, to call this off before you're seen out on a date with a politician."

"I would never do anything like that. I'm going on a date with a brilliant, captivating, and very beautiful woman."

"Who happens to be a politician."

"Technicality. Tonight, anyway."

"Let's go before someone sees you and it ruins your reputation. You promised me carbs smothered in cheese and red sauce. Lead the way."

Reggie opened the truck door for Sophia and stopped in front of the middle door of the three motley, dark storefronts. "Do you trust me?"

"You know that's a weird thing to ask someone right after you promise them dinner, right?"

Reggie laughed. "Come on, you won't regret it."

She opened the door and held it for Sophia. As soon as they were inside, the smell of garlic and comfort filled Reggie's soul. She saw Sophia breathe deeply and then relax and knew she sensed the magic of this place too.

"We have to go back to the kitchen." Reggie walked across the empty room they'd entered and waved Sophia to follow. "No table service."

"It's not much to look at, but it does smell amazing in here."

"The food is better than anything you'll find in the state, no matter what their ratings say. Thank you for giving it a chance."

At the end of the hall, Reggie rang a bell on the wall and waited. A couple of minutes later, Carmen, looking as frazzled as always, dressed in her ever-present chef's hat and apron covered in food stains, bustled over. The moment she saw Reggie her entire body took on the animated exuberance of a bachelorette party finally hearing their favorite song.

"Reggie! Why haven't you been by? When you're gone for so long I start to take it personally. No matter how swamped I am, what good is it if I never see you?" Carmen slapped Reggie's shoulder playfully.

As she bopped Reggie, she noticed Sophia. Her eyes grew wide and she looked from Reggie to Sophia.

She slapped Reggie's shoulder again. "I can tell already she's too good for you. You were right to bring her here to try to convince her you're up to standard. I'll fix you both something special."

Before either of them could say another word, she was gone.

"Carmen, wait." Reggie cupped her hand around her mouth as she called out. "It's not what you think."

Sophia leaned over Reggie's shoulder and spoke close to her ear. "Which part, specifically? The part where we're on a date or the part where I'm too good for you?"

Reggie jumped, then shivered. "I guess it's exactly what Carmen said. I'll introduce you when she comes back."

Sophia put her head on Reggie's shoulder. Reggie shivered again. Damn, if it didn't feel good to have Sophia pressed against her.

It wasn't long before Carmen returned with her arms full of to-go containers. Reggie's mouth watered to the point she worried she was going to embarrass herself by drooling on her shoes. She knew the feast contained in those boxes.

"Here you go, Reggie. She looks like a keeper. I've done all I can. The rest is up to you." Carmen handed Reggie the boxes of food and then gave Reggie a pointed look.

"Jesus, Carmen, she's standing right here. Carmen De Luca, Sophia Lamont. Carmen's the best chef you'll ever meet, even if she hides in this dump of a building."

"Nice to meet you, Sophia." Carmen waved off Reggie's praise. "Don't let her give you any trouble, you hear? Even when I was locked up, I didn't let her get away with too much. But I wouldn't have this place if it wasn't for her, so there's a good heart in there even if she's stubborn as a mule and sometimes dumb as a box of rocks."

"Hey, I can hear you." Reggie's protests were weak. Maybe this hadn't been a good idea after all.

"The food smells wonderful, thank you." Sophia, looking a little bemused, took the boxes while Reggie paid Carmen.

The sun had set while they'd been inside and it was nearing dark. Reggie loved this time of night when the light was settling down for bed and even the daytime noises seemed to understand it was time to quiet for the dusk.

"Did you meet Carmen at work?"

Reggie shifted the to-go containers so she could get back in the truck. "Yes, she was one of my charges for a while. She spent every hour she could in the library learning how to open a business. She peppered me with questions and asked for help finding the answers, so I did what I could to help her get the documents and books she needed. I told her if she opened her restaurant, I'd be sure to come by. She got out and opened her business about five years ago."

"That's impressive. Why an empty storefront?"

"She's never told me, no matter how much I tease her about it, but I will tell you, enough food moves out of that kitchen every night to feed most of the state. Her business hasn't suffered by being under the radar."

Sophia scooped one of the boxes from Reggie before it toppled off the pile and set it on the seat between them. "Maybe she doesn't like doing dishes. I certainly hate them. Where are we going to eat all this, if you don't mind my asking? You do have a plan, right?"

"Of course I have a plan, but you'll have to wait for it."

Sophia stuck out her bottom lip in an exaggerated pout. "I could threaten to raise your taxes or petition for a traffic light right outside your house, you know."

Reggie shrugged. "I work for the state. Raising my taxes won't do you much good, and a stoplight would be great. Maybe it'll slow down the toddler who speeds around the neighborhood on her tricycle."

"Very funny." Sophia steadied the food boxes as Reggie pulled back into traffic. "Do you like your job? Did you always see yourself in corrections?"

Reggie spared a look at Sophia at the question. "You're the second person to ask me that recently." She paused a long time to collect her thoughts before answering. Sophia gave her the time to think without fidgeting or seemingly becoming uncomfortable with the silence. "Let's get set up and then I'll answer whatever you want. We missed the sunset, but the river's still beautiful, even at night. Can I interest you in a truck bed dinner date?"

"It's hard to argue with an offer like that. I should have known you'd be a romantic."

Reggie parked at the riverside, got out, and lowered the tailgate on her truck and then grabbed two blankets from the cab while Sophia waited, her arms full of containers.

"I'm afraid to ask why you have blankets handily stowed in your truck. Do you have picnics under the stars often?"

"Nope. Went snowshoeing after our last big snow and I tossed them in since I had to drive a while in some bad weather. Didn't unpack them and now I'm glad for my oversight."

Sophia took Reggie's hand for assistance into the bed of the truck. "Now I am as well."

They laid out one of the blankets to sit on. The other they wrapped around themselves to ward off the chill of the evening, which also meant they were sitting shoulder to shoulder. Reggie felt like she might be in danger of tachycardia when Sophia practically sat in her lap and tucked the blanket tightly around them.

"So, you promised to answer anything I asked, which sounds like a dangerous promise for you to make." Sophia looked thoughtful. "I'll let you off easy to start. Answer the question about your job."

Reggie bit her lip. "If I'm being honest, I don't like my job. I ended up in corrections a bit by accident. I always thought I'd join the military, but I couldn't take off to wherever the military would have sent me. My mom was sick and needed me to stay. A friend of a friend knew there was a new correction officer recruit class starting up and handed me an application. The money was good and I got the option of working nights so I could take my mom to appointments during the day. I never thought about or cared what was needed to do the actual job."

"Was the military the career you planned?"

"No. Not long term, but it seemed like a good way out. Far away from everything I knew and the burden of my last name, once everything happened around that. Really, I wanted to be an elementary school teacher, but that ship sailed, I think." Reggie worked at opening take-out containers and didn't look at Sophia. Weird, how opening up about wanting a different direction in life could make her feel like she had her underwear on her head and was wearing neon pink assless chaps.

"That's ridiculous. There's this thing called a career change. You should look it up. People do it all the time." Sophia gently turned Reggie's chin until she was looking at her. "You'd be a great teacher."

Reggie nodded and looked away. She didn't mention the internet searching she'd done in the park earlier in the day. Admitting her desire to be a teacher was a big enough step. "What about you? You said you were born for politics?"

Sophia's stomach growled loudly as she dished up Carmen's food. She laughed. "Afraid so. I snuck my parents' laptop into my room at night so I could watch videos of famous political oration. I'd write my own inauguration speeches and then practice them in the mirror."

"I've never thought of a politician as something you could want to be when you grow up just like a doctor or an artist."

"Why not?"

Reggie shrugged. "It always felt like an adult decision, not something for the innocence of childhood. Big societal decisions and what you have to do to make them seem to be something you become aware of with age, not as you ride your bike down the street."

"You know, one of these days, you're going to have to talk to me about why you think so poorly of public servants." Sophia took Reggie's hand and gave it a squeeze.

"You know who my father is, right?"

Sophia nodded.

"Then you must know his reputation and what he's been convicted of. Ask around, do some reading, then trust me when I say, it was much worse than anything you can find out there. And he was far from the only one. Politicians came day and night to work out deals that couldn't be made in an open room with other people watching." Reggie tossed her napkin aside with a growl. "But it seems like you've accomplished your goal. Even I know you're a political rock star. The governor asks you for favors. You must feel on top of the world." She hoped the judgment behind the remark didn't make it into her tone.

"If only that were true. Terrified, more like it." Sophia clapped her hand over her mouth and rolled her eyes. "I did not mean to say that out loud."

"Why are you terrified? If I were to allow the possibility that not all politicians are horrible, you'd be at the top of the nice list." Reggie lifted Sophia's hand and kissed the back with a flourish.

"I'm flattered. I think." Sophia sighed. "Do you know how much pressure comes with being labeled the next big thing, not to mention the first Black woman elected state rep? How much pressure I've put on myself? I've never lost an election I've run in and I love the political gamesmanship, but this time feels different. What if I fail? That wasn't an acceptable outcome in my family growing up."

Reggie pushed her plate of food aside and wrapped her arms around Sophia. She was distracted by how easily Sophia fit in her embrace. How right it felt.

"I can't see you failing at anything you put your mind to, but what worries you most? You've had a lot of expectations and hopes and dreams heaped on your shoulders. Perhaps we can think through some of your worries together. Especially if it relates to the design team. And if, in the unlikely event you do fail? Well, that means you're human after all, which makes you all the more wonderful. "

Sophia looked shocked when she leaned in and kissed Reggie's cheek. "You're a prince."

Reggie felt aflame from the kiss. How was Sophia able to do that with one quick, innocent brush of her lips?

"You're going to have to listen to political machinations. Will your heart take the strain?"

Reggie put her hand on her wrist as if taking her pulse. "I think I'll survive."

Sophia explained the demands of the Speaker of the House and majority leader as well as the governor's request and how she couldn't please them both. She told Reggie about her own campaign promises to deliver practical solutions and work with anyone willing to do the same and Valencia's offer to collaborate.

"Everyone wants a piece of you." Reggie kept Sophia in her protective embrace. Their legs were pressed together from knee to ankle and Sophia rested her head on Reggie's chest. Reggie wished this bed reclined so she could more easily hold Sophia while they talked. "The design team seems like it's going to be your problem. Our group has some ideas I know you're not comfortable with, and we don't know yet what the other groups are working on. Plus the politics are going to get in the way of what is supposed to be an advisory group providing recommendations and nothing more. Since you're able to create legislation, that's what's expected of you, even though that's not your role on the team. Am I right?"

Sophia turned and frowned at Reggie. "Are you sure you're not a politician? You're pretty astute."

"How could you say something so hurtful?" Reggie feigned offense. "We're going to figure this out. I promise."

"I appreciate it, but it's not your problem to deal with. Dealing with the politics of situations is part of my job." Sophia leaned back into Reggie.

"Hey, in this case, I'm sticking my nose right in the middle. We're a design team team. Besides, I can't have a politician messing up all my hard work."

Sophia sat up and gave Reggie a playful push. "You're impossible."

"Hey, come back. No more politician digs, I promise. It felt for a minute like we were the only two in the world and things didn't have to be complicated." Reggie opened her arms.

"Things are always complicated, Reggie."

Reggie wondered if that was a rule or only Sophia's experience. Then again, it was her experience too.

"Maybe, but this doesn't feel it. Maybe your political problems don't have to be either."

"I thought you understood some things about politics. It's always complicated, even when it doesn't have to be." Sophia pulled the blanket tighter.

"So we'll uncomplicate it."

Sophia laughed but there was no humor to the sound. "You make that sound as if it's an easy thing to do."

"Oh no, not at all. I'm not a politician, but I'm not an idiot either and I've had my fill of how it all works. But at the end of the day, you have to feel good about what you're fighting for. You can't change the situation, but maybe you can write rules that work for you. How about a rule that you're just a regular member of the design team with no ability to write laws? You can be Representative Lamont at the statehouse and deal with the politics there."

As they lay there looking at the stars, snuggled together, content, Reggie thought about Sophia, the design team, and the difficult situation Sophia was in. Wasn't this kind of no-win political scenario exactly why Reggie didn't like politics? Sophia needed the courage to fight for what she believed in, even if it cost her politically, otherwise, what good was she to the people who elected her? But what about when the fight turned ugly? In Reggie's experience it always did. She'd already seen Sophia bargaining with the governor. What else would she be willing to do? And could Reggie live within Sophia's comfort zone?

Reggie thought about what she was willing to fight for. She looked at Sophia curled in her arms. Was she willing to fight for a chance at another date with a woman who excited her? Sophia asked her out tonight, but what about when the smudge of her father's reputation started to stick to Sophia? Reggie's chest felt heavy thinking Sophia might regret this night. She didn't want to leave it to fate. Maybe it was time to give fate a nudge in the right direction.

CHAPTER SEVENTEEN

After hours of reading and answering email, Sophia felt giddy when she broke free of her office and exited the statehouse into the late afternoon sun. The weeknight evenings she had the design team made for late nights, but more and more she didn't mind. She told herself it was because the work was invigorating and they were starting to hash out meaningful proposals, which was true, but a large measure of her anticipation was due to seeing Reggie.

While she was waiting to cross the street a couple of blocks from the meeting, the Zookeeper approached.

"Representative Lamont, always a pleasure."

"Zookeeper. How are you this evening?"

The small talk felt awkward, but Sophia didn't know what else, aside from the design team and the weather, they had to talk about. She didn't want to admit there were probably plenty of politicians, businessmen and women, lawyers, doctors, and others she interacted with daily who had plenty to say to the Zookeeper. And probably more than a few who'd been her customers.

"I've been under the impression since the design team started that my presence has disturbed you. Is there some way I can set your mind at ease?"

The Zookeeper gave her a penetrating look that felt like it was as revealing as a Star Trek tricorder.

Sophia felt her face heat all the way to her ears, but she wasn't used to lying. She could deflect questions, omit details, and redirect with the best politicians, but bald-faced lying wasn't something she was comfortable with. "Initially, I wasn't happy you were included as part of the design team. I made an unfair snap judgment, which I regret."

"Your brother is David Lamont, is he not?" The Zookeeper put her hands in her pockets and strolled along as if she hadn't casually identified the source of Sophia's anger.

"He is, yes." Sophia searched the Zookeeper's unreadable expression.

"What happened to him was a miscarriage of justice. He was screwed by the system, by the police, and by his dorm mates. I, too, shouldn't have asked him to take my wares to another customer." The Zookeeper furrowed her brows and the tenor of her voice changed to something closer to menacing.

"I need to know, did you have anything to do with the prosecutor on Davey's case seeing reason?" Sophia put her hand on the Zookeeper's shoulder to stop her before she entered the building where the design team met.

"The prosecutor wanted to announce he'd gotten a drug dealer off the streets. We had one that needed to be cut loose. David wasn't the type of criminal the overzealous prosecutor was looking for, even if he thought he fit the bill."

"But why? Why did you help him? Why *are* you on the design team?" Sophia stepped aside to let other design team members pass.

The Zookeeper propped one foot against the wall and leaned with her back against the building. "The streets are an ecosystem like any other. There is a delicate balance holding everything in stasis, and like any ecosystem there is a hierarchy, a food chain, if you will."

"And you and Parrot Master are at the top?"

"We share cohosting duties with law enforcement. Neither of us exist without the other and both provide balance to the other. I know many in my position would not agree with my assessment, but without law enforcement my enterprise would grow beyond control or devolve into chaos. My time behind bars was a flashing neon sign pointing to the utility of law enforcement's coequal influence. I was dangerously out of control in the midst of my addiction and the illegality of my actions that led to my arrest were to the detriment of the entire ecosystem."

"I still don't understand how this all ties back to my brother." Sophia chewed the inside of her lip.

"Unlike a true food chain, there are some lower down the hierarchy who are under my protection. They are the most vulnerable, and up and down the chain it's clear they are to be left alone. The man who traded places with your brother broke my rules. He preyed on the weak. An ecosystem requires that everyone play by the rules to keep it in balance."

Sophia shook her head slowly. "And what about the design team?"

"Asserting my dominance at the top of the chain by ensuring protection for my flock. The design team is an example of the balance at the top of the chain. I sit in a position of decision-making and perceived importance in a different ecosystem entirely, and one that impacts both my enterprise and law enforcement." The Zookeeper pushed off the wall and held the door for Sophia.

"I'm not sure I understand you any better than when we started this conversation." Sophia half smiled.

"Few do, but I'm not the one who matters. We are united in spirit and profession. We're leaders. Everyone's going to want a piece of you and everyone's going to have an opinion for you. If you know yourself and you've planted your feet deep in your own moral bedrock, you won't be easily swayed from your course. If something is important enough, it is worth withstanding the strongest headwind." The Zookeeper clapped Reggie on the back as they took their seats and looked pointedly at Sophia.

Sophia's knee bounced rapidly as Bert walked to the front of the room. She tried to focus on his glasses, but Reggie sitting next to her, her face, her smell, the feel of her arms around her, was all that filled her mind. But there was no denying that the Zookeeper's strange advice was something she'd need to mull over later.

"You okay?" Reggie leaned close to whisper in her ear. "Is something bothering you?"

Would it be inappropriate to tell Reggie she was what was bothering her and demand she do something about it? What exactly did she hope she'd do, ravish her right there on the worn conference table?

"I'm fine. Long day at work."

"We can make it a short night tonight so you can get home and get some rest. I don't have a big list to go over anyway."

That wasn't what Sophia wanted to hear. She wanted Reggie to have a list a mile long that would take them until the middle of the night requiring a pre-dawn, emergency snack break at Lenny's food truck. She wanted another truck bed picnic. Anything for more time to explore what might become something with Reggie.

She thought about how her constituents or her party's leadership or worse, her parents, if they were still alive, would react and felt queasy. The Zookeeper had told her to plant her feet in her bedrock, but since meeting Reggie, solid ground had started to feel more like quicksand. She was a born public servant. She'd known it since she was a child, but what if her attraction to Reggie diminished her effectiveness? She didn't agree with Reggie being stained with her father's misdeeds, but she wasn't sure she wanted to give up her lifelong dream for his sins either. She looked over at Reggie. How hadn't she noticed that Reggie's eyes sparkled when she smiled? Was she willing to give up Reggie for something as fickle as a political career? She needed to find solid ground soon because the winds of indecision were blowing her off course.

CHAPTER EIGHTEEN

Reggie squirmed in her seat, not even Bert's fire engine red glasses, complete with flame details, was enough to distract her from her discomfort. She and Sophia were meeting for the first time with the four other design team cochairs, and none of them looked happy to see Reggie.

After years of dirty looks and under the breath comments, Reggie's skin should be thick as alligator hide, but the jabs always found her tender spots. Perhaps because she was as sensitive to the association with her father's misdeeds as everyone else seemed to be. The moment Sophia sat down and smiled at her, Reggie felt her chest loosen. What was it about Sophia's presence that set her at ease? Wasn't she supposed to be scared of politicians? To her mind they were the monsters children should fear, not imaginary things in closets and under beds. She mentally rolled her eyes at herself. She was learning generalizations only worked until you attempted to apply them to an individual. Was Sophia proof the job description didn't stipulate duplicitous intent?

"Hi, you." Sophia leaned close as she pulled out her notes. "Everyone looks thrilled to see us. Do you think they have a hang-up about politicians too?"

"Probably. You guys are the worst. I'm sure they've never heard of the Northrups. It was sunshine and rainbows before you walked in."

"It's great to get the six of you in a room together. I thought we should meet at roughly the midpoint of our time as part of the design team and start to scaffold the structure of our future proposals." Bert pushed his glasses up his nose, then shuffled papers in front of him.

"The governor wants all of our recommendations compiled and presented in a written report, right?"

One of the other cochairs, Reggie thought his name was Jackson, emphasized his words with aggressive finger taps on the table.

Bert nodded and looked as if he was going to speak but was cut off.

"That's not all she wants though, right? She asked for specific legislation. She asked you, Representative Lamont, to provide her with specific legislation, right?" Jackson looked like he might rupture something if he kept up the intensity of his stare.

It was subtle, but Reggie saw Sophia tense. She wanted to reach out and take her hand, but that wasn't appropriate here.

"She did, didn't she?" Jackson pointed at Sophia and then tapped the table again.

All eyes were on Sophia.

"I'm not sure what you're alluding to, but the governor and I have certainly discussed her excitement and support for the work we're doing here." Sophia's expression was bland.

Reggie might not like politics, but she'd always admired how so much or how little could be said in a few words.

"I know you don't usually write your own bills, so I want to be involved in crafting this one. Our team has put in a lot of work and I don't want to insult you, but your reputation doesn't scream progressive. My team is looking for generational change." Another cochair, Francis, leaned toward Sophia with his voice raised.

"I always welcome citizen involvement in government."

"Will you commit to bringing our legislation to a vote?" Jackson was leaning back in his chair with his hands knitted behind his head.

Bert held his hands out and patted the air. "Perhaps we can get back on track. Legislation is, believe it or not, outside the scope of the design team. The governor was clear in her expectations for this group. We are to provide recommendations and deliver them to her. What she plans to do with those recommendations is up to her. The fact that we have a sitting representative on the design team is irrelevant, and quite honestly, it is unfair to expect her to sponsor something on our behalf."

Sophia held up her finger asking Bert for a moment. "I can't commit to more than a fair evaluation of any bill that crosses my desk. I can't agree to something I haven't read. Something not even drafted yet, in fact."

Jackson rolled his eyes. "Of course not. It might upset someone if you stuck your neck out and took a position. You call yourself a moderate, but from where I'm sitting, you lack conviction. You're a cowardly pu—"

Reggie jumped to her feet, and even without the uniform became Officer Northrup. "Do not speak to her like that."

"Or what?" Jackson took his feet off the table and sat up in his chair, staring her down.

"I'm happy to show you if you'd like to continue to be a disrespectful asshole." Reggie clenched her fists.

"Go ahead. Then you can get thrown out of here like you deserve. You shouldn't have been allowed to join in the first place. Who knows what kind of shady shit you're doing behind our backs."

Reggie started forward, but Sophia's hand on her shoulder stopped her. She turned and got lost in Sophia's eyes. The kindness and caring she found there melted her anger. As long as Sophia was on her side, she could handle the rest.

"Enough!" Bert's face was as red as his glasses. "You six are supposed to represent the best of your teams. I have half a mind to boot you all out and invite the first six people that walk past the door. They'd likely comport themselves better than this. Five minutes and we come back and get to work. I expect better from everyone."

Reggie saw a lot of averted gazes and deep interest in spots on the floor. They should be embarrassed at the way they'd treated Sophia. She got up and headed for the door. She needed a few minutes to clear her head. She stomped to the windows that overlooked the city. The view was stunning so high up. She put her forearm against the glass and leaned her head on her arm. Why did crap like what the cochairs had slung around still get to her, after all these years?

No, that wasn't it, not really. She'd had far worse thrown her way over the years, and although it was like poking an old wound, she could shrug it off for the most part. If she was being honest, it wasn't what they'd said to her that was boiling her bowels. She still wanted to knock out Jackson's teeth for the way he'd spoken to Sophia. He shouldn't speak to any woman that way, but especially not Sophia. She was remarkable, and kind, and brilliant, and more impressive than he'd ever be.

The more she perseverated the more her innards felt like a firecracker waiting for a spark. So much for coming out to cool off.

Someone put a hand on her shoulder. She spun around, already halfway from zero to sixty with her foot on the confrontation accelerator.

"It's just me." Sophia slid her hand down Reggie's arm. "I come in peace."

"I hope I didn't make it worse for you in there." Reggie hooked her pinkie finger around Sophia's.

"You know I can take care of myself, right?" Sophia jostled their joined hands until Reggie looked at her. "But I didn't mind watching you scorch the earth and threaten everyone in the room to defend my honor. I'm sorry I didn't jump on the table and start breathing fire when they went after you."

"Bert beat you to it. I could tell you were loosening your heels."

"Of course, better traction on top of a desk when you're barefoot."

Reggie looked down at their joined little fingers and up at Sophia's soft, welcoming gaze. She really wanted to kiss her, badly, deeply wanted to kiss her, but now was not a good time to announce to the world that Sophia Lamont had a thing for the Northrup heir.

"You ready to go back in?" Reggie let Sophia's finger go and shoved her hand in her pocket. "They're probably done talking about us. We've given them long enough."

"Don't sell us short, we're plenty interesting to fill up more than the time we've allowed, but let's not give them the pleasure."

Reggie turned toward the conference room but Sophia pulled her back. They held eye contact for a long time, standing inches from each other, Sophia's hand bunched in Reggie's shirt. Finally, after Reggie was sure her nerve endings had worked themselves into retirement, Sophia leaned in and kissed Reggie's cheek.

"No matter what happens when we go back in, I have your back. You belong at that table. You belong next to me. Our team voted for both of us to be here. They say I lack conviction and won't fight for anything? I'll fight for that. I'll fight for you."

Reggie's heart and stomach were beating and flipping and fluttering so wildly she wasn't sure which was making sure she stayed alive and which was cuing her that Sophia might pose a threat to her preconceived notions of the perfect partner. It didn't seem to matter to her internal reference systems that Sophia's speech had been about the design team.

It could have been about the weather or Reggie's right to put pickles on her ice cream and she was certain she'd have reacted the same way. It was the look on Sophia's face and in her eyes as she said she'd fight for her that was turning Reggie inside out.

"Are you coming?" Sophia was almost to the door and looked confused.

Didn't Sophia know what she'd done to her with that speech? How was a woman supposed to get her feet moving after something like that?

Sophia smiled as if she knew why Reggie's feet were glued to the floor. That smile turned out to be all the motivation she needed to get rolling again.

"I'm coming."

The temperature in the room was as chilly as when they'd left, but now there was a heavy fog of petulance. Reggie was curious what Bert had said to the others in their absence.

"Welcome back, you two." Bert was back to his peppy self. "We're going to walk through the major proposals coming out of our teams. Prevention is going to kick us off."

Francis and a young White woman named Colby were the cochairs of the prevention team. The work coming out of their group was focused on children, grades twelve and younger. They were particularly focused on early childhood education, family behavioral health support, and incorporating substance abuse prevention education into public school curricula.

"We have a gentleman on our team who would love some of these proposals. He's very interested in educating young people about the dangers of substance use." Reggie managed to keep her tone neutral as she mentioned Gerald's favorite proposal.

Reggie looked at Sophia who was clearly trying not to laugh. Gerald hadn't stopped harping on the Scared Straight idea since the first meeting.

The treatment team, cochaired by Jackson, who looked to Reggie like a spoiled White frat boy, and a Black woman, Geraldine, who said she'd recently retired as principal of one of the local elementary schools, were next.

They brought up a wide variety of proposals from mobile needle exchanges and drug counselors to transitioning detox programs to methadone or buprenorphine induction programs for opioid users. The idea of involuntary civil commitment to treatment was mentioned as well. From the sound of it, the treatment group brought a lot of ideas to the table and debated them together. They hadn't split off into smaller groups, and Geraldine said more than one meeting got heated.

Bert clapped his hands when Geraldine and Jackson finished their update. "Wonderful. I'm invigorated hearing about the progress you all have been making in your teams. Sophia and Reggie, why don't you cap us off? Then we'll discuss what I'm going to need from each of you as cochairs as we move closer to the end of our time together."

"Our team has broken off into smaller subsets to work on specific topics related to drug policy. Reggie and I, for example, are working on policy changes to make access to treatment less burdensome."

Reggie tried very hard not to stare with moony eyes at Sophia while she talked. They'd been on one date and Reggie felt like a lovestruck teenager. Had it really been that long since she'd been interested in anyone that she'd reverted all the way back to the all-consuming crush?

"Thus far, some of the policy changes that have been proposed include decriminalization of a subset of substances, mandatory law enforcement trainings, a more robust and easily accessible prescription database so a prescribing physician in any system can check recent opioid or pain management scripts, and a supervised injection site." Sophia tapped her pen on her notebook as she spoke.

"That last one is dead in the water since you killed it," Francis muttered under his breath.

Reggie bristled, but Sophia subtly shook her head.

"I appreciate all the power you're tossing my way, but I'd urge you to brush up on your Civics 101. The power of government doesn't reside in a single individual, and if it did, I doubt anyone would choose a freshman state representative from my district, but I'm flattered you think so highly of me." Sophia inclined her head at Francis.

"Which of those proposals are you putting forward?" Geraldine had her hands folded on the table, but there was no malice in her eyes.

Reggie wasn't sure what to do with her hands and shoved them in her lap to keep from balling them into fists while she talked. "We're still collecting data before mapping out our recommendations. Treatment access in prison is an obvious place for reform. Diffusion of resources has come up repeatedly in our discussions. Having one location isn't enough to reach everyone who needs help."

Geraldine looked satisfied with Reggie's answer even if everyone else's expression was still guarded. It wasn't her problem to remove the sticks from their asses about her being at the table. Worrying about them was a waste of precious time.

"Friends, wonderful."

Bert's enthusiastic energy, if harnessed, was enough to power a glittering ball of dazzling sparkle suspended over an all-night dance party.

"As we move to the final phase, as cochairs, the six of you will be responsible for writing the recommendations for your team after consensus is reached. Then the six of you here will have to work out the format and structure of the final document, which will be sent to the governor. I can't wait to move toward our finished product."

As if by agreement, Reggie and Sophia both lingered as the others packed their belongings and one by one headed for the door. They were the last two in the conference room by the time they made their way to the door. They waited for the elevator in silence. Reggie wanted to say something but felt tongue-tied. Why did her words and feelings sometimes flow so easily and other times feel locked away, far out of reach?

"The other night, in your truck. Wait, that sounds like it's going somewhere it's not. The other night at dinner, I had a good time." Sophia rubbed her hands together then wiped her palms on her pants. "A great time, actually. What I guess I want to ask is, will you—"

"Yes, I'll go out with you again. That was what you were going to ask, right?" Reggie took Sophia's hand and ran her thumb over her knuckles.

She brought Sophia's hand to her lips and kissed it lightly.

"Of course it was. Why did I get so nervous asking you that?" Sophia touched her hand where Reggie had kissed and smiled. "I'd love to go out again."

They rode the elevator down in a more companionable silence. On the sidewalk outside Reggie didn't want to part ways and admit the evening was coming to an end.

"On our next date I'm picking the place." Sophia inched closer.

"As long as you're there I'll be happy."

Reggie was distracted by the way the setting sun was casting warm light around Sophia's dark brown hair, making it look surrounded by a ring of fire.

"I like the way you look at me."

Reggie stopped appreciating the view and caught Sophia's eye. "How do I look at you?"

"Like I matter to you. Like I'm beautiful. Like you want to know what I'm thinking." Sophia adjusted her suit jacket while she talked. "Like you see me."

"A very nice summary. But you should take a look at the people you pass. Doesn't everyone look at you like that?"

"Good night, Reggie." Sophia chuckled.

"Good night, Sophia." Reggie took a few excruciating backward steps away from her.

Sophia looked conflicted, but the look was fleeting. She followed Reggie and enveloped her in a tight hug.

The hug caught Reggie off guard, although her body didn't delay its response to Sophia once again pressed against her. "I'm not complaining, but isn't this dangerous for you? Being seen hugging me, I mean." She hated that the words had come out, but they were true and she didn't want to do anything that would jeopardize Sophia's reputation.

She hugged Reggie tighter. Reggie wrapped her arms around Sophia, returning the embrace.

"It's what I want and there shouldn't be backlash because I hugged you in public. If you're lucky someday I might even kiss you where the world can see."

Reggie groaned and playfully pushed Sophia out of her arms. "You can't say things like that when you're plastered all over me. I have a delicate constitution."

Sophia's big, infectious laugh echoed out across downtown. "I'll keep that in mind. Now go, before I insist on starting our second date now. I have to be up early and I'm cranky if I don't get enough sleep. Rodrigo will come find you and yell at you if it's your fault I'm a grump."

"That doesn't sound like something I want. I'm leaving now, but I want it on the record that you're making it very hard on me."

"You and your delicate constitution. So noted. Good night, Reggie."

Reggie managed to walk away, but not without looking back more than once. Each time Sophia was waiting with a wave and a smile. The feelings tingling through her toes, swirling throughout her stomach, fluttering in her chest, and squeezing her brain, felt foreign. So foreign in fact that it took the entirety of the walk back to her truck and the drive home until she recognized what she was experiencing. She was happy.

How long had it been since she could say that? She thought of calling Ava but decided to keep a tight hold of the feeling for the night. What if she described it to someone else and it disappeared? Was it a fleeting experience or something she could build on? Questions sparked and danced with the newly identified emotions, making for a surprising bouquet of possibility. The problem with untapped possibility was that the line between success and failure was razor thin. Could Reggie navigate it? Since her father's fall from grace, she'd never felt she regained her balance and this was a tightrope she didn't want to fall from.

CHAPTER NINETEEN

S ophia parked in front of Davey's job site and cut the engine. He didn't get off work for another ten minutes, but she'd been able to sneak out of work early and hadn't known what to do with herself.

She pulled out her phone and tapped it on the steering wheel before giving in to her desire and texting Reggie to say hi and let her know she was thinking about her.

Reggie wrote back quickly. *At work. Miss your smile.*

It felt like warm candlelight spread from Sophia's toes to her nose as she reread Reggie's words. For the first time, she allowed there could be real feelings building. It scared and thrilled her in equal measure.

Another text came through. *This week is nuts. Haven't forgotten about next date. Soon. Promise.*

Sophia thought about writing back that she couldn't, she'd changed her mind, and nearly choked on her own regret. She wasn't backing out now, even if it was the wiser, more pragmatic choice.

I won't let you forget. I'll see you at the design team if I don't get you sooner. Sophia's hands trembled as she typed.

Davey pulled open the passenger door and dropped into the seat startling Sophia so much she nearly dropped her phone.

"Setting up a hot date?" Davey pointed to her phone suspiciously.

Sophia pulled her phone closer to her chest. "So what if I am."

Davey's eyes got wide. "You are. With who? That mall cop?"

Sophia punched him in the arm, hard. "She's a corrections officer." She narrowed her eyes when Davey started to laugh. "You knew that. You were baiting me."

"Of course I was. You know you give away a lot by how hard you smack me when you're frustrated? You've done it since you were little. You must really be hung up on her to hit me that hard." Davey searched her face but didn't say anything else.

Sophia considered giving him a politically neutral answer or a jokey blow off, but given her own discovery moments ago, either of those felt dishonest. She'd never lied to her brother.

"I can't seem to sort out my feelings for her, but when her name pops up on my phone I can't make myself care that she's a risk to my career. I want to see more of her, even when I just said good-bye."

Davey reached out and took her hand. He only did that when he was about to get serious with her about something.

"A job is something you do, it's not who you are, and it sure as hell isn't something you can tuck yourself in next to at night."

"I think my job is a little different than most. People care a lot about things like who politicians tuck themselves in with at night and a whole lot of other mundane information. You know all the information you always wonder about your doctor or the bus driver you see every day but don't have any right to know? Well, everyone thinks they have a right to know all those details and more about politicians."

"So what? I think I have a right to play my cello in the middle of the street during rush hour because I pay taxes for that road, but everyone else disagrees." Davey shrugged.

"That's not the same thing, but thanks. I think."

"My point is, you don't have to give in just because someone else has expectations for you. You know how damn proud I am of you? Maybe Mom and Pop never let up on us, but even they couldn't find fault with what you're doing now. I tell everyone my baby sister is Representative Lamont, but if this lady makes you happy..." Davey trailed off.

"You make it sound so easy." Sophia pulled away from the curb and headed toward Mrs. Medeiros's restaurant.

"Hell no. You're the one who chose to mix love and politics, the two most volatile human conditions on earth. There are about a million ways this blows up in your face." Davey mocked an explosion with his hands.

"You're one to talk."

"I'm choosing a different route, no mixing. After politics and love, friendship and love is probably next in line for combustion potential. I prefer an explosion-free existence." Davey looked down at his hands in his lap, his eyes sad.

"You know, one of these days I'm going to tell her. Neither one of you is getting any younger. I want to be an auntie and if you aren't going to locate your balls and tell her how you feel, I'll have to take them out for a spin myself."

Davey looked horrified. "You wouldn't."

"Why not? She's my best friend, and we don't keep secrets from each other."

"You've kept this one. I'm begging you." He looked at her with desperation in his eyes.

"For God's sake, Davey, just talk to her." Sophia blew out an exasperated breath.

"Tell me about the work you're doing on the design team. You haven't given me an update in a while."

Apparently, Davey calculated a subject change was in his best interest. Sophia let him off the hook. She was excited to talk to him about the progress she'd made with Reggie and get his opinion. He'd been her sounding board for years. He'd always allowed her the vulnerability and uncertainty her parents frowned upon.

"Reggie and I are working on policies to improve treatment access. I'm surprised how well we've been working together since I think her inclination is for more radical change. I guess increased access is something that spans ideology."

"Was she one of the ones who hammered you on the supervised injection site?"

Sophia smiled back at her argument with Reggie. "We've butted heads more than once, most recently on carte blanche legalization of marijuana. She didn't wave away the concerns about increased traffic fatalities or the impact on adolescent brain development, but she wasn't willing to back down quickly either. She's a worthy sparring partner."

Davey raised an eyebrow. "That sounds promising."

"Remove your mind from the gutter."

"Remove yours. All I was saying is you need someone who's your intellectual equal and likes arguing as much as you do. What were you thinking?"

Davey looked too amused for Sophia's liking. Her face heated.

"We talked to your boss, Kit, about her experience, both personal and from working at Star Recovery. She had some ideas we'll look into. Reggie knows of some glaring need in the prison system. I'm excited about the final proposal we'll put together."

They parked and got out of the car. Davey held the door for her. Mrs. Medeiros, as if she'd been tracking their progress, was waiting for them. She pulled them both into a crushing hug.

"You're table's waiting. Lily's here too." She pushed them away, looked each of them over carefully, then pulled them back for another hug. "I like having my babies all together for dinner."

It was a familiar routine whenever they came for dinner. Since their parents passed, Sophia and Davey had been enveloped into the Medeiros family that had always been a second family to them anyway.

They followed Mrs. Medeiros across the restaurant to their table. Sophia elbowed Davey. "Lily's here. Now's your big chance."

Davey glared at her and put his finger across his lips.

As they approached the table she mouthed "grow a pair." He ignored her and turned his full attention to Lily. Sophia often wondered if Lily was as clueless as Davey assumed.

"Where's Reggie?" Lily looked toward the door.

"Why would she be here?" Sophia looked up quickly. She knew she sounded defensive.

"Be careful, she's wound a little tight on that subject today." Davey stage-whispered behind his hand.

"Is something wrong? I thought you and Reggie were getting along? Didn't your date go well?" Lily put her drink down and gave Sophia her full attention.

"Getting along a little too well." Davey reached for Lily's drink to steal a sip.

Lily slapped Davey's hand away without turning her focus from Sophia. "Hush, Davey. You don't seem to know the first thing about women or relationships or what a woman wants, so put yourself to good use and get us a round at the bar."

Sophia laughed as Davey walked away looking bewildered. She'd always loved how Lily could throw him off balance with barely a glance.

"I don't know how you do that to him. He's going to walk into a wall if he doesn't clear out the cobwebs."

Lily looked Sophia dead in the eye. "You know exactly how I do that to him. He's a damn fool if he doesn't recognize it too. Even stupider if he doesn't know what he does to me in return. How long does he expect me to wait around for him? That man's going to have to step up and show me I'm worth him taking a damn chance."

Sophia sat back and looked at her brother at the bar, joking with the bartender. "You know, it's the twenty-first century, you could make the first move yourself."

Lily looked over her shoulder at Davey and smiled shyly. "Why are we talking about me? Tell me about your Reggie. What's troubling you?"

"Nothing. Absolutely nothing. That's what's concerning me." Sophia put her elbows on the table and buried her face in her hands. "I'm so swept up in the giddy emotions, I'm not thinking rationally. But the not at all subtle threats to stay away from Reggie are still out there. I have my dream job and I'm not worried that I could blow it all up, or at least not worried enough to stay away from her."

"You haven't stayed away from her for months now, and you haven't been impeached or recalled or censured for improper association. Have you gotten any angry constituent letters?"

"Not about Reggie, but I'm more worried about my fellow politicians at the moment."

"I mean this with as much love and respect as possible, but politicians, you know, you guys talk a lot, and sometimes there is a lack of follow-through. Could all that insinuation have been bluster?" Lily reached out and took her hand. "Is it worth risking something that makes you happy on the chance people were blowing smoke?"

"Even if those two guys are all talk, which I doubt they are given their position in my party, what they're threatening isn't hypothetical. Politics is full of sharks and you don't want to be the one to drip blood in the water. Reggie could be a vulnerability for me. I don't have to like it for it to be true."

Lily nodded as Sophia talked then squeezed between her eyes. "I seem to have a death wish tonight and am going to really push my luck. How much of this is you still being scared of not living up to your parents' expectations if someone raises a fuss? It's okay for you to have something for yourself, even if everyone else disapproves."

Davey returned with their drinks. Sophia accepted hers and absently wiped the condensation from the cool surface.

"I don't want to go from rising star to one-hit wonder because I took a stupid chance, you know? I can do good work for the people of this state, but not if I'm blacklisted."

"Sis, you've always put too much pressure on yourself to be perfect. You're going to fail, spectacularly sometimes. I know as a Black woman, you have to work twice as hard and be twenty times as good to be given half the credit, but despite what our parents drilled into us, perfection's not possible, and you're still going to fail at some point."

Davey looked bone deep sad, which always broke Sophia's heart.

"Don't let the guideposts of failure be written for you. Why can't Reggie be your soft landing after a hard day instead of the source of it? You write laws, for God's sake. You should be able to write the rules of your own life and career." Davey picked up his beer and sat back like the matter was settled.

"You're pretty good at pep talks." Sophia blinked rapidly a few times to clear the overabundance of moisture. "I won the brother lottery. But for the record, you'd be a terrible politician."

"Thank you." He saluted with his beer.

"Do you believe any of the things people say about her?" Lily looked thoughtful.

"No." Sophia answered quickly. "I've seen how deeply she despises politics and how much the stain of her father's name hurts. She doesn't want his life or anything to do with what he left behind."

"That seems like it's all that matters. As long as she makes you happy. If you're sure of each other and good to each other, fuck the rest."

Lily rarely swore. It always stood out when she did.

"You make it sound so easy. I'm also noticing you seem to already be planning my happily ever after. Perhaps you can pump the brakes on that. We've been on one date. But maybe you're right. She does make me happy and I don't want to give that up. I put all my political skill to work to solve other people's problems, maybe they can work this problem too."

Sophia was distracted during dinner with thoughts of her job, Reggie, and the intersectionality of the two. New relationships were exciting and daunting. Her job came with reward and great risk of failure, and the political cost of affiliating with Reggie was still unknown. For the first time since childhood, she felt the hint of something new challenging for the top spot on the list of priorities in her life, and that was perhaps the scariest realization of all. If she let Reggie all the way in and it all blew up in her face, what would she be left with then?

CHAPTER TWENTY

Reggie tossed her pen on the table and pinched her fingers on the bridge of her nose. "I agree with you about expanding treatment access in prison. I'm the one who brought it up. What I'm asking is why are so many people in prison for drug related probation violations to begin with?"

Sophia's eyebrows knit together, and she looked at the ceiling. "Once again, that's outside the scope of what we're doing here."

Reggie and Sophia had been going in circles for almost an hour. While things outside the design team were heading in pleasantly warm directions, the current heat between them was the type that could burn.

"Maybe we should expand our scope. If someone's freedom is contingent on abstaining from a substance they haven't been capable of quitting, and once incarcerated there is no option for treatment, isn't that an access issue?" Reggie raised an eyebrow.

"Not necessarily. Why didn't they seek treatment before they were in legal jeopardy? And if they did seek treatment, at what point are you out of chances? I'm not meaning to imply I'm callous to the suffering, but the legal system needs to be able to run its course or laws in this country are meaningless. There can't be endless carve outs for certain populations." The longer Sophia talked, the more animated her hands became as they motioned in the air.

Reggie sighed and tapped her pen on the table. "Of course, but it doesn't feel right to me to tell someone that they're going to prison unless they stop a substance they're addicted to when the use is what got them in trouble to begin with. Holding prison over someone's head when their substance use has already led to a host of negative consequences feels like a stick being wielded with little chance of motivating the sought after behavior. They need treatment access *before* they relapse and end up violating their probation. *Before* they need it in the prison system."

Sophia smiled ruefully. "I get the feeling we could debate all night, but I do think we're off track, although I concede we can't even agree on that. Truce?" She lowered her voice and leaned closer to Reggie. "Even if you're awfully cute when you're fired up and passionate about something."

Reggie felt her eyes go wide. "You know you're not giving me much motivation to drop the argument?"

Before Sophia could answer, Frankie and the Zookeeper rolled their chairs over and interrupted.

"Do you two need a referee?"

"We're fine. If everyone had the same opinions, this design team would be worthless." Sophia looked from Frankie to the Zookeeper and then caught Reggie's eye.

Reggie couldn't be sure, but it felt like the look Sophia threw her way was softer, more intimate, than what Frankie and the Zookeeper got. Even when they'd been strongly disagreeing, Reggie had never felt the rancor growing out of the control. Given Sophia's comment moments ago, she wasn't harboring ill will either.

"I wouldn't usually eavesdrop, but you weren't exactly whispering. Are you still hung up on treatment access in prison?" Frankie looked thoughtful.

"How do you both feel about it? You have different experiences with the system. Maybe you can share some insight." Reggie pulled her notebook close and indicated the Zookeeper with her pen.

"To bring our rep Lamont up to speed, I veered off my sworn path of sobriety and ended up, like so many do, paying for my sins behind bars. Now, Parrot controls the flow of licit and illicit substances in and out of the prison, so I had access to the treatment options of my choice."

Sophia was shaking her head. "I still have trouble wrapping my head around the ins and outs of that economy."

"It *is* one of our more complicated business ventures, but my point is, I was afforded a large degree of privilege not available to everyone, although Parrot and I strive for equity in our business practices."

"You're not suggesting you should be the preferred vendor within the prison system, are you?" Sophia looked horrified.

"Representative Lamont, I'm saying for those that can afford it, we already are. It might be time for a more mainstream solution, although, personally, I trust the job Parrot and I could do more than the mess bureaucrats will make."

"It would have made a huge difference in my mom's life." Frankie picked at a fingernail absently. "She'd only had a few weeks sober when she was arrested for drug possession. Everything she'd been putting in place before was wiped out as soon as she got locked up because there were no treatment programs inside. She went back to what she knew." Frankie reached out and grasped the Zookeeper's arm. "I know you did what you could for her, Zoo. We both appreciate it."

"Every system has its limitations. I know it was rough for her." The Zookeeper put her hand over Frankie's.

"I know what you're doing. Trying to get them on your side to make it three against one might win you the battle but makes your grip on ultimate victory tenuous at best."

Sophia looked long and hard at Reggie. There was no mistaking her meaning. Reggie was ready to surrender this battle and any to come. She'd never wanted to be part of the design team anyway, but a chance with Sophia was something she wanted a lot. Except now the design team meant a lot to her too, and she didn't suspect Sophia would look kindly on her surrender.

The Zookeeper caught Reggie's eye and winked. Reggie remembered the Zookeeper saying she was a good judge of people. Could she know what was going on between them?

Bert called the group back together before Reggie could ponder further. He wrapped up the latest session and dismissed them. The four of them walked out together.

Sophia was quiet as they boarded the elevator. Reggie purposefully positioned herself so she could be close to her on the ride down. She'd looked forward to seeing her all day and they'd spent most of the time arguing. Not exactly the date they'd both been hoping for.

"Zoo, if someone overdoses, out on the street, what happens to them?" Sophia leaned around Reggie to look at the Zookeeper.

"That depends on whether someone has naloxone, whether they're okay calling nine-one-one, mentally and emotionally, and whether they want to risk trying to revive someone in case it doesn't work or they mess it up."

"Aren't there immunity laws and Good Samaritan laws to protect people when they call about an overdose?" Sophia frowned.

"For a law to work, people have to have trust in the system." The Zookeeper shrugged. "And calling for assistance doesn't mean that assistance will arrive in time. Timely naloxone administration is most important, but if it's not readily available the outcome is often tragic."

The elevator reached the first floor and they exited. Frankie and the Zookeeper said good-bye and headed into the evening, but Reggie lingered. She wasn't ready to part. Sophia didn't seem in a rush to leave either.

"Do you have anywhere to be?" Reggie reached out and grazed the back of Sophia's hand.

"Depends on what kind of offers roll in." Sophia made a show of pulling out her phone and checking the display. "What did you have in mind? You'll have to beat what I've already been tempted with."

Reggie didn't want to admit the ball of fire shooting through her veins was jealousy. It wasn't her business if Sophia was seeing other people. At least she was being offered a chance to win the night.

"I was going to suggest ice cream, but if you're busy…" Reggie waved her hand like it didn't matter.

"You're poker face needs work Ms. Northrup. I'm teasing you. Lily texted to ask if I want to discuss the show that came out last weekend that everyone's been bingeing. Apparently, there's a naked ass in the second episode that she still can't get out of her mind."

"Well, I don't want to keep you from talk of naked asses. Ice cream can't compete with that."

The sudden dousing of the flames of jealousy made Reggie a little woozy. Why did the emotions of the heart have to feel so much like a minor medical emergency?

"Oh, I wouldn't be so sure about that." Sophia linked arms with Reggie and steered her toward the ice cream shop a few blocks away. "The ass Lily's offering isn't the one I'm particularly interested in."

Reggie's eyebrows shot up. "Oh?"

Sophia moved her hand into Reggie's back pocket and squeezed. "I hope I'm not being too forward, but I like trying to catch a peek of this one when you're not looking." Sophia removed her hand and linked it again through Reggie's arm.

"You expect me to keep walking like that didn't happen?" Reggie stopped and inadvertently jolted Sophia back into her arms.

"Well, now something happened." Sophia smiled, her face inches from Reggie's.

Sophia smelled like lavender and everything good in the world. Reggie wanted to wrap her arms around her and kiss her, but she hesitated. They were in the middle of the sidewalk, downtown, blocks from the statehouse. The words of the other cochairs about her worthiness still echoed in her mind. Sophia deserved better.

Reggie took a step back, gently releasing Sophia, but keeping a hold of her hand. When did she start worrying about Sophia's political career?

"Not one for public displays of affection?" Sophia shook their joined hands until Reggie looked at her.

"No, it's not that. You shouldn't be. Not with me. Not here." Reggie jammed her free hand in her pocket.

"Wait a minute." Sophia stopped Reggie and stood in front of her. Close in front of her. "Aren't you the one worried about being seen cavorting with a politician? Since when are you worried about me?"

"Maybe you broke me when you grabbed my ass."

Sophia looked delighted. "I wonder what else I could do to you."

Reggie didn't tell her the sky was probably the limit. "Are we getting ice cream?" She tried for a scowl, but she took Sophia's hand and lost her angry look when Sophia dropped her head onto Reggie's shoulder.

"If you insist. One thing I need to say, to clear the air, because I could tell you were jealous earlier. I'm busy and have crazy hours and have people in my business constantly. I'm not interested in juggling a hectic dating schedule. When I like someone, that's who I want to spend time with, and I happen to like you."

"Would your reelection focus groups like it better if you were seen on the arm of a new woman every week or on my arm? What about the fact that I'm White and you're Black? Does that freak anyone out? Does it freak you out? Are there career ramifications about it?"

Sophia wrapped both arms around Reggie's bicep and pulled her close. "Don't know, don't care. I haven't asked and I never will. My personal life is my own. I don't ask my constituents what happens in their bedrooms. As for the fact that I'm Black and you're not, as long as you see me, all of me, and that includes my Blackness, then we're okay. I expect we'll both have learning to do as we go. I'm not naive enough to think this is the last conversation we'll have about it."

Reggie tried to give Sophia an "oh please" look, but she wasn't looking at her. "I do see you and what I see is amazing. But you're a public figure. My reputation has already been brought to your attention, more than once. My guess is the ones who alerted you to the rot on my family tree are the ones who matter a bit more than the family of five counting on you to make their lives a little easier. Which you can't do if you don't get reelected because you're spending time with shadowy people."

Sophia kissed Reggie's cheek. "And yet here we are. We've both stepped outside our comfort zones. Trust that and trust me, okay? And while you're at it, you can buy me some ice cream. Bubble gum or cotton candy, please."

Reggie dropped her arms and stared at Sophia. "Are you serious?"

"Completely. Have you had it since you were a kid? It's delicious. It was my nana's favorite and she passed it on to me."

"That's the scandal that might get you booted from office. It won't be anything to do with me."

Sophia put her hand on her hip and tapped her foot "Are you going to stand there all night judging me or are you going to make good on your ice cream promise because you know I have naked asses as a backup plan."

Reggie shuddered. She could still feel Sophia's hand in her back pocket. What she wouldn't give to have it there again. Although, if she were being honest, she'd give a lot more for those naked asses to be theirs.

She wanted to shove the young family out of line and jump ahead of the high schoolers on an awkward date, but she, appropriately, waited her turn. Impatiently. She was even successful at ignoring the questioning looks when she ordered Sophia's cotton candy cone.

It took her a moment to find Sophia in the early evening crowd. They weren't the only ones enjoying the late spring warm weather and longer days. The sun was low in the sky casting a warm glow over the picnic tables. She finally saw Sophia sitting at the farthest corner of the lawn, her back to the table, her elbows propped behind her, her face toward the last of the sun.

Reggie could have stayed where she was and stared until the dark shuttered the view for the evening, but from here she was only an observer. If she joined her, she got to be part of Sophia's world. As she approached, Reggie remembered, once again, why "beautiful" always seemed so inadequate when describing Sophia.

"What are you doing? Are you going to stand there until our ice cream melts or come sit with me, Hellhound?" Sophia opened her eyes and sat up. She patted the bench next to her.

"I'm trying to remember another time the English language has utterly failed me. I don't think there's a word available to me that describes how beautiful you are. Maybe I'll have to try another one. Maybe Swahili or Farsi. I don't know anything about the languages, and I don't think English has borrowed much from them, so I have high hopes. Latin perhaps?" Reggie handed Sophia her cup and spoon and sat next to her.

"It's always good to try new things." Sophia traced Reggie's eyebrow, along her cheekbone, to her chin.

Reggie shivered. It had nothing to do with the ice cream. She took Sophia's hand before she could meander farther down Reggie's neck. How far was she planning on going? "You may not care about being seen in public with me, but you'd probably care quite a bit if we get booted out of here for groping each other like those two over there." Reggie nodded in the direction of the two teenagers she'd been behind in line.

Sophia looked over Reggie's shoulder and stifled a laugh behind her ice cream. "He needs some guidance. You should pull him aside for a chat."

Reggie sat up straight and looked at Sophia with her spoon halfway to her mouth. "I'm not giving that kid tips on how to feel up his girlfriend in front of toddlers and God and everyone."

Sophia put her hand on Reggie's knee and patted it. She scooted closer and left her hand where it was. "I didn't mean that. You should give him some advice about treating a girl right, cause he's missing a few marks in that regard."

Before Reggie could respond, the young man under review landed on his ass on the ground holding his hands to his crotch. The young woman he'd been getting handsy with stood over him and dumped a milkshake on his head.

"I think he learned a valuable lesson from an excellent teacher." Reggie turned back to Sophia. "Where were we?"

"You were telling me how beautiful you think I am and how worried we should be if someone saw us kissing in public." Sophia moved her hand a little farther up Reggie's leg.

Reggie looked down at her leg and stumbled through a few incoherent utterances. She tried again. "You're beyond beautiful, that was my point. I don't have the words to describe it. And I'm not worried about kissing."

"I'm so glad to hear that." Sophia put her cup on the table, slid her hand behind Reggie's head, and pulled her close. "I've wanted this, and you, for so long."

Their lips were together so quickly Reggie didn't have a chance to think or overthink. She reacted, and that meant she pulled Sophia closer and deepened the kiss. Sophia's lips were soft and urgent and she tasted like cotton candy.

Long before Reggie was ready for it to end, Sophia slowly pulled away, a smile lighting up her face. "That should give everyone something to talk about. It certainly has me buzzing."

Reggie sagged against the table. "I'm so far off balance with you I might as well be standing on my head."

Sophia kissed her again quickly, a light, mostly PG-rated kiss. "Why do I get the feeling you don't mind?"

They finished their ice cream, stealing glances, sharing smiles, and one or two more kisses. Reggie took Sophia's hand as they walked back toward their cars.

"When I'm with you, Reggie, I don't worry about reelection or politics, or how many ways I could fail my constituents or myself. Why is that?"

Reggie laughed to cover the nerves that had sprung back to life. "Probably because I hate politics. Should I write a note for you to keep at the office so you don't worry so much about those things when I'm not around? I'm always happy to remind you how wonderful you are."

"How lucky for me. I know you don't let very many people see this sweet side of you. Thank you for making an exception for me. If you do make a career change and this is who the kids get as a teacher, you're the one they'll talk about twenty years down the road. You'll be the one they say changed their lives." Sophia cupped Reggie's cheek and kissed her one last time before unlocking her car and slipping into the driver's seat.

Reggie closed the door and waved as Sophia drove away. She touched her cheek as she walked to her truck. The evening hadn't gone as expected but had outpaced her wildest hopes. Could she really put aside her fears tied into Sophia's career and see where this led? She could still taste the cotton candy on her lips.

Fear of her father's shadow hadn't stopped her from being crushed under its weight. And now there was Sophia and her career to consider. What if her father's past pulled her under as well? The thought made her ill. But what would happen if she stepped into the light and carved her own path? The possibility of shrugging off the shackles of her family name hadn't ever seemed possible, but maybe it was time. Could she allow the possibility that some politicians used their power for good? Could her heart afford for her not to?

CHAPTER TWENTY-ONE

Rodrigo knocked on Sophia's office door and deposited fresh pastry from his mother and the mail on her desk. She reached for the pastry bag, but he stopped her and pointed to the mail.

"Get those out of the way first."

Sophia looked at his face and frowned. "That bad?"

"Only the two on top. Skim them so you know what's in them, and I'll take them over to the state police and they can add them to the file."

She picked up the letters and scanned the sexist, racist, misogynistic ranting. The second letter was more of the same. She pushed the bag of pastry away and slammed the letters down on her desk.

"I'm not going to eat anything from that bag of heaven while I'm still seething from this."

"Is everything okay?" Valencia knocked on the doorframe and peeked in the office.

Rodrigo sighed. "Hate mail. We send it all to the state police, but people are allowed to write whatever twisted things pop into their heads."

"I can only imagine the tenor of your communications. I don't get a lot but what does come in rattles me and mine don't include every racist name history has cooked up over centuries. I'm sorry."

Sophia grabbed the pastry bag. "Maybe I do need some of this. Was there something you needed, Valencia?" She offered Valencia one of her baked treasures.

Valencia took the offered pastry and a seat. Rodrigo didn't look like he had anywhere he was in a hurry to get to so Sophia waved him to a seat as well.

"Are you going to Lily's grand opening gala this weekend?"

"Of course." Sophia drummed her fingers on her desk. "I know she's thrilled you offered to cohost."

Valencia waved her hand in protest. "No, no. I'm a silent partner. The only one in the spotlight is Lily. I married into a family with more money than they know what to do with. I'm happy to help them find worthy causes, businesses, and people to invest in."

Sophia narrowed her eyes. "And you don't expect anything in return from Lily?"

She thought of Reggie and her distrust of politicians. She would see this as Valencia trying to curry favor with Sophia, but was that what it was?

Valencia grinned. "If I tear my pants or grow five inches, I hope she'll take my emergency call, but otherwise, no. Lily's clothing and Lily herself make the world a more beautiful place. Why wouldn't I want to support that?"

"Well, when you put it like that, I guess I have nothing to worry about." She said a silent prayer on Rodrigo's mother's pastry that Valencia was telling the truth.

"You don't, I give you my word. There was one other reason I stopped by."

Sophia wanted to roll her eyes but kept it to herself. Of course Valencia didn't stop by to chat about Lily's grand opening shindig. Although now that she was thinking about it, she needed something to wear. And a date. Should she bring a date?

"Have you given it any more thought?" Valencia looked at her expectantly.

"I'm sorry, I missed the first part."

Valencia looked puzzled and Rodrigo looked like Sophia had no secrets.

"In our last working meeting, we were stuck on how to get folks linked to treatment within a short time of them having the motivation to enter. Have you solved it yet?"

"Oh, that. No, not yet. Rodrigo, if you needed substance abuse treatment right now, in the next fifteen minutes, where would you go?" Sophia took a bite of her pastry and wiped her hands on her napkin.

"In my own world where I'm the all-powerful ruler of the galaxy or in the real world where you both have to work with some of the idiots whose votes you'd need?" Rodrigo licked baked perfection from his fingertips.

Sophia choked on her next bite as she inhaled some powdered sugar trying not to laugh. "That really is the distinction, isn't it? What you, as an individual, want doesn't ever really matter. God, is that true?"

Valencia nodded. "Sure, to some extent. We were elected to serve the people. We're public servants. Our personal vision is important because that's what we campaigned on, but we're here to do the people's business, not our own. So is everyone else."

"And certainly not everyone's constituents agree on even the most basic ideas or issues. Democracy is truly remarkable." Sophia took another bite. This one tasted slightly less sweet.

"Don't look so blue, I can still answer your question, even if I can't be queen of the world. In the next fifteen minutes, I'd call Star Recovery."

"What about in the middle of the night, when Star isn't open?" Valencia took a napkin to her fingers and tossed it in the trash when she was done.

Rodrigo hesitated. "I don't know. I guess I'd go to the emergency department at the hospital? Is that the right answer?"

"There isn't a wrong answer, but it's not a great solution. I've talked to my sister-in-law Natasha, she's a social worker embedded with the police department in their ride along program, about the fact that emergency room docs aren't trained to get people into treatment. It's not their job." Valencia smiled at Rodrigo.

Sophia tapped her chin. "Add on that anyone coming in with a non-emergency presentation seeking treatment referral would be triaged at the lowest priority. A lot of motivation can disappear after three hours of waiting to be seen for vital signs."

"So what else is open all the time but would see someone as soon as they walked in the door?" Rodrigo looked from Sophia to Valencia. He held up the pastry bag like he was offering a reward for a correct answer. "I'm thinking fast food drive-throughs, twenty-four-hour pharmacies, the strip club two blocks from my uncle's house. What else?"

"Police stations are open all day every day, but the comfort level won't be there." Sophia reached for the bag and turned the problem over in her mind. Where would she be comfortable going?

"Fire stations." Rodrigo looked at Sophia.

Valencia's eyebrows shot up at the suggestion, then she smiled broadly. "Of course. Fire stations. They're safe and don't carry the same level of judgment a police station carries."

"Wait. Safe Stations. I've heard of those. I can't believe I didn't think of that." Sophia bonked the heel of her hand against her forehead. She pulled out her phone and typed and scrolled. "Think we can include something like this, Valencia?"

"Correct me if I'm wrong, but the idea is someone seeking treatment can walk into any fire station day or night and request help?" Valencia put the phone down and looked at Sophia.

"That's right. Fire stations never close so there's always someone there. The individual is medically evaluated and taken to the hospital if needed. Otherwise, they're connected with treatment." Sophia reached for the bag Rodrigo offered. She considered taking two pastries.

"Not to burst your bubble here, but wouldn't fire fighters have the same problem as emergency doctors? They aren't trained to get people clean or sober either, and bringing them to the hospital doesn't get us anywhere we couldn't have gotten on our own." Rodrigo pulled the bag back, looking skeptical.

Sophia pinched the bridge of her nose. "This is going to cost a fortune. Worth every penny, but we'll have to sell the hell out of it. Community partnerships will be the only way it works. Something similar happens now, with Natasha and her partner, right?"

Valencia nodded. "I don't know all the details, but I know they work with Star Recovery. I think they call if they need their mobile team and they're there pretty quickly. Are you saying one of these mobile teams would be available twenty-four seven?"

"That's exactly what I'm saying." Sophia finally snatched the pastry bag from Rodrigo and claimed her prize.

"But you have the 'boring moderate' label. You aren't supposed to have exceptional, transformational ideas. It's not supposed to be in your makeup." Valencia winked.

"I like to keep people guessing."

"You know, you should talk to Natasha and her soon to be wife, Tommy. Natasha's running the ride along program for the police department now and Tommy's one of the officers with a social worker in her car. They started off as partners so they both know what they're talking about with this stuff. They might be able to give you more detail from both the access and options side of things."

"Reggie and I were thinking of getting in touch with someone from that program."

Valencia clapped her hands on her knees and stood. "I gotta run, but I can introduce you this weekend. They're coming to Lily's party. Will Reggie be there too?"

Sophia hesitated. She felt sweat forming on her palms. "Why would you ask if I'm bringing Reggie?"

"I thought I'd heard you were close to her. Am I wrong? I guess I shouldn't believe the rumors in this place." Valencia looked perplexed but was doing a good job recovering.

"It's not that." Sophia wasn't sure what she was planning on saying next. "Reggie and I spend a lot of time together on the design team. I may invite her, especially if Natasha and Tommy will be there."

"Great. I'll see you both then." Valencia waved to Rodrigo and was gone.

As soon as she was alone in her office, Sophia picked up her phone to call Reggie. Then she chickened out and put it down. Her office seemed like the wrong place to call so she grabbed her phone and purse and headed for the door. She'd grab an early lunch at one of the food trucks around the corner. If she was lucky, Lenny's truck would be there today.

The sunshine and warm air filled her with the kind of hope and joy only pristine, cloudless, sunny days could. Before she lost that feeling and let doubt creep in, she dialed.

Reggie answered after a couple of rings. "Hi there. My day off is even better now."

"So is my lunch break. Are you busy Saturday night?" Sophia metaphorically held her breath.

"As you know, my social calendar is jammed, but I think I could clear the books. What did you have in mind?"

"My best friend Lily's having a big party to celebrate the grand opening of her clothing boutique. I'd like you to be my plus one."

There was a long pause on the other end of the line, so long that Sophia thought they might have been disconnected. She checked the display to make sure.

"There are going to be people there, right? People you know? Maybe even political people?"

"Of course. It would be a terrible grand opening if it was you, me, and Lily eating takeout on the floor." Sophia chuckled but couldn't deny the sliver of worry the question caused, especially after her chat with Speaker Spaziano. She shoved it away.

There was another moment of hesitation. "I guess I could make an appearance, since it's not a political party. It shouldn't stain my reputation too much."

Sophia could hear the warmth in Reggie's voice. "Nope, just a boring couture extravaganza."

"So much better. Just to be safe, I'll write 'plus-one' on my name tag so they don't throw me out as an interloper. Will there be name tags? Wait, couture sounds fancy. It's fancy, right? I don't have anything fancy to wear. I can't go." Reggie sounded like she'd talked herself into a knot.

"Can't back out now. Lily's been experimenting with some gender-bending women's suits that I think will look amazing on you. Will you trust me and try out what Lily has? If you don't like it, you can go in your boxers."

It was a mistake to picture Reggie in her boxers. Sophia felt heated in places not touched by the sun. She fanned her face anyway.

"Is this a ruse to get me to a party in my drawers?"

Sophia looked to the sky and took a breath to slow her rapid heartbeat. "Trust me, Reggie, if I get you in your underwear, I'm not going to want a crowd."

"Jesus, it's a good thing I'm not at work right now."

"How do you think I feel? I *am* at work and all I can think about is your underwear."

"You started it, but to aid your imagination, they're navy blue boxer briefs with pictures of flamingoes. In case that's helpful information."

Sophia swore under her breath, which made Reggie laugh.

"You know it's not helpful, but thank you for telling me. I'll let you know when I'm done here and we can meet at Lily's. I'll see you later."

She returned to her office having forgotten about getting lunch and uncomfortably turned on. Since when were flamingoes erotic? Since they were covering Reggie's lady bits, that's when.

Although she was still aware of the reputation that followed Reggie, she was grateful she'd been forced by circumstance to ignore the warnings to keep her distance.

It felt like something real was growing between them, and it would have been tragic to miss that opportunity because of rumor, innuendo, and threat. The more time she and Reggie spent building trust in one another and giving in to their attraction, the more comfortable she felt. Except she'd lied to Valencia, so maybe she was lying to herself. She wanted to believe Northrup was just a name and politician was just a career. Surely there were more sizable obstacles in the world to overcome, but was she ready to believe that and give what she felt for Reggie the chance it deserved?

CHAPTER TWENTY-TWO

Reggie took one last look in the full-length mirror in her bedroom. She smoothed the lapels of the tuxedo and turned to get a look from the back.

"Oh please, stop looking at your own ass. It looks great. She's going to love it." Ava threw a pair of socks at her. "Put those on or you're going to be late, fancy pants."

"I've never had a suit, or anything, that was literally tailored for me. It's no wonder people who can afford it get all their clothes custom-made."

Ava tapped her wrist. "That's great. You look great. Unless you want to spend the night here on a date with yourself, get it in gear. Don't forget who else had a dress custom made for her and not for nothing, but I'd rather be looking at her than me if I was in your expensive dress shoes."

Reggie scowled at Ava but sat down and put on her socks and shoes. She looked at her watch and jumped up. "I'm going to be late."

Ava rolled her eyes but helped her gather the few things she still needed. "Have fun tonight. You look great, as you clearly know, and your date is going to be the hottest woman there. Don't worry about the rest. Feel all the feels. You do remember how to do that, right?"

Reggie stuck out her tongue.

"Those weren't the feels I was talking about, but that's your business. Do you need the safe sex talk? Have you done that sort of thing since college?"

"I'm leaving now. You can stay but you can't drink all my beer. If you go, lock up, please."

Reggie knew Ava would follow her out the door. She was a little surprised Ava wasn't insisting on following her to Sophia's to make sure she got there okay. She'd had a strong mother hen vibe since she arrived earlier in the afternoon.

Ava waved from the driveway as Reggie pulled out and headed to Sophia's house to pick her up. The closer she got, the more her stomach felt like it was filled with tap dancing buffalo.

This was a real date with Sophia, in public, at her best friend's most important night. What if she tripped or said something stupid? What if she spilled an entire tray of food or drinks on someone? What if Lily didn't like her? What if Sophia decided she was better off without her after being around a bunch of people who wore suits like this all the time? What if Sophia's boss was there and everything fell apart?

Reggie shook her head to clear out the doubts. This was the problem with letting any emotions in, they took hold and did whatever they wanted. And they were rude as hell. She thought about Sophia's lips on hers and the feel of Sophia's hand entwined with hers. There was no reason to doubt those feelings. They were real and a foundation to build on. The buffalo settled into a more manageable two-step as she parked outside Sophia's house.

Sophia opened the door and stepped out before Reggie could knock. She was wearing a full-length light pink dress, strapless on one side, and black heels. Reggie wasn't comfortable admitting how close she came to falling ass backwards off the steps at her first sight of Sophia.

"You take my breath away. Poor Lily, it's her big night, but everyone's going to be looking at you." Reggie offered her arm and escorted Sophia to her truck.

Sophia fussed with an earring. "I was a little nervous getting dressed tonight. Lily made this for me, but I never saw it before she handed me the garment bag. Are you sure it's okay?"

Reggie pulled Sophia into her arms and kissed her softly. "It's more than okay. A pretty pink dress isn't why you're beautiful to me, but that is a stunning dress on a gorgeous woman. The combo is a level fifteen on a one to ten scale."

Sophia kissed Reggie one more time and then climbed into the truck. "You know, you're awfully good for my ego. I like kissing you too."

Reggie practically skipped around to the driver's side of the truck. She thought Ava would be proud of her. She was definitely feeling the feels. She climbed in the truck and realized she wasn't sure how to get where they were going.

"Don't worry, I'll direct you. We'll get there safely." Sophia ran her hand down Reggie's arm and squeezed her hand before returning her own hand to the passenger's side of the cab.

"I'll follow wherever you lead. For tonight at least." Reggie winked.

"That's a dangerous offer with you looking so good in that tuxedo. You better be ready to back up such bold promises."

Reggie swallowed hard. What had she agreed to? She was looking forward to finding out.

After parking and making their way to the door, Reggie felt out of her element. Or more precisely, she felt thrust back into an element she never wanted to revisit. This big swanky party filled with beautiful people, tiny food, fancy drinks, and lots of air kisses was somewhere her father would have been extremely comfortable. As a result, suddenly she was not. Childhood memories of old men in bad cologne with cruel smiles made her stomach turn.

"Hey, are you okay?" Sophia pulled Reggie aside as soon as they were through the door.

"Yes, it's nothing." Reggie looked at the floor.

Sophia lifted Reggie's chin. Her eyes were piercing but kind. "Don't pull that 'it's nothing' crap. It's me you're talking to. We're all dressed up at this fancy party and I don't want to spend it standing against the wall like it's my high school prom all over again."

Reggie half smiled. "I'd never leave you standing all night against the wall."

"You're cute, Reggie, but I like to dance. If you're going to pout in a corner and not talk to me, I'm going to spend the night regretting my shoe choice."

"You don't make the most convincing case for my getting my ass out of the corner if I'd get to watch you dance all night. Which now that I say it out loud sounds way creepier than I meant." Reggie face-palmed.

"If you're over here I can't do this." Sophia put her arms around Reggie's neck and her hands in the hair on the back of Reggie's head. "Or this." She kissed Reggie's neck. "Definitely not this." She kissed her way to Reggie's mouth.

Reggie moved her hands around Sophia's waist and held her loosely. "You win. I'd never willingly be so far from you. This party caught me off guard. It felt like events my father brought me to when he was in his prime, although the décor was significantly less classy."

"You looked spooked. I wondered if it might be something like that. Look around." Sophia stepped out of Reggie's arms and pointed around the room. "This is about fashion, not politics. I'm not Representative Lamont tonight. I'm Sophia, a very proud friend here to support the insanely talented Lily Medeiros. Valencia Blackstone is cohosting a big-ass party so the world can finally see what I've known about Lily since we were kids. She may have brought the politicians and the money, but there are plenty of people here just for the fashion and fun of it, too."

"You're always Representative Lamont, but I can see past my own fear. It was a momentary jolt to something I'd rather forget, that's all. I'm exactly where I want to be, with the only person I want to spend the evening with." Reggie offered her arm. Childhood baggage be damned, she wasn't going to blow this.

Sophia took her offered arm and led her across the room, toward Lily who was holding court in front of a display of clothing and jumbo photographs. She squealed when she saw Sophia. They ran to each other and hugged years' worth of pent-up joy, pride, and friendship.

"You must be Reggie."

Reggie turned at the sound of her name. Valencia Blackstone, who Reggie had only briefly interacted with in the middle of the night at Lenny's food truck, but knew by sight from television and magazine features, was smiling warmly at her.

"Guilty."

"Sophia speaks highly of you and the work you've been doing on the design team together."

A spark of jealousy threatened to ignite until Reggie remembered that Valencia was also a state representative.

"It's been a great opportunity. I wasn't sure what to expect, but it's surprised me at every turn."

"I'm looking forward to reading your recommendations, which reminds me, I told Sophia I'd introduce the two of you to my sister-in-law Natasha and her fiancée, Tommy. They're involved in the social worker ride along program in the police department. They're around here somewhere." Valencia scanned the crowd.

Sophia rejoined them. She snaked her arm around Reggie's waist. Reggie put her arm around Sophia. Would her system ever stop feeling like it switched to overload when she was this close to Sophia? Or was this her new state of being?

Valencia looked from Reggie to Sophia. She raised an eyebrow but didn't comment. "I was telling Reggie that Natasha and Tommy are here somewhere. If I can find them, I'll introduce you."

Sophia looked at Reggie. She seemed tense since Valencia started talking. Reggie squeezed Sophia's waist gently and she seemed to relax.

"Is that okay? To talk business at the party?"

Reggie kissed the top of Sophia's head. "Thank you for checking. I'd love to meet them."

"Ah, there they are." Valencia picked her way through the crowd.

They approached two women, standing close, with eyes only for each other. Even from a distance, Reggie could tell they were very much in love. She wondered what people thought when they saw her looking at Sophia.

Valencia spoke with the women and gestured to Reggie and Sophia. The blond-haired woman smiled while the buttoned-up, butch one evaluated them coolly. She was obviously the cop.

Valencia made introductions all around. Once that was done, she took her leave and let them chat.

Tommy and Reggie eyed each other. Normally, Reggie would chalk it up to a normal butch territory-marking situation, but there was extra wariness in Tommy's eyes. Reggie figured it was better to lay her cards on the table.

"Out of curiosity, which one of us are you worried about?" Reggie held eye contact and indicated between herself and Sophia.

"Who said I'm worried?" Tommy squared her shoulders.

"Valencia speaks very highly of you, Sophia." Natasha smiled warmly.

"So me then?" Reggie crossed her arms.

"Don't mind her." Natasha snaked her arm into Tommy's. "If she'd stubbornly refused to budge from her first impression of me, we wouldn't be planning a wedding."

Tommy's frown had no bite behind it. The love showed through.

"I don't care what your reputation is, Reggie. I know a thing or two about living in a parent's long shadow. Mine happens to be a positive glow. I'm lucky, but I worried for years what people thought about me because of my family name." Tommy was still sizing Reggie up carefully. "The thing I learned was my mistakes and triumphs were my own, no matter who my mother is."

Reggie squirmed under Tommy's scrutiny. Perhaps the direct approach was backfiring.

"If you want to be a dirty scoundrel, don't ride on your father's coattails, make a name for yourself. But it sounds like you don't want that, and you've gone the other way entirely. Valencia's a good judge of character and she speaks highly of Sophia. Sophia seems fond of you. So, if you're as good as you seem to be, then the people who matter already know it. Politicians talk. It's what they do." Tommy's shoulders relaxed and she smiled slightly.

"Because we're the worst," Sophia interrupted.

"Ignore them." Tommy nodded as if that ended the debate.

"But don't ignore all of us," Sophia whispered in Reggie's ear.

Natasha watched them with a knowing smile. "How long have you two been together?"

"It's not really like that."

"We're sort of only starting to figure it out."

Tommy laughed and looked at Natasha. "That sounds familiar."

Sophia looked intrigued. "It's clear how much you two adore each other. You didn't fall into each other's arms and live happily ever after the moment you met?"

Natasha nearly spit out a sip of champagne. She coughed it down instead. "Buy her a drink sometime and get her to tell you what she thought of me when we first met. Our jobs weren't conducive, my parents were 'ruin your life' against it, but we were meant to be." She slipped her hand into Tommy's. "There're all kinds of obstacles and noise out there. Some you can't change, some you can with a little bit of fight."

"See." Sophia playfully jabbed Reggie in the side. "Someone trying to ruin your life is all part of the relationship maturation process."

"I don't think that's a universal rule." Reggie squirmed away from Sophia's jab.

"I think Nat's point is, don't let go easily if you care about each other. There's plenty of bad in the world, but loving someone isn't one of those things." Tommy clapped Reggie on the shoulder in buddy cop fashion.

"I don't think Valencia introduced us so we could badger you about your relationship. She said you're involved in the governor's substance use task force."

Sophia nodded. "They're calling it a community design team and we've been tasked with looking at every aspect of substance use in the state and recommending changes. Reggie and I are on the policy team and we're looking at treatment access. We were hoping to pick your brain."

"Pick away. Although I'm sure Natasha could give you a list of treatment access barriers off the top of her head."

Tommy might as well have slipped into her uniform, as it was obvious to Reggie she was now fully in work mode.

"This is going to sound strange, but stick with me." Natasha looked from Reggie to Sophia. "The biggest access barrier is access. Tommy and I have been building the ride along program and that's been a facilitator to those seeking treatment and who happen to intersect with one of us. But how many are out there who don't want to talk to anyone associated with the police? Or don't stumble across a social worker and cop at the moment their motivation is pointing toward making a change?"

Sophia's eyes lit up. "I'm guessing you don't have twenty-four-hour coverage either."

"I need my beauty sleep."

"Can someone make an appointment to see you guys? Or at Star Recovery?" Reggie tried to think of other places she'd heard mentioned at work.

"Not with us, not directly, but the other places, sure. Although most of their clients access them on demand. We refer to them and they're on call to meet us in the community as needed."

Natasha nodded along as Tommy spoke. "They have limits too. Folks have to get to them, or wait for the mobile team if we call. If they make an appointment who knows what factors will be in play by the time that meeting rolls around, whether it's an hour, a day, or a week later."

"So the barrier to access is access at the very moment it's needed." Sophia laughed. "No problem. Easy fix."

"She's here to protect, I'm here to serve. Glad I have another happy customer." Natasha gave a dramatic half curtsey.

Tommy shook her head with a grin. She fake-whispered behind her hand. "She's mostly here to cause trouble and she's really good at it, but she's also right."

"Of course I am." Natasha gave Tommy's arm a squeeze. "You two get in touch about anything else we can help with. There's lots of work to be done in this area, and I'm glad good people are putting thought into it."

Reggie watched Tommy and Natasha walk away, hand in hand. Her own hand tingled. She missed the feel of Sophia's hand in hers, the feel of her body.

"I believe you promised me dancing." Reggie wrapped her arm around Sophia's waist and pulled her close.

Sophia searched her face. "I don't know why, but I didn't think you'd be interested in spending the night on the dance floor."

"I can't let you and Lily have all the fun tonight. And was that your brother I saw in the middle of the dance floor?" She closed the distance between them and kissed her slow and deep.

Sophia's hands roamed up her back urgently and her lips and tongue were demanding. Reggie didn't break the kiss until the heat between them rose to near critical, until she felt in danger of melting into the dress shoes that were so beautiful they deserved better than melted horny human goo all over them. Who knew she had any self-control left at all?

She took Sophia's hand and maneuvered them through the crowd to the dance floor.

"You still care about dancing? After what you started back there?"

Lily appeared next to them as soon as they arrived on the dance floor. She flung her arm around both of them never breaking the rhythm of the current song as she pulled them farther onto the floor.

Reggie leaned closer to Sophia as they followed Lily. "Tonight's about Lily, and I wouldn't keep you from dancing with your best friend. This is where you belong."

"Thank you."

Reggie was sure she'd do almost anything to keep that look of happiness on Sophia's face forever.

They danced for what could have been a decade, the music certainly spanned that amount of time. After a while, thirst forced Reggie to the bar for water for the three of them. She scanned the crowd as she waited. Although she'd been completely wrapped up in Sophia all night, stepping back now she was able to see what a huge success the event was for Lily. She made a note to congratulate her before the end of the night.

Reggie collected the water and was about to head back to the dance floor to find Sophia and Lily when Sophia emerged from the crowd looking shell-shocked and close to tears.

Reggie practically threw the drinks back on the bar and ran to Sophia. "What's wrong?" She pulled Sophia into her arms, then held her at arm's length so she could see her.

Sophia collapsed into her and buried her face in Reggie's neck and chest. Reggie held her. She was content to hold her until she was ready to talk.

Finally, Sophia pushed out of Reggie's arms and pulled out her cell phone.

She grimaced as she unlocked the phone and showed Reggie a text.

"Speaker and minority leader are demanding a meeting tomorrow morning at seven. What trouble have you gotten into?"

Reggie didn't know who Rodrigo was, but she did have a pretty good idea of the kind of trouble Sophia had gotten herself into.

"Do you want to throw your drink on me and make a big scene telling me off? That might work to your advantage."

"I would never do that to you." Sophia wiped angrily at her eyes. "I don't know why I'm shocked or so upset."

Reggie tentatively cupped Sophia's cheek. "Because no one should be watching you at your best friend's party. Because someone here is reporting who you're kissing to your bosses. Because from what you've said they can control your career and I assume might make you choose between your career and me."

Sophia looked Reggie in the eyes with fire in her gaze. "I won't let them force that choice. We"—she pointed between the two of them—"aren't doing anything wrong. You aren't wrong."

The fluttering in her chest was unfamiliar. Reggie wouldn't have known what it was except it was the same feeling she got when she thought of Sophia unexpectedly in the middle of the day or caught sight of her for the first time after a few days apart. It was a feeling only Sophia could elicit, and it was one Reggie liked. A lot.

"If it's okay with you, I think I'm ready to go. My buzz has been killed, and apparently, I have to be up early."

While Sophia said good-bye to Lily, Reggie collected their things. She met her at the door. Sophia looked deflated as they walked back to the truck.

"Is there anything I can do?"

Reggie wanted to keep Sophia with her all night. She wanted to chase the sadness and anxiety radiating off Sophia like a tsunami as far away as she could, but spending the night with her wasn't likely to help.

"I won't know much until the morning. You gave me a wonderful evening. What else could I ask from you?" Sophia took Reggie's offered hand as she climbed into the truck cab.

"You can ask anything." Reggie rested her hand on Sophia's knee for a quick moment, then closed her door and jogged around to the driver's side.

It was a quiet ride back to Sophia's house. Reggie walked her to the door. Sophia kissed her good night, but it was a chaste kiss absent all the passion and fun from earlier. It felt, a little, like good-bye.

Reggie drove home with her mind filled with unhelpful "what-if" scenarios and angry screeds for Sophia's colleagues. She'd hoped her worst assumptions about politics would remain paranoid suspicions. Sophia deserved better than getting caught up in the worst of her profession.

The further she got from her last interaction with Sophia, the more doubt crept into Reggie's thoughts. Sophia was a politician too. What if, in the end, her career was more important to her than Reggie? What if she was threatened with something she couldn't say no to? Or offered something she couldn't turn down?

Reggie slammed her hand on the steering wheel. No, Sophia had said they hadn't done anything wrong. That Reggie wasn't wrong. Surely she'd fight for them? Right? But what would that fight cost Sophia? Surely Reggie and all the political baggage she carried would ruin Sophia's career if she did fight to keep what they had. Politics might be awful and she might strongly dislike politicians, but Sophia was exactly the type who should be serving the public's interests. She couldn't do that if she was dragged down by Reggie's last name. How could she ask her to make that kind of sacrifice? Reggie had a long night of worry and an anxious morning before she had any hope of an answer. God, she hated politics. Why'd she have to fall for a politician?

CHAPTER TWENTY-THREE

Sophia straightened her suit jacked for the hundredth time since she arrived at the statehouse, tried a silent Jedi mind trick on the occupants of the Speaker's office telling them she wasn't the one they were mad at, and knocked on the door. It was exactly seven. She hadn't had her coffee yet and she was oscillating between nerves and anger at being called to this meeting, at the ass crack of dawn on a Sunday no less, presumably to be yelled at.

When acknowledged, she opened the door and took the offered seat. She was still nervous, but the place for nervous tells and tics was outside. In here she wasn't giving anything away.

"Good morning, Sophia. I'm sure you know why we asked for this meeting." The Speaker was noticeably less jovial than usual.

"If you're interested in a design team update, I still don't have the final recommendations. As for the other part, I think the governor has the same goal as you do. Getting legislation passed and signed shouldn't be a problem. You can fight it out with her and the public to see who gets the credit in the end." Sophia folded her hands over her knees. She wasn't about to mention the work she and Valencia were doing together, which was coming along nicely.

"Do you think, at seven in the morning on Sunday, I give a fuck what you're talking about during your design team meetings?" Red crept up the Speaker's neck.

Sophia counted to five in her head so she didn't impulsively say something politically stupid. "Honestly, Mr. Speaker it's early, as you mentioned, and I don't know what fucks you give."

The majority leader barked a laugh which he turned into an awkward cough. He put his hand on his knee and pounded on his chest with his other hand. Sophia offered him the water that had been set for her.

"Let me enlighten you then. The fuck I give has nothing to do with what you're talking about in those meetings. It's who you're talking to. We warned you about keeping company with the wrong people, then I tried to make it crystal clear in case you weren't picking up on the subtlety." The Speaker jabbed his finger in Sophia's direction.

Sophia had known her association with Reggie was why she was here now, but it still shocked her to hear it said out loud. What could these two men possibly have against Reggie? Had they ever met her?

"With all due respect, sir, both of the women you suggested I stay away from are part of my four-woman group. It would be nearly impossible to participate in the design team without interacting with both of them." Sophia's heart was racing, and her mouth felt as dry as a sawdust and peanut butter sandwich.

"And was kissing Reggie Northrup at Valencia Blackstone's clothes party last night part of your small group assignment too? Or playing grab ass all over the damn city? Perhaps your career isn't as important to you as I thought. I expected more from you, Sophia." The Speaker's good-natured, happy uncle routine was replaced with the venom of a pit viper.

"It was a grand opening celebration for a hot new fashion designer, Lily Medeiros, not a clothes party, and what I do in my personal life is none of your business." Sophia balled her fists in her lap.

"You don't get a personal life. Everything is the people's business now." The majority leader had the decency to look sympathetic.

"It might be the people's business, but it's none of yours. I haven't heard any complaints from my constituents about who I'm spending my afterhours time with."

"Sophia, be smart about this. You were offered the chance of a lifetime. No freshman rep rises to the kind of leadership position we're offering you. All you have to do is ditch the Northrup heir. And you should trust us on this one, you want to do that anyway." The majority leader leaned forward in his chair, his expression earnest and concerned. "Bartholomew Northrup's not as retired as his prison sentence would lead you to believe. You think your reputation's in danger now, being seen with Gina? Wait until father dearest let's everyone know the way to his heart is to do a favor or offer up a sweet deal to his daughter's girlfriend."

"So you're afraid Bartholomew Northrup will make me too radioactive for you to promote or that he'll drive up the price so high you won't be able to afford the kind of bribes you think it'll take to get me under your thumb? Are we done here?" Sophia stood up.

"Are you sure you want to do this?" The Speaker stood as well and drummed his fingers on his desk. "I'm not afraid of the Northrups, Bart and I go back a ways, but you should be. You're new to this game and don't have very many cards. I have the power to help you rise to meteoric heights. I can also bury you in a well so deep you'll never dig yourself out."

Sophia wavered. She'd dreamed of this job her entire life. What if everything came crashing down? If she took his offer, was that how she wanted to succeed?

"You won't though. It's not a good look for an old White guy to keep a capable, intelligent, popular Black woman from advancing because I kissed someone you don't like. You can try and spin it however you want, but I'll make sure that's how it's reported in every news story and all over social media." Sophia forced the Speaker to look away first before grabbing her purse and walking out the door, head held high. She gripped her purse hard so they wouldn't see that her hands were trembling.

She really hoped she was right. The voice of her mother was ringing in her head telling her turn around and apologize, grovel if she had to, but keep her job prospects secure. Her heart was telling her to run for the door. She'd taken a big gamble, but even if she crashed and burned, she wouldn't have been able to live with herself under the Speaker's thumb. Something didn't feel right about any of this and she wasn't going to be beholden to him for the rest of her career.

What she needed now was to figure out who *her* friends were. Where *her* power came from so that she had her own alliances and backup should the Speaker move against her. Valencia seemed like a good bet, and the governor's enthusiasm for legislation from the design team had seemed genuine. It was a start.

She pulled out her phone as she walked out of the statehouse. It was only seven thirty. Drawing lines in the sand and pissing off the most powerful members of her political party had taken less time than a children's cartoon. If she needed to brush up her résumé she'd list "efficiency" as a special skill.

It was too early to call Lily. She was likely still buzzing from the night before, and there was no telling who was sharing her bed. She texted her to tell her they needed to talk later. Her phone pinged a minute later, but it was from Davey.

We have some things to talk to you about too, but in about four hours. Why are you awake?

Sophia stared at her phone. We? Did he mean Davey and Lily? Things? What things? She wanted to write back and demand answers, but she knew her brother would turn his phone off and make her wait longer if she badgered him.

She was about to put her phone back in her bag and go home, or in search of coffee, but that wasn't what she wanted. She wanted to see Reggie. She wanted, it felt like she needed, to reach out to her, have some connection to her, which felt weird since Reggie was the reason her career might have just imploded. She didn't question it though, she knew the feeling of calm that flowed through her veins when she was with Reggie. She needed that right now.

She didn't know if Reggie was a morning person or slept until noon. She didn't even know if Reggie was working today. She didn't care, she sent a text anyway. If she was asleep or at work, she could ignore it.

I miss you. How is that possible?

She responded quickly, as if she'd been waiting for Sophia to get in touch. *How was your meeting?*

It's poor manners to threaten someone before they've had coffee. Can I fix the coffee problem? I just made a pot.

Sophia smiled at her phone. She could picture Reggie in her kitchen, or what she imagined her kitchen looked like, dutifully readying the coffee.

I'd love that. And seeing you.

Reggie gave her directions and Sophia made it to her house easily. God-awful early on a Sunday was thankfully traffic-free. Reggie was waiting on the porch with two mugs.

Sophia made it halfway up the walk then stopped to admire the view. Reggie was wearing athletic shorts and a well-loved T-shirt. Her hair was still sleep tousled and the morning light framed her in a warm glow. She looked like every happy thought Sophia wanted to get lost in and damned sexy as the cherry on top.

"Hug or coffee first? You look like you could use both." Reggie put down her mug and stood, arms open.

Sophia realized coffee was in danger of losing its crown as her beacon out of bed in the morning. Reggie's arms were likely to detour her from any cup, mug, pot, or shop no matter how carefully brewed.

"Do you know how terrible politics are?" Sophia nuzzled into Reggie's neck.

"That's a total shock to me. Pull back the curtain and tell me more." She guided them to the porch. Reggie sat one step up and wrapped her arms around Sophia. She handed her the steaming cup of coffee.

"Well, you see, there's this woman."

"There always is." Reggie kissed the top of Sophia's head.

Sophia looked around. Was anyone watching? She looked down at the sidewalk at the step below. Her eyes felt heavy with tears. Why did she care?

"What's wrong? Did I do something wrong?" Reggie swung down to sit next to Sophia, lifting her chin gently.

She shook her head, not trusting her voice. She took a breath. "No, of course not. I'm the one who's wrong. Can we go inside?"

Reggie looked confused but she nodded and gave Sophia a hand up. Sophia followed her inside to the dining room table.

"Can I get you something to eat?" Reggie rubbed the back of her head and shifted from foot to foot.

"No. Sit with me. I'm sorry I'm being weird. My meeting this morning has me jumbled up."

Reggie nodded more than she needed to and finally sat. "Was it what we thought? I mean, you and me, from last night?"

Sophia smiled sadly. "They didn't seem to think the night was as magical as I did."

She couldn't get a read on Reggie; her face was impassive. It occurred to Sophia that this morning must have been hard for Reggie too. But she was here with her now. She'd stood up for them, but Reggie didn't know that.

"The Speaker of the House thought my fraternizing with you was a personal affront after he told me to stay away from you."

Reggie cut in. "I told you I wasn't popular in the statehouse."

"I'm probably not either, at least not with him. I told you last night, this"—she pointed between the two of them—"is not wrong. You're not wrong."

A smile slowly crept across Reggie's face. "Please tell me you didn't say that to the leadership of your party."

"I answer to the voters, not to those guys." Sophia's voice was stronger than her conviction.

"Maybe you aren't really a politician if you believe that." Reggie shook her head looking shocked, but still smiling. "Thank you."

Sophia took a sip of coffee and waved her off. "I'm still the bloodthirsty politician of your nightmares, or theirs, but I'm on the hunt for new allies. Ones who won't tell me who I'm allowed to kiss. Speaking of which, I know this is asking a lot and is probably going to piss you off, but do you mind if most of our kissing is indoors for the next week? Just until I get a feel for the new landscape?"

She knew that request was going to push all of Reggie's buttons, and she felt guilty making it. She wasn't ashamed of being with Reggie, but she knew it would come across that way. She'd made her choice to see where these feelings for Reggie were taking her when she gave the implied middle finger to the Speaker on her way out the door.

"Oh." Reggie stood up abruptly and took her mug to the kitchen. She roughly poured more coffee and spilled some on the counter. "Sure. Whatever you need."

"Can I explain why?" Sophia joined Reggie in the kitchen and stood shoulder to shoulder next to her.

Sophia took Reggie's silence as consent. She interpreted Reggie's stiff shoulders and locked jaw as a sign she needed to talk fast. Was this the time to mention the new information about Reggie's father?

"Politics is about power, among all the other things, and I need to figure out where mine is. Now I have friends in the House, and I hope in the governor's office too. I need to consolidate some of that power right now."

"What does that have to do with us?" Reggie still looked out the window above the sink.

"Everything. I'm a freshman representative. No one expects me to be challenging the Speaker for dominance of our caucus, but I don't want to be dependent on him for my rise or fall, or to get things passed that I really believe in. So I need my own coalition, independent of his influence." Sophia reached out and tentatively slid her hand over Reggie's.

Reggie turned to her. There was deep hurt in her eyes. "So while you shore up your career, you want to hide me away? I'll be the skeleton in your closet, hopefully never to find the light of day?"

"What? No." Sophia took a step back. "Babe, never. I'm worried things are going to get ugly for a little while and I don't want you to be a target, and, honestly, I don't want to provide any more ammunition until I have people at my back to help me deal with the onslaught. In my experience, people in power don't give up any of it, even a tiny slice, without a fight. And I took their advice about you and told them they could shove it up their ass."

"You didn't really tell them that, did you?" Reggie tentatively stepped to Sophia and put her hands on her waist.

"I think they were clear on the message." Sophia looped her arms around Reggie's shoulders. "I'm not ashamed of you, or this. I'm sorry I made you feel that way. I just need a bit of slow motion until I can put myself out there without losing everything I've built."

"I'm sorry I jumped to conclusions. Ava said I need to get in touch with my emotions more, but they go a little haywire on me sometimes." Reggie pulled Sophia closer.

"Not haywire. Perfectly normal." Sophia risked a kiss.

She was rewarded when Reggie let her hands roam freely and deepened the kiss. Standing in Reggie's kitchen, bodies tangled, kissing and caressing, Sophia had never been happier.

Reggie broke the kiss, her breath coming heavier than usual. "I still wish you'd let me onto the front lines with you. I'm tougher than I look."

Sophia slipped her hand under Reggie's shirt and across her abs. Reggie shivered under her touch. "I hope not. I like your soft parts and look forward to exploring more." Sophia trailed one finger past Reggie's waistband but stopped just short of the apex of her thighs.

Before she fully processed, Reggie's mouth was back on hers, more insistent this time. Reggie walked her backward as they kissed, out of the kitchen. Sophia didn't know if they were headed for the couch or elsewhere in the house, but she didn't care. She wanted Reggie, right now, anywhere Reggie was leading.

"Is this okay?" Reggie stopped their motion and their kissing and made sure she had Sophia's full attention."

Sophia cupped Reggie's crotch and squeezed. "Get moving, hot stuff."

Reggie took Sophia's hand and started down the hall. Sophia's stomach tumbled with nerves, anticipation, and lust.

They stepped into what Sophia assumed was Reggie's bedroom and Reggie closed the distance between them. She pulled the shirt from Sophia's tailor-made dress pants and slid her hands under the turquoise fabric.

She was moving too slowly for Sophia's taste, and she was about to take Reggie's hands and move them to her breasts when Reggie's phone rang. Reggie glanced at the bed where she'd tossed it. Sophia redirected Reggie's gaze to the task at hand, but Reggie stepped toward the bed instead.

"I'm sorry, it's work. I'm on call and I have to answer it."

Sophia wanted to be mad, but she understood the call of duty.

"I bet kindergarten teachers don't get calls interrupting Sunday morning foreplay." She rubbed her hands up and down her own torso, pausing a few extra seconds on her breasts before sitting serenely on the bed, waiting for Reggie.

Reggie barely said three words during the short call. She looked annoyed as she ended it.

"I have to go in. They're short staffed."

Sophia stood up and kissed along Reggie's neck. "Tell them you're busy all day and are unavailable."

Reggie intercepted Sophia's next kiss and delivered a searing one of her own. "I wish it worked that way. Perhaps a small consolation for you, I'm going to be wet and uncomfortable because of you all shift."

"No consolation at all since I'm going to suffer right along with you. Do you really have to leave now?"

"Afraid so." Reggie moved to the closet and pulled out her uniform.

Sophia made no move for the door or any coy nod to covering her eyes as Reggie changed. From the look of it, Reggie enjoyed her watching. Her ballsiness backfired, however. A mostly naked Reggie was a lot to take in. Her muscles were defined enough to make Sophia want to demand a feat of strength, but she hadn't lost her feminine curves. A delicate tattoo of branches and birds surrounded one of her upper forearms and bicep. Today's boxer briefs were forest green with red chili peppers. Sophia was certainly feeling the heat.

"You okay?" Reggie looked amused.

"Don't act like you don't know what I'm feeling." Sophia pouted.

"I wish I didn't have to go. I'd do almost anything to stay and get you to look at me again the way you did when you saw me in my underwear." Reggie pulled Sophia to her feet and led her back to the kitchen. She put the mugs from earlier in the sink and walked Sophia to her car.

"We're outside. Can I kiss you good-bye?" Reggie looked around.

"You better." Sophia pulled her in, not caring if there were cameras around. At least, not right now. "Call me later if you get off work before tomorrow."

Sophia saw Reggie waving in the rearview as she drove away. She felt more solid in her refusal to bend to the Speaker's demands earlier. Reggie, more than any political carrot dangled in her face, felt like the future. Maybe it was political suicide to grow a mind of her own, but the seed was planted. Political greatness didn't come to the meek.

CHAPTER TWENTY-FOUR

R eggie waited for the heavy prison entry door to slide closed and lock. She never liked these brief moments when she was trapped between the inner and outer doors, in the confined space, unable to get in or out until one of the two doors buzzed open. The confinement was a reminder, every time she entered, that the inmates she guarded spent their days in a space roughly the same size with no chance of exit.

The second, inner door buzzed open and she walked through the metal detector and onto the women's unit where she worked. Before she turned toward the locker room to drop her things, the lieutenant warden flagged her down.

"Northrup, come in, please." He waved her into his office.

"What can I do for you, sir?" Reggie stood inside the door stiffly.

She was wary of being hailed so quickly. Being called in to work after a shift had already started was odd, and this was adding to her unease with the situation.

"You're needed on cell block D this morning. Special assignment." The warden moved papers around his desk and didn't look at her.

"Cell block D?" Reggie dragged the words out, the taste of them bitter. "I thought you were short-staffed here. Isn't that why I was called in?"

"Things change, Northrup. Get your ass over to D."

"Yes, sir." Reggie stayed put an extra beat, trying to catch the warden's eye.

The warden continued to look at his desk. What was going on? He wasn't the greatest boss, but his biggest fault was an over infatuation with the sound of his own voice. The clipped tone and short answers had her on guard.

Since there didn't seem to be additional answers to be pried from the warden, Reggie continued to her original destination. She dropped her things in the locker room. She might be assigned to D, but she wasn't going to navigate unknown territory

"What are you doing here? I thought you were off today." Ava opened the locker next to Reggie.

"Got called in. You guys short-staffed today?" Reggie slammed the locker shut and leaned against the door facing Ava.

Ava looked confused. "Not today. We're fully staffed and now you're here so I think that makes you the awkward third wheel. Can't you sneak out the back and pretend you weren't here?"

"We work at a prison. Sneaking out the back isn't supposed to be something you can do. Besides, I've already been given a special assignment to cell block D." Reggie leaned her head back against the locker harder than she meant to. "Ow. Fuck. You have no idea where I was when that damn call came in."

Ava looked at her intently. "I have a few guesses given how grumpy you are. I'm more interested in why you're getting sent on a special assignment to your father's neighborhood."

"You and me both."

"Well, you aren't going to find out in here." Ava grabbed Reggie by the shoulders, spun her toward the door, and gave her a shove. "Get your ass moving. I can't wait to find out what's going on."

"Yes, I *am* a little apprehensive about it, thanks for asking. Something *does* feel suspicious to me too. I don't know how I'd feel if I ended up face-to-face with him after all this time." Reggie picked at one of her nail beds.

"Now's not the time for that, Reggie. Shove your daddy issues back in their deep dark hole and get moving." Ava gave her another little push.

Reggie looked back over her shoulder with a glare. "You're the one who told me to start exploring my feelings. You send extremely mixed messages."

She stomped out before Ava could answer, but she could hear her laughing. The walk to cell block D felt endless and too fast. She checked in with the officer in charge once she was on the cell block. They were clearly expecting her and led her to one of the large visitation rooms. This was one used for attorney meetings or other confidential business and didn't have audio surveillance.

"Have a seat, he'll be right in."

Reggie wanted to run back into the hall and demand to know who she was meeting, but she knew. Why her father wanted to meet with her was beyond her, but he was the only one who could possibly care enough to go to all this trouble. And he was the only one who still had enough power to get visitation when he asked for it.

She didn't have to wait long for confirmation. An officer she didn't know led her father in, had him sit, and uncuffed him.

"Anything else you need, Mr. Northrup?"

Reggie took the officer by the arm and herded him to the door. "No, he doesn't need anything. This isn't a restaurant and you don't work for him."

The officer skittered out the door and pulled it shut behind him. Reggie turned around and stormed back toward her father.

"You don't need to be rough on him, Gina, he's only doing his job."

Reggie put her hands on the back of the chair across from her father and leaned toward him. He looked older, more haggard since she'd last seen him, but his hair was still neatly combed and shiny with pomade, as always. The prison coveralls made him look too skinny, but even in clothes meant to rob individuality, he hadn't lost his ability to fill up a room with his presence.

"His job is to keep you locked up, not chauffeur you around. What is all this? Why am I here?" Reggie pointed between the two of them.

"Can't a father spend some time with his only child?" Her dad smiled the big winning smile that, in Reggie's experience, got him whatever he wanted most of the time.

"That's what visiting hours are for, just like everyone else in here."

"And yet you've never come to see me in all the time I've been here." He shrugged.

"That should tell you something, Dad." Reggie crossed her arms.

"It tells me plenty, but I needed to talk to you, so I had to make other arrangements. You're as stubborn as I am. Sit, Gina, it's about your Sophia." Her father indicated the chair across from him.

Reggie's fingers tingled and her neck muscles tightened. "How do you know about her?"

"Relax. Sit. I'm on your side and I mean her no harm, but I need to talk to you to make sure she isn't a threat to you." He tried again to point to the chair.

Reggie yanked the chair back and slammed into it. She dropped her forearms heavily onto the table and leaned forward. "I doubt you're on my side unless there's something in it for you. What do you know about Sophia?"

Her father kicked his feet up on the table and laced his fingers together behind his head. "You know, Gina, I always assumed you'd follow me into the family business. You were a whip smart kid. You could have been governor by now. I pictured us running this state together. Do you know the difference we could have made? Can you picture it?"

"I wasn't interested in politics, I was never going to be governor, and I didn't want any part of what you were offering."

"There was a time you did. There was a time you still looked at me like I meant something to you. Do you remember? That's when you started coming with me to the political events. But look at you now, wasting your life in here. Doing what?" He looked around the room, disgust etched on his face.

"Even if I'd wanted to run for president, it wouldn't have mattered. Your getting locked up in here ruined my good name out there. No one wants anything to do with me, thanks. And how would you and I have possibly run the state with you doing time? You can't run anything from in here."

Reggie wondered if that was true. He certainly seemed to have orchestrated their current meeting. She wasn't interested in revisiting family history. So what if she'd thought, once upon a time, that she'd join the family business. That was before she knew what politics really was.

"No more wandering down memory lane. Tell me about Sophia." Reggie slammed her hand on the metal table.

Her father held up his hands as if to appease her. "I'm getting there. Would it surprise you to know someone is trying to get you kicked out of the community design team?"

"No, it wouldn't. Again, thanks to you. What does that have to do with Sophia?"

He raised an eyebrow. "What if it's her?"

"Is it?"

Reggie knew it wasn't. She didn't have proof or any reason to be so confident, but she knew it wasn't Sophia.

"No, at least I don't think so. And before you ask, I don't know who it is, but someone is gunning for you."

"Geez, I wonder what anyone could find objectionable about me?" Reggie crossed her hands on the table and glared at her father.

"Enough. You might not agree with my methods, you might think I was a lousy father, but everything I did was in service to the people of this state. There are plenty of people who want a piece of me because they think I'm weakened locked up in here, and blacklisting you is a way to get at me." He accentuated each sentence with his finger jabbed in Reggie's direction.

Reggie bit her tongue. She wanted to argue, yell, or bang her hands on the table, but it was important to hear him out. She'd never heard his perspective, and maybe doing so would allow her to move out of his shadow.

"I'm sorry you have to deal with the political bottom-feeders using you to get to me, but I'm not apologizing for the rest. If I walked out of here today and put my name on any ballot, I bet you dollars to donuts I win." He looked completely certain it was true, the arrogant surety of a privileged White man, even as he sat there in his prison uniform.

She decided not to point out there were a few elections he'd be ineligible for due to a felony conviction, but his point was valid. He still had a devoted following and had always been a political genius. It was part of the reason she distrusted politicians. No matter how crooked some were, others continued to follow them.

"I think you're giving yourself too much credit. Getting me thrown off some committee isn't blacklisting me. It's not like it's going to boost my career. Sophia. Let's stay focused here. Why do you want to talk about Sophia?" She tapped the table to emphasize her point.

He nodded, his expression serious. "She's in a bit of trouble. Francis, the Speaker of the House, offered her a bribe a few months ago. I don't know all the particulars, but I know she never agreed to the terms and this morning she gave him a double middle finger and told him to fuck off."

"A bribe? I don't understand." Reggie pushed back in her chair and ran her hand through her hair. Why hadn't Sophia told her?

"Focus, Gina. Being offered a bribe isn't the same as accepting. I'll show you. Gina, I'll give you a million dollars if you help me break out of here. Now you've ben offered a bribe too." Her father looked too nonchalant.

"That's not the same. I'd never consider accepting your bribe."

"Do you think so little of your Sophia that you think she would?" Her father frowned.

Sophia wouldn't, would she? Reggie knew her, trusted her. Right? The most important thing was that she'd said no. Twice and emphatically, apparently. That must have been at her meeting with the Speaker this morning. But why did it take months for her to tell him no? Damn it.

"Gina, let's focus on what's important here. Her leadership's going to turn on her. Francis will try to bury her in career purgatory. It will happen quickly if she lets it. She's going to have to fight her way out."

"She knows that." Reggie wanted to pick up the chair she was sitting in and throw it through the wall.

"She needs to choose her friends carefully, but move quickly. Francis looks like Santa Claus, but underneath he's vindictive, vengeful, and power hungry. It's why I chose him to rise to Speaker. I wanted someone who wouldn't relinquish power and would fight for what I needed."

Reggie opened her mouth to say something, but it took her brain a few beats to process what her father said. "Did you say you put him in power? From here?"

"Telecommuting is an option for many businesses these days." A small smile played at the corners of his mouth. "Look, I can't call him off in his pursuit of her. She stood up to him and refused to bow to his will. He's not going to let that stand without a reason to back down. She has to give him a reason."

"If you put him in power, surely you control him. Isn't that your thing?" Reggie shook her head trying to get the pieces of this mishmashed puzzle to fall into place. "And he's threatening Sophia because she's dating me. That's okay with you?"

"Actually, he's threatening Sophia because he's scared of her and of me. The fact she's dating you is a convenient way to sully her name and get to me. I'm sorry your reputation could use a spit shine, but there are bigger power plays happening behind the scenes here. Francis is a shark and as such he was always a risk. But I needed a shark to take care of some other business. He wants to strip Sophia of her power because she's a threat to him. She refuses to back down and play the game. He's exactly the kind of guy I needed in power. Now it's biting me in my family's ass, but these things happen. Short of retiring him permanently, which isn't off the table, I can't fully shield her from his political self-preservation and power hungry instincts."

"Why are you getting your sticky fingers back in this mess now?"

"Gina, you're smarter than this. My fingers never left the levers of power. This is a courtesy call because I love you, whatever you think of me. You're my daughter and you seem to care about Sophia Lamont. Guys like Francis Spaziano understand strength and they understand power. She has access to both, but she needs to move fast." He reached across the metal table and patted Reggie's hand.

"Is she like you? Like the rest of them?" Reggie's shoulders sagged and she looked at her hands.

He flinched and moved back. "No, she's nothing like me. There's an old guard that did things a certain way, but now?" He shrugged and gestured in the air. "Now there's a whole class of idealists invading the statehouse. They'll never get anything done, but they stand by their convictions. History will be the judge of who better served the people. Maybe us old guys got it wrong after all." He winked, showing just what he thought of that possibility.

"Where is she supposed to turn if it's not to you or the leadership of her party?" The air felt too thick to breathe in the small room.

"Who has their own money and isn't beholden to campaign cash? Who's offered to work with her but hasn't asked for anything in return? Who has different priorities but has still reached out seeking compromise? Who's been given shitty committee assignments and has still consistently been passed up for leadership positions? Those are the people she should reach out to."

He got up and knocked on the door. It opened and the same officer came back in.

"All done, sir? I'm sorry, but I'll have to put these back on while we're out there." The officer indicated over his shoulder toward the hall.

He put his wrists out. He turned and winked at Reggie once again. "One of many indignities in here."

"This isn't a country club, Dad."

"Of course, of course. But even at this fine establishment, they allow visitors, you know."

"It doesn't seem like I need to make an appointment to see you. One will be made for me." She looked at the young officer until he ducked his head and looked away.

"That's only because you work here and it's easier this way." He paused and looked at her seriously, his expression more open than she'd ever seen it. "You've done your duty long enough, Gina. I'm confined and serving my time. You don't need to continue watching over me, nor should you. This life doesn't suit you. Besides, the politicians hate you because they think you and I are planning an uprising in here. Get some distance from me and your life may ease up a little. Since you were little you'd tell your mother you wanted to be a teacher. Yeah, I know, you didn't think I was listening. But I was. It's time to go make your own dreams."

He saluted with his shackled hands on his way out the door. Reggie didn't move for a long time. What the hell had just happened?

Since her call into work seemed to have been a ruse to get her in the room with her father, she assumed she was free to clock out. She double-timed it back to her locker, collected her things, and buzzed out the double doors. She hadn't realized how tense she'd been until the fresh air hit her lungs and she took a few big, lung-expanding breaths. The kind that felt like they could crack ribs and oxygenate your toenails.

As she started her truck and pointed it toward home, a Star Wars style recap scroll rolled through her mind. Her father had never let go of the levers of power, except now he seemed to have lost control of one of his lieutenants. Sophia was the target of said lieutenant, a vengeful, power hungry, man shark. Sophia, who'd been offered a bribe, but hadn't taken it and seemingly didn't play the same political games, but she had to if she wanted to save her career.

It was easy for Reggie to separate Sophia from politics, but Representative Lamont was a different story. She seemed destined to be dragged into the world Reggie hated. She hadn't even gotten to the part where popular opinion had her plotting with her father for years. She'd always known people distrusted her because of the link to her father. That they'd think she'd be in league with him even now was nauseating.

She thought about calling Sophia. She could easily fall into her arms and get lost in her touch, but her head felt like it was being squeezed in a vice of past and future and she needed to relieve some of the pressure before she talked to Sophia. And the bribe was still nagging at her. Why hadn't Sophia told her?

When she got home, she pulled on running clothes and her sneakers. It was a beautiful day and she had hours of free time ahead of her. She locked the door and set off at a blistering pace. If only she could figure out if she was running toward her future or away from it.

CHAPTER TWENTY-FIVE

S ophia tried to keep still and not fidget while Jackson and the other cochairs presented their teams' final recommendations for inclusion in the design team's report to the governor, but she was failing. She'd known this meeting was going to be difficult, but it was proving there was no bar too low to slip below.

"Well done, everyone. Just superb work. You and your teams should be tremendously proud of yourselves." Bert's glasses were, if possible, more enthusiastic than he was, given their vibrant hue and firework motif.

It turned out Bert's glasses were prescient.

"Representative Lamont, you've heard all our proposals. Can we trust you to follow through on the governor's request and help transform our work into legislation?" Jackson leaned forward, his elbows planted firmly on the table.

Sophia sighed. "You know as well as I do, Jackson, the goal of the design team wasn't ever legislative action. We've fulfilled our responsibility as soon as we deliver these recommendations to Governor Seeley."

"If there were to be legislation to come from our recommendations, would we get any credit for our work?" Geraldine looked up from her notes. Her eyebrows were furrowed, but she looked curious, not angry.

"Of course. The design team would be mentioned as a key incubator, but by the time anything became law, I would expect there would be a number of amendments and alterations." Sophia ignored Jackson's sputtering and addressed Geraldine.

"What you're saying is you get all the credit and we're a footnote." Jackson half stood and raised his voice.

Bert tried to jump in, but Reggie was faster.

"She gets the credit because it's her job and she'd be doing the work. If you can get a bill signed into law, then do it yourself. She gets the credit the same way you'd get all the credit if you had a courier service and biked over to deliver the recommendations yourself. I wouldn't ride along with you shouting that I helped too." Reggie's face was flushed and her jaw was tight.

"Fine. Will you guarantee, right here, in front of all of us, that you'll take our recommendations and push ahead with legislation as written? I'll write the first draft with you, so it doesn't fall down your list, given what I'm sure is a busy schedule." Jackson's sickly-sweet voice oozed with condescension.

Sophia looked at Reggie and said a silent prayer she'd understand. "No. As I said to you during our first meeting, I always welcome citizen involvement in government, but if you want a bill passed based on *these* recommendations, you'll have to find someone else to sponsor it. Or allow the governor to do with it as she will."

Jackson slammed his hand on the table. The rest of the cochairs looked somewhere between angry, uncomfortable, and apologetic.

"You're a coward." Jackson spit out the words as if they tasted of excrement.

Sophia could tell Reggie was ready to come to her defense again, but it wasn't necessary. She put her hand on her arm. She also caught Bert's eye and shook him off. She could handle this on her own.

"We've all put in hours of our time and a great deal of our heart into these recommendations. They'll be delivered to the governor as intended. As for my role after I walk out the door, I'm a politician, Jackson. I have more to think about than these recommendations when I calculate what projects to sponsor. As written, I don't believe in these, they're too far reaching for my comfort, and politically it doesn't make sense for me to champion something I'm lukewarm on and something I don't think has a chance of passage. If that makes me a coward, so be it. If you live in my district you're welcome to make your voice heard at the ballot box."

"Fuck you." Jackson got up and slammed the door on the way out.

The rest of the cochairs filed out after a few parting words from Bert. A few stopped by to offer encouragement, and Geraldine gave her a reassuring shoulder squeeze, but Sophia wanted to be away from all of them. The only comfort she needed was from Reggie's gentle words and strong arms.

Once she and Reggie headed to the door, Sophia could tell that comfort would have to wait. Reggie nearly pushed the elevator button through the wiring and the swiftly closing doors weren't enough to shut out the cloud of doom and gloom hanging over her head. If they weren't sharing the elevator with other design team cochairs she'd have called her out, but now wasn't the time.

"Maybe we should rain check dinner tonight. We've both had a long day." Reggie shifted from one foot to the other once they'd left the elevator and were alone once again.

"Oh, I don't think so. Something ugly's churning up your gut and if you and I are going to work, you need to share the ugly with me, not just the sappy stuff that makes my insides dance." Sophia stepped into Reggie's space and cupped her cheek. "What's going on?"

Reggie leaned into her touch then seemed to remember she was upset and stepped away. "Guess we might as well have full bellies while we talk. Where're we going?"

"I was planning on Mrs. Medeiros's restaurant, but it seems like we have serious business to discuss. I don't want an audience tonight. Rumor has it Lenny's food truck is parked by the river tonight. Can I tempt you?" Sophia tentatively moved her hand to Reggie's hand.

She took it as a good sign that Reggie didn't shove it away. Something about their meeting had Reggie tied up in a knot and they needed to untangle it. She hoped the quiet evening and a chance to talk would help clear the air. She wasn't naive enough to think the sign of a strong relationship was never disagreeing, but this felt different, and it was unsettling. What if Reggie was having second thoughts about their relationship? If this crisis of confidence had laid anything bare it was that her feelings for Reggie were strong, and if Reggie walked away now, Sophia would be heartbroken.

Lenny's truck, as promised, was parked at the river. They ordered and Reggie led the way toward the water.

"I run this way sometimes. There's a bench tucked down here, right along the riverbank."

Sophia was sure Reggie was going to walk them straight into the shallows, but as she was preparing to roll up her pant legs, the aforementioned bench appeared. It was nestled between two trees and looked like it was waiting for them.

"I don't know how you saw this on a run from the path, but it's perfect." Sophia turned in a circle taking in the view.

A smile tugged at the corners of Reggie's mouth. "I might have seen a disheveled couple stumbling back to the path from down here and detoured to see where they'd been." Reggie's eyes got wide. "Not in a weird way. It's just that it looks like this goes straight into the water so I was curious."

Sophia grabbed Reggie's head and pulled her in for a kiss. "I love the thoughtful, romantic side of you, and you're pretty cute when you're embarrassed too."

She let Reggie go and moved to the bench. Even though the kiss had been spontaneous, she was still pleased to see fewer rumbles of thunder threatening in Reggie's eyes.

Reggie sat close to her, so their legs were pressed together. Then she turned so she was facing Sophia. "Why did you tell the cochairs you wouldn't even consider writing and sponsoring a bill with Jackson?"

"Because it's based on the design team's final report. You heard what's going into our recommendations to the governor. I can't put my name on those and push for a vote." Sophia put her hand on Reggie's knee and searched her face.

"Why not?" Reggie put her food behind her on the bench and propped her elbow on the seat back.

"Because it'll never pass." Sophia threw her hands in the air. "And I'm not in the position right now to waste political capital on something that will be all for show."

Reggie exploded out of her seat. "It's not all for show if you fight for it. Real people's real lives would be changed for the better if those recommendations were made the law of the land. You campaigned on the promise to improve the lives of your constituents. Now you have a chance to do that and you're turning your back."

Sophia took a deep breath and unclenched her jaw. "I'm not serving anyone by grandstanding with legislation that has no chance of passing or straying from my ideals. Babe, I'm a practical politician and I'm interested in results. I've been labeled a moderate like it's a bad thing, but more often than not, we work in a divided government so no one's going to get what the far end of their party's political spectrum wants."

Reggie was shaking her head. "Why not start the negotiation at the far end, where the most good can be done and only concede ground when you're forced?"

"I'm not giving up on anything. Don't forget, though, there are two sides to every coin. What you believe will help is someone else's nightmare, but middle ground exists between two points along any spectrum. All you have to do is look for it. A good compromise usually means no one leaves completely happy, but both sides get at least a small win." Sophia reached out her hand.

Reggie took it. "I don't know that I agree. If you know something is right for the people you serve, why stop fighting for it?"

Sophia tugged Reggie back to the bench. "You're forgetting that sometimes what you know is right, isn't obvious to the voters. You say decriminalize drug use and someone else hears 'everything's legal, it's a free-for-all.'"

"Again, so what?"

"So then the law you passed is controversial and has low approval. Groups mobilize to repeal it or weaken it with other laws.

It becomes a rallying cry for political opponents and a wedge issue when it didn't need to be any of those things. The loser in all of those scenarios is the people who are struggling with the disease of addiction."

"I get it, but I still think it's worth fighting for some of these recommendations. What good is being the voice of the people if you can't use it?" Reggie looked defeated. "How much of your calculation on these decisions is about your own political survival? You told me you need to grow your power base to stay in the game."

Sophia played with the short hair on the back of Reggie's neck. "Is that what this is about?"

Reggie looked at the sky. "No. My father arranged a visit. When I got called into work Sunday, it was his doing."

"What?" Sophia sat up straight. "How could he possibly arrange that?"

"It seems like he never let go of the levers of power. Your friend, the Speaker of the House, is one of his puppets who turned into a real power hungry asshole and is out to get you. This is the shit that makes my politician trust issues seem too lax. He said the Speaker offered you a bribe. Did you think about taking it?" Reggie put her elbows on her knees and her head in her hands.

"No. He wanted to me to walk away from you. You know me. You can trust me." Sophia's insides churned. Why hadn't she told Reggie about the Speaker's offer? She knew she wouldn't take it, but what must Reggie be thinking? "You've known who and what your father is for a while. This development is surprising but not what I'd call a shocking plot twist."

"He said you're in a tough spot right now and you need to consolidate power quickly so the Speaker can't sweep you down some dark political hole. Apparently, I'm also a liability to you because rumor has it he and I are plotting an overthrow of the political order with a prisoner army or something." Reggie stood again and paced in front of the bench.

Sophia couldn't help it, she laughed. "This all sounds a little bit like the plot of a low-budget thriller. I've never heard the rumor that you were plotting to overthrow the government."

"Not kissing me in public, not bringing this bill forward, sitting on the Speaker's bribe for months until you made sure it wasn't what you wanted...tell me those aren't actions to help you? To position yourself to better take on the Speaker or get reelected." Reggie flopped on the bench again, her face twisted in conflict.

"I've already told you they are, Reggie. I'm not hiding that, except the bribe. I wasn't ever going to accept his offer." She reached out and traced a line along Reggie's knee. "And I didn't say no kissing in public, just not in the middle of the street during rush hour and only for a week or so."

Reggie sighed heavily. "So how is this any different from what my father did? Aside from the killing and assault, obviously. He looked out for his self-interest in the name of staying in power to *help* people. That seems to be what politics is about. Now he's in prison and he's still doing it."

This time Sophia stood up and moved away from Reggie. "So what are you saying? Suddenly because your father points out that I'm doing my job, doing what I believe is right, by the way, I'm no better than a murderer? Your father did a lot more than look out for his own interests and I resent the comparison."

Reggie looked at the ground.

"I don't know when the focus of the design team became legislation. That wasn't the original intent, and everyone clearly would have been better served had it never been broached. No one seems able to get over my job long enough to remember this was a *volunteer* position for all of us."

"But it was brought up and—"

Sophia held up her hand. "We've beaten this topic into the ground. I don't have much else to say. Reggie, I've been scared of failing or letting my family or myself down as long as I can remember. Because of you I've taken the biggest risks of my life recently. The first was falling in love with you and the second was not giving up on that love even when my career was threatened because of it. I can't move forward if every decision I make at work leads to a crisis in our relationship."

Reggie stood and moved closer to Sophia. She reached out tentatively and touched Sophia's face. "I've almost singlehandedly torched your career, gotten the entire cochair group to hate you by association, and you can't take me out in public, and you still can look me in the eye and say you're in love with me?"

Her heart hammered in her chest. "Yes, Reggie. How you don't already know that is beyond me. But I'm serious about the other part. It will break my heart to walk away, but you have to decide if you can commit to being with a politician because I can't be in a relationship where that's being constantly held against me. I know what I'm getting with you and I've tried to make it clear that I'm okay with you and everything that comes with your last name. It's up to you to decide if you're okay with everything that comes with my job title."

"I'm not holding your job against you." Reggie stopped and looked thoughtful. "I am doing that, aren't I?"

Sophia indicated a little with her thumb and index finger.

Reggie blew out a breath. She looked frustrated. "What happens the next time someone threatens your career because of me? What if the bribes get bigger or you don't have friends who can withstand the pressure like you do? What if you run out of power to consolidate and suddenly your career, the one you've wanted since you were a kid, is gone, because of me? Politics is fun for you, but it's what my childhood nightmares are made of and they've followed me into adulthood. You won't always get to play with only the good guys if you want to get things done. What then?"

"God, you're stubborn. You trust me, Reggie, and you trust us. That's how we answer all those questions. We trust each other. I'm going to go home now before this turns into an argument we both regret. I'm not kidding about deciding if you can be with Sophia *and* Representative Lamont because you can't choose only one." Sophia kissed Reggie's cheek and walked back up to the river path.

Her heart was heavy as she walked to her car, thankful they'd taken two cars for once. It took a strength she didn't often have to access not to look back. She'd told Reggie what she needed to, now it was up to Reggie to decide if she could give it to her.

She dialed Lily a few hundred feet down the path. She answered after a few rings, sounding happier than Sophia felt she had a right to given how miserable she felt.

"I thought tonight was date night with Reggie. Why are you calling me?"

Sophia tried to explain what had happened, but all that came out was one big loud sob.

"Oh, sweetie, I'll meet you at your place."

On the ride home the reality of the last hour began to sink in. Until the words were out of her mouth Sophia hadn't put a label on how she felt about Reggie, but there was no denying her feelings. She was in love with her, and it would be some kind of shitty if the moment she realized it was also the moment she and Reggie called it quits.

Lily was waiting for her when she pulled into her driveway. Sophia was barely out of the car before Lily had her wrapped in a hug.

"What are we dealing with here? Broken heart? Trouble at work? Life crisis?" Lily held her at arm's length.

"Do I have to pick?" Sophia half smiled.

"Oh, it's worse than I thought. Not to fear, I came prepared." Lily led Sophia to the front door and picked up a grocery bag.

The clink of bottles was unmistakable. Sophia peeked in the bag. In addition to an impressive variety of alcohol, there were chocolate chips, ice cream, and gherkins, which for some reason Lily felt were appropriate for every occasion.

"What exactly did you think was happening over here tonight and how many of me were you expecting?" Sophia pointed at the bag.

"I needed to be able to make the appropriate pairing so I brought it all. You'll thank me later."

Two mojitos and a bowl of ice cream, for Sophia, and a daiquiri, a bag of chips, and gherkins, for Lily, later, Sophia was less forlorn.

"Should I call her?" Sophia looked around for her phone.

"Hell no. She's got to come to you. Unless she doesn't and then I guess you have to make some decisions." Lily tried to swipe Sophia's ice cream spoon.

"Get your pickle fingers off my spoon." She slapped Lily away. "I don't know what I'll do if she decides to walk away. Spend a lot more time on the couch with you, trying not to smell gherkins with every bite of ice cream, I guess. She's not going to walk away, right?"

Lily took her hand. "I don't know, sweetie. She's a damn fool if she does, but there are idiots all over this world."

Before Sophia could respond, Davey hollered from the front porch. Lily jumped up to let him in.

"What's going on in here?" Davey looked over the remnants of operation cheer up. He looked concerned.

Lily pulled him down on the couch next to her and kissed him. "Thanks for coming over. All hands on deck on this one."

Sophia choked on the sip she'd taken. "I think I've missed a thing or two."

Davey looked shy. "I told you we had something to tell you. Later. This"—he pointed to the ice cream and gherkins—"needs some explaining."

Lily filled him in while Sophia nursed her drink, head back against the sofa cushions. She missed Reggie and that made her heart hurt. What was she doing right now? Was she hurting too?

"Look, sis, Reggie's a moron if she leaves the best thing that will ever be a part of her life." He pointed at her. "But I can see why that design team thing hurt. You told us how miserable people make it for her and she stuck her neck out to be part of that group. I'm sure she wanted to make a difference even if it meant some misery for her personally."

"We all made a difference. The governor got a one-hundred-and-forty-seven-page report with over sixty recommendations. We spent months arguing and researching and working our asses off." Sophia felt like a little kid again trying to convince her parents her efforts were worthy of their praise. "But that's not really what she's so spooked about. I was offered a leadership position at the start of the new legislative session if I stayed away from Reggie. When she looks at our future together, I think that's what she sees, my career blowing up all around us because of her and me being dragged into the worst version of a nefarious political stereotype."

"Well, damn. When you put it like that, I wouldn't date you either. And to be clear, you said no to the bribe, right? This family only has room for one felon and I cornered that market." Davey grabbed a handful of chips and crunched one loudly.

"Of course I said no to the bribe. I'm in love with her. I couldn't stay away from her any more than a bee could stay away from a beautiful flower."

"Did she tell you she's scared of ruining your career and you breaking bad?" Lily grabbed the dirty dishes and carried them to the kitchen.

"Yes. I told her she needs to trust me and us and she can't only date Sophia, Representative Lamont comes along too." Sophia followed Lily to the kitchen with their empty drink glasses.

"Ouch." Davey leaned against the counter and swiped a gherkin.

"Ouch? What do you mean, 'ouch'?" Sophia resisted the urge to fling the closest heavy object at her brother.

"She told you all the things she's freaked out about and you basically told her to trust you, it's fine, and take it or leave it, this is who I am. Did she know about the bribe?" Davey leveled a stare that cut right through her.

"I told her I love her and we need to trust each other. Then I told her if she wants to be with me she has to be with all of me. I didn't tell her about the offered bribe. I don't know why. You should see the way people react to her. It's awful. She hasn't done anything wrong and she's treated like she should serve time alongside her father." Sophia felt the tears she'd mostly kept at bay threatening a new offensive.

"Sweetie, that's what she's worried will happen to you, you know." Lily slipped her arm around Sophia's waist and pulled her close.

"I know." Sophia couldn't force her voice higher than a meek whisper. "I'd be stupid not to see the possibility of it happening. It's not like more than one person hasn't tried to warn me away from her. I've risked a lot for us."

Davey slid the empty gherkin bowl down the counter to the sink and wiped his hands on his shirt, then looked guiltily at Lily. "Bet she feels like she's risking a lot too. You said she hates politics and politicians, but she hasn't run screaming from you. That's got to be scary as hell."

"Does she know what you do?" Lily turned so she was facing Sophia. "Don't give me that look like I've lost my mind. I mean does she know what you actually do, not what she thinks all politicians do? Her only point of reference is her crooked ass father, right? You might want to consider a 'take your girlfriend to work day.'"

"You're right, both of you. I don't know what's gotten into me. Is love supposed to do this to you?" Sophia leaned heavily against the counter.

"I think the possibility of losing love might. Look, you and Reggie are going to work this out. You love her and only an idiot would walk away from your love. Reggie seems like a pretty smart lady to me." Lily pulled Sophia into a crushing hug.

Davey joined the squeeze until Sophia felt smothered. She pushed them away but couldn't help smiling.

"Thank you. When did you two get so wise?"

"Always have been."

"About time you noticed."

It was late, but as if by silent agreement they all settled onto the couch for a movie. Sophia couldn't concentrate on the television because she was distracted by thoughts of Reggie and the design team. She wanted Reggie, desperately, but Reggie had to want her, all of her, too.

She thought of Reggie and the look of disappointment on her face by the river. The tears threatened again. Was there a way to reverse the course they'd veered onto? She wanted to blame Jackson and his insistence on legislation but she knew that wasn't really what Reggie had been upset about. At least, it wasn't the only thing she was upset about.

For months she'd been so worried about her own career, her own reputation, she'd barely stopped to consider the toll this was taking on Reggie. How selfish was that? Maybe Lily was right and showing Reggie what politics—clean, above board politics—looked like would set her mind at ease. It was surely much less exciting and illegal than what Reggie was likely imagining. To do that though, Reggie needed to make the choice to come back to her. She knew with certainty she couldn't be with someone who would hold her career against her or constantly question her motivations. She knew with equal certainty her heart might never recover if Reggie walked away and didn't look back. How was she supposed to reconcile two opposing truths so powerful they felt like they might tear her in two? She hoped she found relief before the pain became unbearable.

CHAPTER TWENTY-SIX

Reggie took a deep breath and held it while she hit "submit" then exhaled with a whoosh. It felt like her heart skipped a few beats when she realized she'd applied for a post-baccalaureate teaching degree program.

It would be a little while until she heard if she'd been accepted, but it already felt as if she'd moved on from her current career. She was toying with the idea of resigning now, living off savings for a month, and finding temporary employment until she hopefully started graduate school. Corrections officer was wearing on her like an endless, starless night. Lately she'd found herself staying up later and later in an attempt to delay the inevitable coming of the dawn and the new workday. It was time to lift the fog of despair she felt when she slipped into her uniform and set off down a new path.

She jumped when the doorbell rang. She checked her watch and realized that it was much later than she thought and it was probably Ava at the door for weekly game night. She'd considered canceling since she wasn't in the mood for fun after the way she and Sophia had left things, but seeing her best friend was probably good medicine. She'd already called and given her an extra brief rundown of the implosion, and Ava had been unusually quiet about the whole thing.

Before she could get to the door, Ava strolled in and deposited two pizza boxes on the kitchen counter.

"Most people wait for the door to be answered after they ring." Reggie opened the lid on one of the boxes. "How many people are you expecting tonight?"

"The ring was a warning to put pants on in case part of your moping process was walking around in your underwear." She pointed at the pizza. "I'm hungry."

"I'm not moping and I do have pants on." Reggie looked down at her sweatpants.

"Good enough for me, but you're going to have to do better if you want to win her back." Ava grabbed beer, napkins, plates, and pizza.

Reggie looked around the room. "Where's the game?"

Ava shook her head and pointed to the dining room table. "No game tonight. We're going to talk."

"No, no, no. It's game night and I don't want to talk."

"Yep, I know, but you need to. I'm your best friend and I'm not going to let you make the biggest mistake of your life. Your father's taken a lot from you already. I'm not letting him take her too. Now sit your ass down or I'm going to crawl into your bed and fart in your sheets."

"Did you ever evolve past twelve?" Reggie did as she was told.

"Talk to me, Reggie." Ava didn't touch her food and looked at Reggie intently.

"I applied to a teacher's program today and I'm thinking of quitting my job." Reggie peeled the label on her beer.

"Yes!" Ava practically shouted. "About damn time. You've put in your time watching over your father and making sure he's locked up tight long enough. One point for you. You're still pretty far in the red, but that's a start. What about Sophia? Have you called her?"

"What would I say?" Reggie was practically whispering. Just the sound of Sophia's name made her shake.

"How do you feel when I say her name?"

Reggie pulled the label fully off the bottle and crumpled it. "Like someone is wringing out my heart. Like I'm being repeatedly punched in the stomach. Like I'm surrounded by a hundred sous chefs chopping onions."

"My suggestion would be that you call her and tell her you love her and you're sorry for standing there like an asshole when she took a chance and told you how she felt. But I'm not you." Ava shrugged.

"I can't call her up and tell her that without having an answer to the other part about her job and whether it's okay with me."

"Jesus, Reggie, she's not asking for your blessing. You don't get a say in whether it's okay for her to do her job. She's asking if you're going to be the kind of partner she can count on to stand by her and support her even if you don't agree with her. I don't understand why you can't answer that. You love her." Ava leaned forward and tapped the center of Reggie's chest.

"You know what my father did, what he still does. He arranged for me to get called in, on my day off. He's been pulling strings on Capitol Hill from prison. Someone tried to bribe Sophia to stay away from me because they're scared of her and of him. Can you imagine how much worse it could get for her if more people know about us?" Reggie shoved her pizza away.

"Let's set your father aside. He's not a good yardstick. He's a criminal. No profession should be judged by the worst of its members." Ava's face softened. "You've been through hell because of him, but maybe it's time to stop fighting the fight you can't win. What happens if you worry less about distrusting him and focus more on trusting her?"

Reggie let Ava's words percolate. What was it she distrusted? Was she unfairly punishing Sophia for something that wasn't her fault?

"I do trust her." Reggie's eyes widened as the words came out of her mouth. "But she's part of a system that breeds…I don't even know what."

"The system she's part of is called the government. It's rather consequential and her role in it is, I'd say, important. The system is as good as the people in it. She's good people. If she stands up to the nut sack your father put in power, all the better."

"I know all that." Reggie pinched the bridge of her nose.

"Then stop putting an asterisk after 'I trust her' or 'I love her.' Either you do or you don't. She has a hard job, that's why we elect people to govern for us. I sure as shit don't want to do it. Everyone's out for blood and no one's ever happy with her. If you can't stand by her and support her, then for her sake, walk away." Ava got up and grabbed more pizza.

"But how do you really feel?" Reggie pulled her plate back and took a bite of her dinner. "I take it you're team Sophia? If you are, shouldn't you be more concerned about what I can do to her career?"

"Did you not listen to me telling you to get your head out of your ass? The only team you should be worried about is team Reggia? Normont? Lamrup? Those are all terrible combinations. The point is, why are you trying to pit yourself against her? Or find reasons to keep away from her. When have you run away from a fight?"

Was that what she was doing? It was easier to keep Sophia from completely stealing her heart when she thought of her as Sophia the Politician, but that wasn't fair. Politics was what she did, not who she was. Sophia was thoughtful, intelligent, caring, and principled. That's who she was. It also wasn't fair to push Sophia away because of Reggie's baggage when Sophia had already put herself on the line repeatedly to show she was willing to fight for them despite the risks.

"I know that look." Ava circled her finger in the direction of Reggie's face. "Are we done here?"

Reggie nodded. "Thank you."

"Don't lose sight of the fact that she's the best thing that's ever happened to you. I can see it every time your eyes light up when you say her name."

Sophia knocked on Governor Seeley's office door. She was getting tired of standing outside the most powerful offices in the statehouse with her nerves playing out of tune jazz standards.

Brenda Seeley opened the door and ushered her inside. "Don't sit. I thought we could take a walk. I rarely get a chance to stroll. Do you mind a walking meeting?"

Sophia snuck a look at her shoes and the governor's footwear. The governor might be progressive in politics, but she leaned conservative when it came to footwear. "No, ma'am. Walking sounds great."

Once outside, they walked the sidewalk that looped around the statehouse's large lawn. It was a sizable stroll. Sophia glanced over her shoulder at the two state police officers trailing behind them.

"You'll forget they're there in a few minutes." Brenda nodded toward her protection detail. "Unless we need them. Darcy's my go-to lady if there's trouble, but they aren't interested in our conversation. Tell me about the design team. I read the recommendations. I was disappointed it wasn't followed by an announcement of a legislative push. You and I had a nodding agreement to move it forward together, did we not?"

Sophia looked at the ground. "I knew you would be, ma'am. While there are things in the design team recommendations I agree with, I couldn't get a bill passed based on that alone. It's too far."

Brenda looked pensive. "Sophia, I followed your campaign enthusiastically. I've prayed for you to take the statehouse by storm. You promised to be a change agent and get things done. Real, tangible, practical things and you said you'd work with whoever was willing to help."

"I'm still that person. I stand by what I campaigned on. That's why I'm here telling you that following those recommendations to the letter isn't a prudent path forward." Sophia searched Brenda's expression looking for a spark of understanding.

"Help comes in a lot of ways, Sophia. Don't you think a bill that had the backing of the governor and the Speaker of the House could get through, even if, as you put it, it was 'too far'?"

Brenda didn't look angry exactly, but she didn't look happy either. Sophia wiped her palms on her pants. How many political enemies could one freshman rep make?

"Practicality and caution are all well and good, but if you're looking for the perfect opportunity, you're in the wrong business. Never making the decision to get in on the action and open yourself up to failure is, in and of itself, a choice. It's the wrong choice, if I can give you some advice." Brenda put her hand on Sophia's shoulder.

They stopped walking. Sophia felt tears welling, which was mortifying. "I do worry about a large crash and burn." Sophia turned away slightly to get herself together.

"Big swings and misses are risky. They'll win you friends and enemies, but the friends will be the devoted, ride or die types. Every politician needs them."

"Friends are few and far between right now." Sophia outpaced Brenda for a couple of steps as her anger surged.

Brenda chuckled. "I heard about your dustup with Francis. See, that's what I'm talking about. That's a big swing. So is your relationship with Ms. Northrup. Despite many warnings to keep your distance, you pulled her close. Tell me about her."

Although she felt like Schrodinger's cat, simultaneously broken and joyful, with only Reggie able to resolve reality, love was still the first thing she felt when Reggie crossed her mind.

"The oversized role perception plays in everything we do is the worst part of our job." Sophia looked Brenda square in the eye. "Reggie is nothing like her father. She despises politics and everything we do that can be taken advantage of. You'd like her, she was furious I'm not willing to make a legislative push from the design team's work too."

Brenda raised an eyebrow. "Perhaps I've been guilty of exactly what you said. I admit to knowing very little of Ms. Northrup and a great deal about her father's misdeeds."

Sophia wiped sweat off her palms again as she looked for the courage to take another big swing. They walked in silence long enough that Sophia talked herself in and out of taking the risk more than once.

Finally, she took a deep breath, pushed her hands in her pockets, since she didn't know what else to do with them, and turned to face

Brenda. "How wedded are you to the specific proposals in that design team recommendation document versus getting some new policy addressing substance use on the books? How would you feel about middle ground? Not throwing away all the design team's work, but revising the proposals to create plausible action? I've been working with Valencia Blackstone and we've started outlining a bill you might be interested in. It wouldn't be hard to pull off as many of the design team's recommendations as we can."

Brenda's eyes sparkled as a smile lit up her entire face. "I've been waiting for you to ask me that question. I want the legislation, Sophia, and if you can keep a lot of the team's work intact while writing a bill that you feel is viable, then that works for me. I want your name on it and if we can screw Francis Spaziano out of getting any credit and make him watch you get the glory, I'm not going to turn down a gift like that. There aren't many ways for me to have fun in my job, but watching that old jack wagon squirm would be diverting."

Sophia stared for a few paces and then laughed. Brenda joined her.

"So what do we do now?"

"We've done about all we can in this meeting I believe. Plenty of folks have seen us together and my feet are starting to hurt. I still have twenty minutes before I get dragged off to something else. I assume you have a group of people you think will take your side in a fight with the Speaker?" Brenda gave her a look that said this was not the time to play coy.

Sophia listed a few of her House colleagues, including Valencia Blackstone. Brenda suggested two more.

"Let's meet in your office. Yell out nice and loudly to your chief that you need an emergency meeting with that group you just named. There are ears all over that building so everyone will know something's happening."

Sophia's footwear was impractical for jogging, but she wasn't opposed to pulling off her heels and cutting across the lawn to make things happen.

"What will you be up to?"

"Since I'll be in the neighborhood, I might as well pay Francis a visit, inquire as to his health and the state of things. I'm sure the very important emergency meeting in your office will happen to come up." Brenda winked.

"Ma'am, you're scary good at this."

"I'm a politician, Sophia. The people's business is a cutthroat one. Are you ready to get out of the slow lane and live up to your potential?"

"Yes, ma'am, I am. Thank you."

Sophia and the governor parted ways in the hall outside her office. As instructed, she hollered for Rodrigo from her desk and loudly announced the need for an emergency meeting with her chosen colleagues. She could see Rodrigo's curiosity was piqued, but he took "emergency" seriously.

While she waited, Sophia pulled up a picture of Reggie on her phone. It was from Lily's gala. It felt like her ribs contracted squeezing everything in her chest too tightly. Would Reggie see what she was doing as more political manipulation or her attempt to follow her compass to a political position she was proud of? Either way, she knew in her heart she was doing what she needed to do.

Valencia was the first to make it to her office. She looked overjoyed at the invitation. Sophia took one final look at her phone and set it back on her desk. She'd told Reggie it was up to her to take the first steps back in her direction. No one had told her how much it would hurt to wait.

CHAPTER TWENTY-SEVEN

The day after game night was Reggie's day off. She'd been up since dawn, revisiting Ava's admonishments. The walls of her house started to feel judgmental too so she pulled on sneakers and running clothes and took off at an unsustainable pace.

Although she'd never be able to keep running so quickly, for the moment she appreciated the need to focus on drawing breath and urging her still sleepy body to keep pushing. It felt better than going around and around in her head about Sophia, her father, and the fact that life was nothing like she'd thought it would be when she got to this age.

She sprinted down one street and up another, running from troubles of her own creation. When she finally stopped, gasping for breath, hands on her knees, she was in the Zookeeper's park standing in front of the library. What did it say that she was the one who ran toward the criminals?

Reggie stumbled toward the nearest bench and slumped to a seat. She leaned her head back, her lungs screaming for more oxygen. After a few minutes, she couldn't feel her heart roaring in her ears anymore and her lungs didn't feel like they were trying to claw their way out of her chest. She sat forward and looked around.

"I was ready to call for an ambulance if you couldn't work that out on your own. You get chased in here by something nightmares are made of?" The Zookeeper was leaning against a tree about fifteen feet away appraising her.

"Do you have some kind of perimeter alarm in this park that alerts you to outsiders?" Reggie swiped at the sweat dripping into her eyes.

"Walk with me, I'm on my way to check on my flock." The Zookeeper pushed off the tree and motioned for Reggie to follow.

Reggie stood up tentatively, hoping her legs were still functional after what she'd put them through. She still had to get home.

"You pissed about Sophia shoving the design team recommendations in a drawer?" The Zookeeper glanced at Reggie quickly, but her eyes were intense.

Reggie shrugged, noncommittal. "I'd hoped more would come from our work. Didn't you?"

The Zookeeper didn't answer for a while. She looked like she was choosing her words carefully. "I'm surprised you've written off the possibility more will come from it. I'd gotten the impression you and Sophia were closer than colleagues."

Reggie stopped walking. "What do you mean?"

"I told you, I'm pretty good at taking the measure of people. I thought you and Sophia were more than mere acquaintances. There seemed genuine fondness between you. I'm sorry to be wrong." The Zookeeper put her hand on Reggie's shoulder.

"No, you're not wrong about that. I wasn't sure what you meant about the outcome of the design team." Reggie started walking again to keep her legs moving.

The Zookeeper looked at her quizzically. "I can't figure you out, Reggie. You and Sophia butted heads about many of the things in the final report, but why did you assume she'd jump at the chance to put her name on a piece of legislation she didn't stand behind? She has never struck me as disingenuous. That however is but one of many possible iterations, I suspect."

"It never occurred to me that laws could still be made, even if they didn't look exactly like what we recommended. I was too hung up on…other issues I guess." Reggie nearly slapped herself on the forehead. "I'm my own worst enemy sometimes."

"We all often are."

"Can I ask you a personal question?" Reggie waited for consent before continuing. "Was there ever a time you weren't sure you could be with Parrot Master because of the work he does?"

The Zookeeper laughed. "You should bring this inquiry to him. He was not overly enamored with the idea of keeping company with a lawyer. But we came to an understanding that satisfied both of us. You know my moral compass is guided by a different lodestar than most."

"You never had any hesitation?"

"Of course I did. So did he. What kind of fools would we have been if we didn't? Relationships aren't fairy tales and we knew what we were getting with each other. I defended him while doing pro bono work for the law firm I'd joined out of law school. That's when I fell for him. I knew what he did and who he was. It was all out on the table." The Zookeeper swept her hands out in front of her.

Reggie wasn't sure she'd ever understand the Zookeeper.

"I didn't fall in or out of love with his job, but that trial showed me what kind of man he was. He was arrested for assault. The man he put in the hospital had run afoul of Parrot's rules related to the treatment of those vulnerable on the street. Parrot could have had one of his guys take care of the matter, but he handled it personally. To me, the man was more important than the job."

The Zookeeper stopped Reggie with her hand on her shoulder. She looked Reggie in the eye. Her expression didn't give Reggie the warm fuzzies.

"I like you. I like Sophia too. The fact that you have to ask me about Parrot means Sophia doesn't deserve the bullshit you're wrestling with. Clean up whatever's cluttering your head before you go back to sort it out with her." She spun Reggie around and gave her a shove. "You have more important engagements than accompanying me on my errands."

"You don't even know what I'm wrestling with." Reggie turned and watched the Zookeeper lope off, already out of earshot. She might not ever have a full measure of the Zookeeper but despite it all, she'd grown to respect her. She wouldn't go so far as to say she was fond of her, but she did grudgingly like her.

She pulled her phone from her pocket and moved it from hand to hand. Her heart rate kicked up again. At this rate she might not survive the day.

There was another park bench a few hundred feet up the path. Reggie headed for it and took a seat. She stared at her phone another minute, then dialed before she lost her nerve. If her father could summon her, she should be able to return the favor. If the world had any order remaining the officer-inmate relationship should retain some meaning. Hopefully, this wouldn't make things more challenging for Sophia, but she needed some answers.

Her voice felt annoyingly small when she explained who she was and asked to speak with her father. It was stronger when she pushed past the initial resistance. By the time she demanded she speak to the officer who escorted her father in to their original meeting, her nerves were gone and her tone was commanding.

She spoke with her father's chaperone, who sounded terrified. He agreed to get a phone to her father. Five minutes later, her cell rang.

"Hello, Dad."

"Gina, to what do I owe the pleasure? I'm impressed by the means of communication. Very flashy. Very against the rules. Either you've decided to join the family business after all or you need fatherly advice. Either way, I'm here for you."

Reggie took a deep breath and shut her eyes tight. She opened them and asked the question she'd been afraid to have answered her entire adult life. "I need to know why. Why did you do what you did?"

"That's why you called? Oh, Gina, that's like asking me to call and order you a pizza. I've told you all this before. I did it all to help people. Did I cut some corners? Sure. Did I work with the wrong kind of people? Maybe."

"No." Reggie squeezed the phone so tightly her fingers ached. "Cut the bullshit. Maybe that's what you told yourself, but what's the real reason? There are public servants up and down the government who help people and somehow no one ends up dead or in jail. So this time, don't lie to me, why'd you do it?"

The silence dragged on so long Reggie thought he'd hung up on her.

"Deep down, despite deluding myself into thinking otherwise, I always knew you'd never be able to take over the family business. You don't have the stones for it. You're too much like your mother. You want to know why I did it? Because I wanted the power. Helping people was fine, but it was better to have them know that I was the only one who could. And more than that, I wanted them to know that not only could I help them but I could hurt them too. When you have all the power, a business, a career, a life, it's all yours for the taking."

Reggie felt sick. How had she missed this side of her father? How could she have sat down to dinner every night with a man so comfortable with destruction and ruin? A man who was no better than a mobster and murderer? She'd heard the rumors and knew what he'd been charged with, but until now she'd never fully believed he'd been capable of the worst things flung his way. Now she knew it was more sinister than most people probably knew.

"I wanted the power, the control, and the money. Do you have any idea what people would come and offer me so I'd help solve their pissant problems? I'm not saying solving problems wasn't gratifying, but in the end that was better for me than whoever benefitted from my work. And if the ants didn't want to pay for my help, I was fine being the boot to snuff them out." He sighed softly. "That's the truth. I like power, and I'm not apologetic about it. And sometimes keeping that power means getting my hands dirty. I'm sorry it hurt you, and I'm sorry it hurt your mother. Does that answer your question, Gina?"

"That tells me everything I need to know. Good-bye, Dad." Reggie hung up and put her phone away.

She stayed on the bench a long time watching the activity of the park. Hearing her father spell out his true motivations had been like getting hit with a two-by-four. A wave of guilt and shame crashed over her. How could she not have seen what was happening? How many times had he brought her along on one event or another? Had he been planning murder or other life-altering destruction in front of her and she'd been unaware?

Then, to her surprise, the wave crashed and slowly receded. Ava was right, he was a criminal and his actions were driven by selfishness and cruelty. That wasn't her. She was not her father. And no matter how many years she stood guard, sacrificing her happiness, she couldn't undo his crimes or change the way she was perceived and, she was beginning to realize, it wasn't her job to do so. She wondered what those coming out of a cycle of polar night felt like at seeing the sun for the first time. She expected it felt a great deal like what she was experiencing now—jubilation, rebirth, relief.

Eventually, her thoughts turned to Sophia. How could she have compared Sophia to Bartholomew Northrup? Reggie might not agree with the political decisions she made or the positions she took, but Sophia would never clear a restaurant to set up a receiving line for bribery. She wasn't about power, and she wouldn't be tempted by it. She enjoyed her job and the machinations that went with it, but she'd never cross that line and she certainly would never use the power she had to destroy people.

Her chest seized when she thought of her last interaction with Sophia. How could she have been so stupid? There was nothing she could do about the past except beg for forgiveness. If Sophia was willing to put her career and reputation on the line to be in a relationship with Reggie, then who was she to turn that down? Too many decisions had already been based on fear. It was time to be brave.

Reggie got up to make her way back home. She expected her legs to feel leaden from the sprint to the park earlier, but she felt light as a feather. The weight of the Northrup name seemed to have been lifted and all she saw in the future was Sophia. The only question remaining was whether Sophia was willing to take her hand and walk into that future together.

CHAPTER TWENTY-EIGHT

S ophia had been staring at her computer screen for fifteen minutes and had read and reread the same sentence multiple times. She had no idea what it said. She'd been distracted and irritable the further out they got from the moment she and Reggie parted ways at the river.

She was beginning to fear that the two of them were a lost cause. Her heart seemed intent on hope, but she was a rational woman. She *had* expected more than to be ghosted though. She pulled out her design team notebook and read over the notes she'd taken, and each time she'd highlighted something worth revisiting in her meetings with Valencia. The design team that had brought so much excitement then was like a clap of thunder now, promising a deluge of tears on the horizon.

She had a second meeting with the new group she and the governor had put together to continue refining the bill she and Valencia had started. More than a few of the ideas in her notebook were weaving their way into the bill since she and Reggie had worked so hard to produce their piece of the recommendations. If only Reggie were interested in hearing about the direction their work was taking now.

She wanted to throw something to relieve the pressure of so many emotions—anger and sadness primarily. It was good she didn't since Rodrigo was on his way in the door.

"Hope you're not busy. You have a constituent, or a voter, or a someone here to see you. I cleared your schedule." He looked at her desk skeptically as if he knew she hadn't done any work yet today.

"A voter or someone? That doesn't sound worth clearing my schedule."

"Trust me." Rodrigo mouthed the words as he waved in her unscheduled appointment.

She sat back in surprise and nearly toppled her chair when Reggie walked in. Rodrigo looked like he wanted to stay, but Sophia waved him out. He closed the door reluctantly as he left.

Reggie looked nervous standing in her office. Sophia thought she ought to have a hat in her hands the way she seemed about to launch into an earnest speech. She also looked so damn good Sophia was almost willing to skip whatever Reggie had to say and beg her to kiss all the turmoil and angst away.

The inconvenient fact that Reggie was the source of those feelings kept her in her seat.

"I'm sorry I've been out of touch." Reggie didn't seem to know what to do with her hands. "I couldn't call you until I knew what to say. That took a little time to sort out."

"But you know now?" Sophia leaned forward.

"Yes. I love you." Reggie took a hesitant step forward.

Sophia stood up and came around the desk. "That's it?"

Reggie shook her head. "Oh no, not at all. There's more, but that's the most important thing. Even if you're not interested in hearing the rest I wanted you to know that."

"Which one of me do you love?" Sophia crossed her arms.

"I love Representative Sophia Lamont. And Astronaut Sophia Lamont. And Sophia Giraffe. Whoever you want to be and exactly who you are." Reggie half smiled.

Sophia studied Reggie's face. "That's a pretty good answer. How long have you been working on it, Hellhound?" She returned Reggie's grin.

"Not sure if I want to reveal that. I'm sorry, Sophia. Please don't kick me out of here before I can say that a few more times."

"You've got some explaining to do and so do I, but I'm not kicking you out. I'm pissed it took you this long to get over here though." Sophia took Reggie's hand and led her to one of the seats in front of her desk. "Start talking."

"To start with, everyone I've talked to thinks I'm an idiot for making you doubt my love for you and that I'd be here to support you. To stand proudly next to you. My best friend, Ava, was not shy in her disapproval of my behavior, and the Zookeeper didn't seem impressed either."

"How many people know our business?" Sophia crossed her legs and put her hands on her legs.

"Just those two. I didn't think I needed to reconvene the design team for their input, and I left you out of it when I called my father." Reggie ran her hands through her hair, making it stick up wildly.

"That conversation reverberated through these hallways. Did you really demand a cell phone be brought to his cell so you could speak with him?"

"No, I didn't demand that. I didn't care at all how they got him on the phone, a landline would have been fine. I needed to talk to him. It was important." Reggie picked at her nail. "How does anyone here know about that call?"

Sophia patted Reggie's knee. "Remember how you said the Speaker was put in place by your father and there are rumors you're plotting with your father to stage a coup? Well, throwing your weight around and demanding instantaneous access to Bartholomew Northrup made a few people around here quite nervous. The hallways are alight with gossip. Rodrigo is in his element."

"It never occurred to me how it would look. Did it cause problems for you?"

Sophia shrugged. "It hasn't hurt. The Speaker still hates me, he's still trying to break free from your father's grip, and my friends are still loyal to me. People know we're together, but so far the sky hasn't fallen. Actually, not much has changed except Rodrigo has a lot to talk about."

"Are we? Together, I mean?" Reggie leaned so far toward she looked in danger of toppling out of the chair.

"You're the one I want. I thought I made that clear. If you've decided I'm who you want too, then I think we'll find our way through this. I feel like I've finally found something worth fighting for." Sophia took Reggie's hand.

Reggie squeezed Sophia's hand. "Me too. It took me a while to come to peace with the things I can't change. Maybe I can't change who my father is, but I don't have to live in his shadow either. You've shown me it's possible to understand the risks and still take them. But if you need to talk to my father, you'll have to stick to regular visiting hours. I quit my job right after I hung up."

"I was wondering how you avoided being fired. I can't imagine breaking all those rules gets you a merit badge. Are you happy to be unemployed?" Sophia searched Reggie's face.

"It feels like I unloaded a backpack full of rocks I didn't know I was being forced to carry. I'm going to take a few weeks off and then look for something else while I wait for word on graduate school. I applied to teacher programs." Reggie toed at the carpet.

"Reggie, that's amazing. I'm so happy for you." Sophia pulled their joined hands closer and kissed Reggie's knuckles.

"Thank you. We're off topic though. I still have a couple of apologies to make. You said you resented being compared to my father and you're right. I shouldn't have made that comparison. I'm sorry."

Sophia nodded. She wanted to interrupt and tell Reggie it was okay, she didn't need to say more, but it was important that they aired this out. When Reggie was done, Sophia had a few apologies of her own.

"I called my father for you. For me too, I guess, but I needed to know why he did what he did. He needed to hit me over the head with his greed, selfishness, power seeking, cruelty, and narcissism. Those are traits he possesses in spades and none of which afflict you, and I like to think I've avoided them too. It felt like as soon as he told me why he did what he did, I felt free. I think I've always thought I should have known what he was doing and stopped it. Like it was my fault somehow. It's not though. He is who he is and he didn't need my permission to hurt people. I gave myself the power to feel responsible for all these years so I also had the power to walk out of my self-imposed confinement." Reggie traced her fingers along Sophia's cheek with her free hand.

Sophia leaned into Reggie's touch. How hard that must have been for Reggie to hear and process.

"For the record, I also looked back at your campaign promises and the characteristics you highlighted as essential to a good public servant. You said an open mind, willingness to listen and compromise, never falling in love with your own ideas, and integrity. My father would hate every one of those. You two are nothing alike."

"I could have been lying." Sophia moved closer to Reggie.

"But you weren't." Reggie leaned in and whispered in Sophia's ear. "Because I know you."

Sophia shivered. She wanted to be done talking. She wanted to kiss Reggie, maybe test the boundaries of upstanding public servant and the weight limit of her desk. Would she ever be able to work on that desk again if Reggie made her come on top of it?

"Did you hear me?" Reggie looked amused. "I was trying to offer my second apology, but it looks like your mind was elsewhere."

"I'm listening now." Sophia's face felt hot.

"As I said, I know this is a small one, but I'm sorry for freaking out about the design team legislation and not trusting you. I know we didn't see eye to eye on some of the issues that came up during the meetings, but you can't move forward with something that impacts your career. At the end of the day, the rest of us go back to our lives without any consequences if the legislation fails, but that's not true for you." Reggie swung their joined hands and smiled.

Sophia took a breath. "My turn for apologies too. I should have been more sensitive about how stepping back into the political arena was for you. I saw how our design team and the cochairs and my colleagues reacted to you, but I still brushed it off. I was more worried about my own career, and that wasn't fair. You were concerned about my job, and I should have been looking out for your heart."

Reggie leaned forward and snuck a quick kiss. "My heart has always felt safe with you."

"Hey, no kissing. I'm in the middle of an apology." Sophia frowned but it didn't look like Reggie was taking her seriously. "Lily suggested I bring you to work with me one day so you can see what I do and don't have to fill in the blanks with some of the criminal activities your father filled his calendar with. I want you to trust me and what happens in this office. And I should have told you sooner about the Speaker's offer. The bribe."

"Thank you. I'd love to learn more about what you do. I don't have a very good idea how you spend your days." Reggie leaned forward again but seemed to catch herself before she kissed Sophia again. She sat back but looked a little grumpy.

"I'm almost done. I know how much the design team meant to you, and I believe deeply in the work we did. Maybe the recommendations as written can't be implemented right now, but that doesn't mean changes can't be made. I've been working with Valencia and the governor, and I put together a larger team to draft a bill that can actually get passed."

"Really?" Reggie sat up straight, practically bouncing in her seat.

"I've been calling it 'operation middle ground.' I know it's not what you were hoping for, but it has the backing of the governor and will make a difference. I hope once you read it, you'll be proud of it. Of me." Sophia looked at her hands.

"I'm already proud of you, Sophia Giraffe." Reggie took both of Sophia's hands in hers and smoothed her thumbs over Sophia's knuckles. "What now?"

Sophia pulled Reggie to her. She paused when their faces were inches from each other. "Please don't make me miss you so much again."

She closed the distance and sighed as Reggie's lips met hers. She fell into the kiss. It hadn't been that long, but it felt like the experience was brand new.

Reggie's lips were soft and demanding. Sophia slipped her hands under Reggie's shirt and dragged her nails lightly across Reggie's back. Reggie went still.

Sophia traced the contours of Reggie's torso, from her back, to her side, to her stomach. Reggie's abs twitched under her touch, but otherwise she let Sophia explore. Sophia tried to kiss her but Reggie didn't react.

"You're playing with fire. I'm wound awfully tight." Reggie looked pained.

"Who says I don't know exactly what I'm playing with?" Sophia bit down on Reggie's neck. "Go lock the door."

Reggie looked from Sophia to the door as if not believing what she'd heard. Sophia nodded and Reggie sprang across the room. Sophia's clit was throbbing as she thought of what they were about to do. It had always been a fantasy. Reggie stalked across the room desire written all over her face. She didn't touch Sophia, but the look in her eyes was commanding enough to walk her backward until Sophia's ass hit her desk.

When Reggie demanded access, Sophia arched her neck. Reggie kissed her way down. Sophia shivered and felt her nipples grow hard. She wrapped one leg around Reggie's calf.

It felt like an entire legislative session passed before Reggie worked the first button of her shirt free. Sophia was going to offer to help until she saw the look on Reggie's face. She was teasing her.

The problem was Sophia wasn't in the mood to be teased. She'd waited too long for Reggie. Her body'd been ready at the first touch.

"Pick up the pace, Northrup, or you'll lose your privileges." Sophia directed Reggie's hand to her breast and squeezed both their hands.

She leaned into Reggie's neck and moaned against her. She pulled Reggie's other hand to her chest. Sophia started to protest when Reggie immediately moved her hands, but quickly quieted when Reggie grasped her by the hips and lifted her onto the desk.

Sophia grabbed Reggie by the ass and pulled her close, between her spread legs. Reggie's hard stomach rubbed pleasurably against Sophia's clit. She arched back, supporting herself with her hands behind her on the desk.

"I'd planned on being more of a gentleman and taking my time." Reggie worked the buttons free on Sophia's shirt.

"Fucking on the desk in my office doesn't lend itself to slow and romantic, Reggie. I want hours of that, but right now, I want you inside me until I come." Sophia hooked the heel of one shoe into the waistband of Reggie's jeans.

"Jesus Christ."

Reggie trailed her hand from Sophia's ankle along her calf and up her thigh. As she moved up her leg she pulled Sophia's skirt with her until her lacy bright pink underwear were exposed.

Sophia had been wet the moment Reggie started kissing her, but now she was aching for Reggie's touch. Even though she'd said no teasing, Reggie took the time to pull her bra down and suck each nipple into her mouth.

Pleasure moved so quickly from her nipples to her clit and back Sophia was worried there would be a ten-million-neuron crash and her system would short out. She'd never experienced anyone's touch that felt so electrifying.

Her concerns and ecstasy were amplified when Reggie directed her other leg onto the desk, heel flat on the desktop. Sophia didn't have time to feel vulnerable or relish the fact that she was spread eagle on her desk awaiting fantasy fulfillment. Reggie moved inside her underwear, stroked along the length of Sophia's clit, and then swiftly pushed first one, then two fingers inside.

Sophia dug her heel into Reggie's hip and leaned back on her hands, her head thrown back. She drove down on Reggie's fingers.

"You're so beautiful." Reggie kissed the inside of Sophia's knee.

"Enough sightseeing. This feels incredible and you need to finish the job." Sophia moved her hips, trying to find a rhythm.

Reggie grinned. She leaned forward and crawled onto the desk, on top of Sophia. Sophia was forced onto her back. She could feel paperwork and a pen under her. Luckily, she'd moved her laptop. She nearly came as she felt the full weight of Reggie on top of her while being filled by her. She clawed Reggie's ass and stroked her arm.

Reggie kissed her, hungry and possessive. It was ferocious. Sophia met the kiss and deepened it. Reggie started pumping her hand in a slow rhythm at first, then faster. Sophia rolled her hips to meet her.

When she was close to coming she broke the kiss and squeezed her eyes shut, focusing on the immense pleasure that was rapidly building to crescendo. She wrapped her leg around Reggie's thighs and scratched down her back.

She was vaguely aware of Reggie kissing and biting along her neck and shoulders as her pleasure built and then she tumbled over the edge with a thunderclap. It felt like an explosion throughout her body, and she would have happily stopped time to feel like that forever.

Reggie was looking down at her when she opened her eyes. "Did it live up to your fantasies?"

Sophia playfully pushed Reggie off her and sat up. "How do you know it was a fantasy?"

When Sophia got to the edge of the desk, Reggie stopped her. She stepped back between her legs and kissed her, gently and lovingly this time.

"I told you, I know you, and earlier you were definitely not looking around the room thinking of ways the two of us could redecorate. The question I have is, does your fantasy end there? Or is there more we should be exploring?"

Sophia pushed Reggie away from the desk and backed her around to the other side. She reached for Reggie's belt and pushed her pants and underwear to her ankles.

"There's definitely more. Would you like to find out the rest?"

Reggie licked her lips. She nodded. Sophia gave her a soft push back into her own chair. She pulled Reggie forward until she was at the edge of the chair and she knelt in front of her.

"The fantasy ends with my getting a hot woman in my chair and making her come for me." Sophia licked the full length of Reggie's clit. "Can I make you come?"

"I'm so primed it won't take much. I need slow and romantic next time so I can last longer than a first-timer."

Sophia traced Reggie's clit again and thrilled when Reggie gripped the armrests tightly and leaned her head back against the headrest.

"I hope you're coming over tonight. I'll make sure there's music and candles and elegant snacks on the menu. And when we're done I'll order dinner."

Reggie groaned. Sophia smiled and took Reggie fully in her mouth. Reggie was right, she was primed and came quickly. Sophia laid her head against Reggie's thigh and then kissed her way up her torso.

"I have more fantasies. Maybe we can make a list."

"I'm the woman for the job."

As Reggie buckled her pants Sophia wrapped her arms around her from behind. She never would've been brave enough to explore this fantasy with anyone else. She'd wanted Reggie and Reggie made her feel safe. Sexy, desired, and loved, but also safe.

"Do you have more work to do today?" Reggie sounded unsure of herself.

"No, there's nothing else for me in the office today." Sophia squeezed Reggie tightly. "I have everything I need right here."

She paused. That was true and that surprised her. Even if everything else fell apart, she had Reggie and she'd be happy. Their love was enough. But, she suspected, it wouldn't need to be. Now that they were a team, there was no telling what they could accomplish together. First though, she wanted to burn through a few candles giving slow and romantic a try.

Reggie paused at her back door and took in her backyard. She knew Sophia was waiting for her. It had been a few weeks since they'd patched things up, and in that time, Reggie had grown accustomed to a feeling of utter contentment in her life. She knew, down to her marrow, that she'd finally found her place in the world. Kit had once had a look of serenity on her face when she thought of her wife. Reggie had been jealous then. Now, she felt kinship.

Reggie used her elbow to open the glass sliding door to her back deck enough to jam her foot in and open it the rest of the way. She shifted her armful of precariously balanced snacks before they tumbled to the ground. Sophia was lying in the wide cloth hammock stretched between two poles in the middle of the lawn. She had one arm thrown over her face, shielding her eyes from the sun. One of her legs was draped off the side lazily rocking the hammock back and forth.

Reggie stopped halfway across the deck, dropped the snacks on the patio table, and stared. Would there ever be a time when the sight of Sophia wouldn't cause an earthquake to rumble from her stomach up through her chest? Sophia's shirt was pulled up exposing her stomach and Reggie's fingers tingled at the memory of Sophia's skin reacting to her touch.

"Is there room for me?"

Sophia opened her eyes and turned toward Reggie. "I suppose I could share with someone as sexy as you. Do you think your neighbors would talk too much if I asked you to strip down naked before you joined me?"

"The four-year-old next door got binoculars for his birthday, and Gertrude, in the house behind me, keeps regular track of the watering schedule of my lawn. But if you come inside with me, I'll take off anything you like." Reggie raised her eyebrows suggestively.

"I plan on lots of that later." Sophia slid carefully over on the hammock. "Right now though, come swing with me. I want you to hold me for a while. I need to memorize how it feels so I know if you feel different once you're officially a graduate student next week."

Reggie laughed as she settled onto the hammock and pulled Sophia into her arms. They lay together swinging in comfortable silence. Reggie couldn't remember a time she'd felt so at peace.

"How'd your meeting go today?" Reggie traced slow circles on Sophia's stomach, inching her shirt farther up as she did.

"The Speaker seems to have accepted reality. My group started small, but our numbers are growing. If he keeps fighting me so openly, he's in considerable danger of losing the Speakership. I could probably push for a vote next year and I don't know if he'd survive. I don't know who would step up to replace him, but there's always someone who wants power. Since he and I both know that now, I don't think he'll be bothering you or me for a while." Sophia stopped Reggie's upward progress before she reached her breasts.

"Do you think my father has anything to do with the Speaker's new precarious political position?" Reggie let Sophia guide both their hands to her chest.

"Are you sure you want to talk about him when you could be focused on this?" Sophia put Reggie's hand on her breast and squeezed.

"Truthfully, I don't want to talk to, or about, him again." Reggie rolled so she was on top of Sophia. The hammock swayed wildly making them both laugh and stretch their bodies to find the balance.

"When we met that day in the coffee shop, was there any part of you that pictured this?" Sophia kissed Reggie's neck and propped herself on her elbow.

"Who doesn't fantasize about the most beautiful woman they've ever seen choosing them? Looking back now, I don't know why I spent so much time fighting what was already written in my heart. There were battles to be fought, but they were never against you." Reggie kissed her.

Sophia pulled Reggie down and deepened the kiss. "You are my safe harbor." She placed her hand over Reggie's heart.

"You are my anchor in any storm." Reggie traced down Sophia's neck.

"Then there aren't any waters we can't navigate together. Now get inside, I'm done basking and metaphoring."

Reggie jumped out of the hammock, careful not to flip Sophia to the ground. "Aye-aye, Captain."

"Oh, I like the sound of that." Sophia took off for the house looking back over her shoulder at Reggie with a wicked grin.

Reggie took off after her, not sure how life could get any better. Except she knew it could and would because their life together was just leaving the harbor. And she'd finally developed the wisdom to chart her own course.

EPILOGUE

Sophia slipped into her latest Lily Medieros masterpiece and walked over to Reggie for help with the zipper in the back. Reggie was in front of her closet in her underwear, phone in hand, a dazed look on her face.

"What's wrong, babe?" Sophia took Reggie's phone and turned to give access to the zipper.

"You usually aren't asking me to zip these up." Reggie kissed her neck as she finished and pulled Sophia close.

Sophia spun and put her arms around Reggie's neck. "I'm also not usually able to resist you when you're strutting around in your underwear, but there isn't anything, even your sexy ass, that's going to make me late today. Or let you be late, so get moving."

"The governor's going to be there and she's always late. Everyone will wait for her. We have time." Reggie kissed down Sophia's neck.

"Hands, lips, and everything else to yourself." Sophia stepped out of Reggie's arms. "And put some clothes on. My iron will is only so strong."

Sophia moved out of the bedroom and away from Reggie since she talked a much better game than she was comfortable she could deliver if pushed. Her phone, which she'd left on the kitchen counter, was alight with texts and missed call notifications. It seemed she wasn't the only one excited about the day.

"Okay, I'm ready. How do I look?" Reggie skidded to a halt in the kitchen in her socks, smoothing down the nonexistent wrinkles on the shirt Lily had made for her.

Sophia had no words. They'd certainly be late if she stood around searching for the right ones so she pulled Reggie close and kissed her deeply. When she'd had her fill and was confident her feelings had been communicated, she took half a step back, smoothed Reggie's shirt, and wiped the lipstick from her lips.

"You look very nice."

Reggie looked down at her socked feet. "I'm nervous. So many people are going to be there today."

"They're going to be there for you. Because they're as proud of you as I am. The Zookeeper's going to make everyone there extremely nervous."

"See, now I wish I could sit with you guys." Reggie looked at her watch. "Shit. We have to get to your thing first. It's time for the state to adore you."

Sophia followed Reggie out to her truck. "How are these two things scheduled on the same day? Did you remember your cap and gown?"

As they headed downtown, Reggie nodded. "I put it in the truck last night. I feel like I've been so wrapped up in my own stuff I haven't told you how proud I am of all you've accomplished getting the Brighter Future bill passed and ushering the policies from paper into the real world."

Sophia took Reggie's hand. "It wouldn't have mattered if I didn't have you."

When they arrived at the downtown fire station, the pomp and circumstance of a large-scale news event was already ramping up. Reggie tried to hold back, but Sophia reached for her hand and walked, proudly, with her by her side to the front of the crowd.

Valencia and the fire chief greeted both of them warmly. Additional members of Sophia's squadron were milling about. The Speaker was there, but there wasn't a place for him in the center of attention.

As soon as Brenda arrived, the official ceremony opening the first Safe Station in the state began. Reggie drifted to the edge of the swarm of activity and fanfare, but Sophia appreciated her desire to remain a supportive girlfriend, not a main political player.

After the ceremony, once the press packed up their cameras, and most of the crowd had dispersed, Brenda waved Reggie and Sophia over.

"Sophia, amazing accomplishment. This is going to help so many of our citizens, and I know you're only getting started." She looked at Reggie and raised an eyebrow. "Now, Ms. Northrup, time to fete you. Are we caravanning over? Is there a party bus?"

Reggie looked shocked.

"Education of our youth is a topic very close to my heart. I wouldn't miss an opportunity to celebrate the newest crop of teachers graduating today." Brenda put her hand up to her face and spoke behind it to Reggie. "I hope you don't mind I demanded a gubernatorial privilege in the ceremony today."

"I think that's your right, ma'am." Reggie swallowed hard.

Sophia wanted to reach out to her, but Reggie didn't need her riding to the rescue, especially not from Brenda.

"It's my right, but today it's also my honor. I asked if today I'd be able to hand the diploma to a friend as she crossed the stage. I hope you don't mind, Reggie. It'd mean a lot to me."

Reggie straightened and Sophia felt her breath catch.

"Of course I don't mind, ma'am. But my father—"

"Hush. Today isn't about him. You aren't him. I know that and my handing you that degree will alert the world they should accept that too. Besides, I've worked with Sophia quite a bit on this project and I feel like I know you from how much she gushes about you." She indicated the fire station behind them. "And from the few times we've interacted, I like you."

Sophia wanted to wrap both of them in a crushing hug. She'd already felt filled to bursting with emotions as soon as she'd woken up next to Reggie this morning, but somehow, Brenda had crammed a few more in.

"I'll see you two over there if there's no party bus for all of us." Brenda waved as she rejoined her handlers and security.

"I know that look." Sophia touched Reggie's cheek. "Today, all the work you've done earning your degree is yours and he has nothing to do with any of it."

"I wasn't thinking about him, actually. I was thinking about my mother. She would have loved today. She would have loved you." Reggie took Sophia's hand and led her toward the truck. "Do you mind if we walk over to the graduation?"

While Reggie retrieved her cap and gown, Sophia looked at the fire station and the new "Safe Station" sign hung near the door. If this was what middle ground looked like, she was happy to seek it over and over. It was a haven, a place of refuge and help for those searching for it. Staffed with people who understood the needs involved, it was a major win for the community. There was still so much more work to be done, but this was real, tangible progress. Today she felt she'd served the people well, but now she was off the clock and serving a different role. Now she was the exuberant girlfriend of a soon-to-be teacher.

They walked hand in hand toward the convention center. The closer they got the more they were surrounded by the shared spirit of celebration.

"Thank you for sharing today with me." Sophia squeezed Reggie's hand and put her head on her shoulder as they walked.

Reggie laughed. "Today wouldn't have been possible without you. When I watched you today at the ceremony I saw your passion. When I look at this"—Reggie held up her cap and gown—"I see my passion. When I look at you, I see my happily ever after."

"When I was a kid, I wanted to know what happily ever after looked like. I needed a sequel. Reggie, you're my happily ever after and my sequel." Sophia pulled them out of the line of foot traffic.

"Happily ever after and the adventurous journey through life and love."

"Now that sounds like something worth reading."

"And writing."

"Together."

Sophia sat with new friends and old as she watched Reggie receive her diploma, handed to her by the governor, a woman she'd come to respect and even call a friend. Cheers went up with the caps, and she could swear her heart would burst with happiness. Her parents had pushed her hard; maybe too hard, sometimes. But here she was, making a difference, living a life of love, and immersed in all the world had to offer. As Reggie made her way toward her, she knew she was right where she needed to be.

About the Author

Jesse Thoma wishes that Swiss Army Knife were an official job title because she would use it.

Although she works best under the pressure of a deadline, she balks at being told what to do. Despite that, she's no fool and knows she'd be lost without her editor's brilliance. While writing, Jesse is usually under the close supervision of a judgmental cat or a snoring dog.

Jesse loves to write what she knows or what she wishes was true in the world. Someday she hopes to write a book where someone wears a cape and can fly.

Wisdom is Jesse's seventh novel. *Seneca Falls* was a finalist for a Lambda Literary Award in romance. *Data Capture* and *Serenity* were finalists for the Golden Crown Literary Society "Goldie" Award.

Books Available from Bold Strokes Books

A Fairer Tomorrow by Kathleen Knowles. For Maddie Weeks and Gerry Stern, the Second World War brought them together, but the end of the war might rip them apart. (978-1-63555-874-6)

Holiday Hearts by Diana Day-Admire and Lyn Cole. Opposites attract during Christmastime chaos in Kansas City. (978-1-63679-128-9)

Changing Majors by Ana Hartnett Reichardt. Beyond a love, beyond a coming-out, Bailey Sullivan discovers what lies beyond the shame and self-doubt imposed on her by traditional Southern ideals. (978-1-63679-081-7)

Fresh Grave in Grand Canyon by Lee Patton. The age-old Grand Canyon becomes more and more ominous as a group of volunteers fight to survive alone in nature and uncover a murderer among them. (978-1-63679-047-3)

Highland Whirl by Anna Larner. Opposites attract in the Scottish Highlands, when feisty Alice Campbell falls for city-girl-about-town Roxanne Barns. (978-1-63555-892-0)

Humbug by Amanda Radley. With the corporate Christmas party in jeopardy, CEO Rosalind Caldwell hires Christmas Girl Ellie Pearce as her personal assistant. The only problem is, Ellie isn't a PA, has never planned a party, and develops a ridiculous crush on her totally intimidating new boss. (978-1-63555-965-1)

On the Rocks by Georgia Beers. Schoolteacher Vanessa Martini makes no apologies for her dating checklist, and newly single mom Grace Chapman ticks all Vanessa's Do Not Date boxes. Of course, they're never going to fall in love. (978-1-63555-989-7)

Song of Serenity by Brey Willows. Arguing with the muse of music and justice is complicated, falling in love with her even more so. (978-1-63679-015-2)

The Christmas Proposal by Lisa Moreau. Stranded together in a Christmas village on a snowy mountain, Grace and Bridget face their past and question their dreams for the future. (978-1-63555-648-3)

The Infinite Summer by Morgan Lee Miller. While spending the summer with her dad in a small beach town, Remi Brenner falls for Harper Hebert and accidentally finds herself tangled up in an intense restaurant rivalry between her famous stepmom and her first love. (978-1-63555-969-9)

Wisdom by Jesse J. Thoma. When Sophia and Reggie are chosen for the governor's new community design team and tasked with tackling substance abuse and mental health issues, battle lines are drawn even as sparks fly. (978-1-63555-886-9)

A Convenient Arrangement by Aurora Rey and Jaime Clevenger. Cuffing season has come for lesbians, and for Jess Archer and Cody Dawson, their convenient arrangement becomes anything but. (978-1-63555-818-0)

An Alaskan Wedding by Nance Sparks. The last thing either Andrea or Riley expects is to bump into the one who broke her heart fifteen years ago, but when they meet at the welcome party, their feelings come rushing back. (978-1-63679-053-4)

Beulah Lodge by Cathy Dunnell. It's 1874, and newly engaged Ruth Mallowes is set on marriage and life as a missionary…until she falls in love with the housemaid at Beulah Lodge. (978-1-63679-007-7)

Gia's Gems by Toni Logan. When Lindsey Speyer discovers that popular travel columnist Gia Williams is a complete fake and threatens to expose her, blackmail has never been so sexy. (978-1-63555-917-0)

Holiday Wishes & Mistletoe Kisses by M. Ullrich. Four holidays, four couples, four chances to make their wishes come true. (978-1-63555-760-2)

Love By Proxy by Dena Blake. Tess has a secret crush on her best friend, Sophie, so the last thing she wants is to help Sophie fall in love with someone else, but how can she stand in the way of her happiness? (978-1-63555-973-6)

Loyalty, Love, & Vermouth by Eric Peterson. A comic valentine to a gay man's family of choice, including the ones with cold noses and four paws. (978-1-63555-997-2)

Marry Me by Melissa Brayden. Allison Hale attempts to plan the wedding of the century to a man who could save her family's business, if only she wasn't falling for her wedding planner, Megan Kinkaid. (978-1-63555-932-3)

Pathway to Love by Radclyffe. Courtney Valentine is looking for a woman exactly like Ben—smart, sexy, and not in the market for anything serious. All she has to do is convince Ben that sex-without-strings is the perfect pathway to pleasure. (978-1-63679-110-4)

Sweet Surprise by Jenny Frame. Flora and Mac never thought they'd ever see each other again, but when Mac opens up her barber shop right next to Flora's sweet shop, their connection comes roaring back. (978-1-63679-001-5)

The Edge of Yesterday by CJ Birch. Easton Gray is sent from the future to save humanity from technological disaster. When she's forced to target the woman she's falling in love with, can Easton do what's needed to save humanity? (978-1-63679-025-1)

The Scout and the Scoundrel by Barbara Ann Wright. With unexpected danger surrounding them, Zara and Roni are stuck between duty and survival, with little room for exploring their feelings, especially love. (978-1-63555-978-1)

Bury Me in Shadows by Greg Herren. College student Jake Chapman is forced to spend the summer at his dying grandmother's home and soon finds danger from long-buried family secrets. (978-1-63555-993-4)

Can't Leave Love by Kimberly Cooper Griffin. Sophia and Pru have no intention of falling in love, but sometimes love happens when and where you least expect it. (978-1-636790041-1)

Free Fall at Angel Creek by Julie Tizard. Detective Dee Rawlings and aircraft accident investigator Dr. River Dawson use conflicting methods to find answers when a plane goes missing, while overcoming surprising threats, and discovering an unlikely chance at love. (978-1-63555-884-5)

Love's Compromise by Cass Sellars. For Piper Holthaus and Brook Myers, will professional dreams and past baggage stop two hearts from realizing they are meant for each other? (978-1-63555-942-2)

Not All a Dream by Sophia Kell Hagin. Hester has lost the woman she loved and the world has descended into relentless dark and cold. But giving up will have to wait when she stumbles upon people who help her survive. (978-1-63679-067-1)

Protecting the Lady by Amanda Radley. If Eve Webb had known she'd be protecting royalty, she'd never have taken the job as bodyguard, but as the threat to Lady Katherine's life draws closer, she'll do whatever it takes to save her, and may just lose her heart in the process. (978-1-63679-003-9)

The Secrets of Willowra by Kadyan. A family saga of three women, their homestead called Willowra in the Australian outback, and the secrets that link them all. (978-1-63679-064-0)

Trial by Fire by Carsen Taite. When prosecutor Lennox Roy and public defender Wren Bishop become fierce adversaries in a headline-grabbing arson case, their attraction ignites a passion that leads them both to question their assumptions about the law, the truth, and each other. (978-1-63555-860-9)

Turbulent Waves by Ali Vali. Kai Merlin and Vivien Palmer plan their future together as hostile forces make their own plans to destroy what they have, as well as all those they love. (978-1-63679-011-4)

Unbreakable by Cari Hunter. When Dr. Grace Kendal is forced at gunpoint to help an injured woman, she is dragged into a nightmare where nothing is quite as it seems, and their lives aren't the only ones on the line. (978-1-63555-961-3)

Veterinary Surgeon by Nancy Wheelton. When dangerous drugs are stolen from the veterinary clinic, Mitch investigates and Kay becomes a suspect. As pride and professions clash, love seems impossible. (978-1-63679-043-5)

A Different Man by Andrew L. Huerta. This diverse collection of stories chronicling the challenges of gay life at various ages shines a light on the progress made and the progress still to come. (978-1-63555-977-4)

All That Remains by Sheri Lewis Wohl. Johnnie and Shantel might have to risk their lives—and their love—to stop a werewolf intent on killing. (978-1-63555-949-1)

Beginner's Bet by Fiona Riley. Phenom luxury Realtor Ellison Gamble has everything, except a family to share it with, so when a mix-up brings youthful Katie Crawford into her life, she bets the house on love. (978-1-63555-733-6)

Dangerous Without You by Lexus Grey. Throughout their senior year in high school, Aspen, Remington, Denna, and Raleigh face challenges in life and romance that they never expect. (978-1-63555-947-7)

Desiring More by Raven Sky. In this collection of steamy stories, a rich variety of lovers find themselves desiring more, more from a lover, more from themselves, and more from life. (978-1-63679-037-4)

Jordan's Kiss by Nanisi Barrett D'Arnuck. After losing everything in a fire, Jordan Phelps joins a small lounge band and meets pianist Morgan Sparks, who lights another blaze, this time in Jordan's heart. (978-1-63555-980-4)

Late City Summer by Jeanette Bears. Forced together for her wedding, Emily Stanton and Kate Alessi navigate their lingering passion for one another against the backdrop of New York City and World War II, and a summer romance they left behind. (978-1-63555-968-2)

Love and Lotus Blossoms by Anne Shade. On her path to self-acceptance and true passion, Janesse will risk everything—and possibly everyone—she loves. (978-1-63555-985-9)

Love in the Limelight by Ashley Moore. Marion Hargreaves, the finest actress of her generation, and Jessica Carmichael, the world's biggest pop star, rediscover each other twenty years after an ill-fated affair. (978-1-63679-051-0)

Suspecting Her by Mary P. Burns. Complications ensue when Erin O'Connor falls for top real estate saleswoman Catherine Williams while investigating racism in the real estate industry; the fallout could end their chance at happiness. (978-1-63555-960-6)

Two Winters by Lauren Emily Whalen. A modern YA retelling of Shakespeare's *The Winter's Tale* about birth, death, Catholic school, improv comedy, and the healing nature of time. (978-1-63679-019-0)

Busy Ain't the Half of It by Frederick Smith and Chaz Lamar Cruz. Elijah and Justin seek happily-ever-afters in LA, but are they too busy to notice happiness when it's there? (978-1-63555-944-6)

Calumet by Ali Vali. Jaxon Lavigne and Iris Long had a forbidden small-town romance that didn't last, and the consequences of that love will be uncovered fifteen years later at their high school reunion. (978-1-63555-900-2)

Her Countess to Cherish by Jane Walsh. London Society's material girl realizes there is more to life than diamonds when she falls in love with a non-binary bluestocking. (978-1-63555-902-6)

Hot Days, Heated Nights by Renee Roman. When Cole and Lee meet, instant attraction quickly flares into uncontrollable passion, but their connection might be short lived as Lee's identity is tied to her life in the city. (978-1-63555-888-3)

Never Be the Same by MA Binfield. Casey meets Olivia and sparks fly in this opposites attract romance that proves love can be found in the unlikeliest places. (978-1-63555-938-5)

Quiet Village by Eden Darry. Something not quite human is stalking Collie and her niece, and she'll be forced to work with undercover reporter Emily Lassiter if they want to get out of Hyam alive. (978-1-63555-898-2)

Shaken or Stirred by Georgia Beers. Bar owner Julia Martini and home health aide Savannah McNally attempt to weather the storms brought on by a mysterious blogger trashing the bar, family feuds they knew nothing about, and way too much advice from way too many relatives. (978-1-63555-928-6)

The Fiend in the Fog by Jess Faraday. Can four people on different trajectories work together to save the vulnerable residents of East London from the terrifying fiend in the fog before it's too late? (978-1-63555-514-1)

The Marriage Masquerade by Toni Logan. A no strings attached marriage scheme to inherit a Maui B&B uncovers unexpected attractions and a dark family secret. (978-1-63555-914-9)